Plea~ ~urn ~

The James Version

For Andrew

Back
Front

Published by Back to Ftont
www.back-to-front.com

The James Version

Ruth Dugdall

I

Ann

I am walking up Barnfield Hill, and my feet are bare. The coarse stub of cut corn scratches at my ankles, but still I keep walking in spite of the pain. It is like treading on shattered glass. My small, quick steps take me up the beckoning slope, my body going onward despite my unwilling heart. I want to scream, 'No, no, not again!' but no words come.

I know where I am going. Already a sickly sweet stench fills my nose—rotting hay and rats' nests. I try to stop, urge my eyes to look away from what is ahead, but every step takes me closer.

Suddenly I am blind. Everything around me is black. I am in its spell once more. The shadow of the Red Barn surrounds me.

I stare into blackness, seeing nothing, but sensing in front of me the heavy timber door. My heart hits against my chest like the wings of a caged bird. I want desperately to wake up, to know this is only a dream.

But then I see chinks of light between the timber and I think that after all everything will be well. I am safe. This is not the bad dream I dread. The light comforts me and I am warmed with happiness, for I feel sure that I am meant to be here.

I see, rather than feel, my hand reach for the wooden door, but I do not touch it; the door yields freely; I have been called to this place. The brightness is as blinding as the midday sun.

Dazzled, my hands cage my face. As I become accustomed to the glow I unlace my fingers. I see dark timbers criss-crossing the space, like the skeleton of a huge animal. The walls of its stomach are slippery-wet. Reaching out, I press against hot stickiness, and when I take my palm away I see that it is stained with blood. Blood courses down the walls, veins the timbers and spreads in clotted pools on the floor. Soon the tide of blood swallows my toes, eats up my feet and ankles.

Bracing my body against the flow, I am pulled backwards as if a child is clasping my skirt, but it is a rat, griping the hem in its jaws to keep from being swept away. Other animals are desperately swimming, a rabbit, dog, and then a deer with terror in its eyes. But now I see that it is not a deer at all, but Maria. She is drowning. She implores me to help her. I turn my head and look away but on the wall I see a form in shadow. I see that it is holding her by the throat, pulling something tight around her neck. I touch my own neck in fear, and then see the shadow bearing up a knife. Lunging, bending it again and again makes stabbing motions into the lifeless girl, her face in profile, her gaping mouth silently screaming.

I did not save her. I sob with the heaviness of guilt. But still, my thighs ache from resisting the blood and the swell of thick, sticky liquid. My white cotton slip is now drenched in red. Blood rises from my waist and then to my chest. I am drowning, here in the Red Barn. This is my hell. I want to scream but when I open my mouth the warm clotted liquid pours down my throat. Maria's blood.

I thrash my arms in terror, and discover that I am already awake.

II

Rectory Journal
3rd January 1851

Travelling does not suit my temperament. I have a headache from the continual striking of hooves on stone roads, repeating in my ears even now. Unfortunately, a journey of two days travel was necessary to bring me here. I left my familiar but bleak Cambridgeshire Fens, passing through the vast flatness and onto the stretches of patchwork fields.

The Christmas festivities required me to remain at my parents' home, the Four Elms in Ely, over December, and this was a mixed blessing. My mother had organised the arranging of red-berried holly above mantles and candles next to crystal, so that the house looked even more splendid than usual. She supervised the kitchen, an area in which she normally has only minimal involvement, and there were plumped plum puddings and extravagant slabs of marzipan amid piles of black and green grapes. (Too rich for me; I could appreciate the aesthetics of the spread but resisted being pressed into the cloying taste of indulgence.) Yet all this excess counted for nothing as I sat with my parents in silence, waiting for the goose to be carved, all of us avoiding the empty chair where my brother once sat. The atmosphere between my parents was chilled like the weather, making me feel that a walk in the frozen grounds was preferable to staying indoors.

And so it was without regret that I turned my back on the home of my youth and strode into the world, as a man should who has strong vocation. My bags had been packed with all that I require for my future life, and behind me I have left the relics of my childhood. I will not need them now. My books had been sent ahead so I travelled with just one box containing only the minimum necessary.

My route was to take me away from the windswept land of my boyhood and on to this small village in Suffolk where I am to commence employment as Rector. I had made my farewells to my parents at the house. I was relieved that my mother did not cry, or insist on joining me on part of the journey, as I recalled her doing when Henry had travelled from home.

Seeing Cambridge again after more than a month was a pleasure greater than that of being with my family, and in my two-hour wait for the stagecoach I had arranged to see my dear friend Peter Coombes. We had agreed to meet outside of our old college, and then go to dine. As I took the short walk to Trinity I thought how I had missed him in the month I had been at home. He himself has no family in the vicinity and I had thought of asking him to Four Elms, but I was able to predict the atmosphere there and felt it would be unkind to inflict melancholy on my good-natured friend. Besides, he had not seemed to mind that he would remain in Cambridge when most of his fellow graduates had already left.

When I saw him I noted the red scarf wrapped around his mouth, and thought how only Peter could wear such a colour without looking like a dandy. His dark hair hung to the bridge of his nose and thus, being denied sight of eyes or mouth, I could not initially see his expression. In the crook of his elbow was a brown package, which he moved to his other arm as he stamped his feet against the cold. As I drew closer he pulled down the scarf and called to me. I saw then that he was smiling with his usual warmth, but there was more colour in his cheek. We slapped each other's backs and shared a breath of cold air before Peter declared that it was too cold to stop—we must retire to a tavern—and without more ado, pulled me towards the nearest hostelry.

I am not a man who appreciates the taste of ale and so asked for a whisky, thinking it would serve to warm me. The drinks had not even arrived before Peter blurted out his good news—he had found employment! This in itself was no shock to me as Peter is a gifted student of medicine who had graduated with honours, humbling my own second-class degree in theology. But instead of choosing the respectable path of administering to bodily afflictions he wishes to apply himself in the service of the feeble-minded. Although this "science" is apparently well established in Europe, the new group of practitioners in this country guard their work fiercely and do not let outsiders into their group willingly, as Peter has often told me. But this was not the only news,

'I have yet to tell you the name of the asylum—it is the Suffolk County Lunatic Asylum! I too shall be in Suffolk. Why, James, we shall be neighbours. Ah, now I see you are pleased.'

'In which town is the asylum?' I hardly dared hope that it would be Bury St Edmunds, the nearest large town to my destination.

'It is in Melton, near Woodbridge.' I frowned and shook my head, 'I did not expect you to know the name—it is a village location. But it is a progressive place. The Director allows no bindings or corporal punishment, only cold baths and isolation. And he shares my interest in dreams theory. Isn't that marvellous?'

'Yes, yes, truly. But how near to my position is it? Do you know?'

'It is not so far. Some thirty miles—an easy journey in half a day. We can visit regularly. Are you pleased?'

Indeed I was—more pleased than I could decently reveal. I asked him some more about the asylum.

'It is quite old—it opened in 1829, and was as punitive as any other. But since then directors have changed and it now moves in the enlightened spirit of the York Retreat. I am to start in just two days time.'

I listened to Peter, gestured for our drinks to be replenished, watching his face flush with excitement as he spoke of his post. His enthusiasm made the modest pleasure I had felt at gaining my first employment seem lack-lustre and as he attempted to glean information from me I heard my flat voice and knew that I was fooling no-one.

'I confess it; I had hoped to be Rector in a city such as Cambridge, or even, in my wilder fancies, London. But I am going to minister in a place nobody has heard of in rural Suffolk, one of the most unfashionable shires in England. But forgive me. I sound like a child.'

Peter put his hand on my shoulder briefly, and then reached for his drink. 'You do not need my forgiveness, James. It is natural that a man of your background should desire more. For me, I was not raised to expect much and gratefully take any advancement as a gift. But you are from a good family, and it should have been reflected in your post. Is Mr Coyte unhappy?'

I answered truthfully, my tongue loosened by drink, 'I cannot say. My father said little enough before Henry's death, but now he seems quite insular. My vocation was his choice. Coming from a good family, as you put it, brings responsibility as well as privilege. He chose the Church for me, and medicine for Henry.'

'Ah, Henry. He would have made a good doctor, I grant you. But you? I always thought that you would be a fine one.'

'You flatter me.'

'Indeed no, I speak my mind. And this seems the moment to give you your gift... here.'

The brown package, which I had forgotten about, was lifted from the floor and placed in front of me. I gingerly tugged at the paper, which was loose, and unbound the gift. It was a stone head, the size of a large man's, with writing on it. Peter was laughing, 'I don't know how much use it will be in Suffolk, but we are bound to have several at the asylum. It is a Phrenology skull. Have you seen one before?'

I shook my head, my hands navigating the smooth porcelain and reading the curious words written on it. Then Peter did something peculiar. Taking my hand, he placed it on his brow and moved my finger to a bony bump, 'Feel this? Now look to your stone skull and find the exact place. What does it say?' I looked—the word 'humour' was written in exactly the spot where Peter's head is angled. My jaw dropped in wonder as I exclaimed, 'But this is magnificent. And can everything about a character be told from it?

Peter laughed, 'So Phrenologists would have us believe. But I doubt that your flock would allow you to examine their heads to discover the truth of it! Which is a shame. You have always taken such an interest in all my studies, and I have seen what a precise mind you have. I believe you would have excelled as a man of medicine. But I see I have spoken out of turn. Forgive me, I have been too blunt once more.'

I did not want my friend to feel embarrassed for speaking honestly, and sought to re-assure him, 'It is not your words that cause offence. It is the thought that, now Henry is gone, there will be no Doctor in this generation of my family.'

'But, you could always re-train...'

I had to interrupt him. Some things should not be spoken. 'No, Peter. Do not think it. It is too late. I have had my time as a student. My parents have supported me enough. I must continue as I was, and not let thoughts of what might have been sway me. But believe me, I am happy for you. You have worked hard for this. Let us drink to your good fortune.'

Before we had tired of each other's company our time was spent and Peter walked me to the stagecoach, and shook my hand.

'We are both to be in Suffolk, old boy. I shall visit—you can take it on oath. And you must come to see the asylum, if you have a mind to.'

I found that the idea did interest me, but I was reluctant to show this. I had said too much about my childish dreams of an alternative vocation so I merely nodded, and boarded the coach. Fortunately the seat nearest the window was unoccupied and I turned for a final time. Peter pulled his scarf over his mouth and turned tail.

The coach jerked suddenly as the horses moved off out beyond the city. Familiar places went by. And then the scenery became foreign, and the stretches between towns grew.

I spent the night in Bury St Edmunds and from the little I saw of the town it seems that it is not quite the backwater I had imagined it to be. When I arrived at dusk I perceived that the dwellings were modest but adequate, and the streets, although littered by the usual disgraceful vagrants and low women, boasted those dressed in a finer cut of cloth than I had expected.

My stay with my superior, the Bishop, was brief. I arrived too late for a full meal, but the supper provided was ample. In truth, my one desire was to sleep although I cannot claim to have felt very rested. The room was adequate enough, but I do not adjust well to a strange bed and the unfamiliar noises from the foreign surroundings disturbed my dreams.

If the first half of my journey was a departure from civilisation, then the second part was a descent into a wild landscape over which a permanently grey sky looms like the wrath of God. Two of us boarded the stagecoach at Bury St Edmunds, and sat as far apart as space would allow. I wiped away the mist from the window and viewed the fields lying under their thick coat of frost. On and on they stretched, with just a few sorry slopes scattered with black-faced sheep enlivening the featureless landscape. At one point the other traveller pointed to a fork in the road, grimly informing me that, 'Last month a boy hung his-self from that tree, too ashamed to tell his master that he'd lost a sheep.' I looked at the tree and thought of the young shepherd, saying nothing. I was glad when the traveller left the coach at the next stop and I was alone in the carriage. For miles I saw no one, the only evidence of habitation being the occasional poorly thatched cottage painted a dull reddish brown, a colour reminiscent of clotted blood.

The stagecoach went no farther than Hadleigh, some four miles from my final destination, and it was here that my journey became even more wretched. By now evening was drawing in and I was hungry. The local blacksmith by the name of Simon Stowe, of similar age to myself, had agreed to convey me for the remainder of the journey. He stood with his head resting against his horse's neck, their joined breath rising on the cold air. I pulled my tired body up to the seat next to him, as I did not want to ride into my parish like a common labourer in the back of a tradesman's wagon.

I tried to engage Simon in conversation, 'So you are a blacksmith?'

'Yup.'

'And do you own your own forge?' I asked, turning my collar up as it had begun to drizzle. To that he laughed but made no response other than a brief shake of the head and a clicking noise that I assume was to the horse rather than myself. I took from this that he is a man of few words, and spoke no more than was necessary for the remainder of the distance. As we travelled I mused on the coincidence that the man at my side shared the name of the disciple later called Peter, like my own dear friend. Two men, alike in age with a shared namesake yet so opposite. The man I had left was genial and good-natured, wanting to make a mark on the world. The man at my side was as dull as his horse, and not even civil enough to make minor conversation. I hoped that this was not a sign of things to come.

Through the darkening sky I could make out no landmark save the occasional skeletal tree. A blanket of night fell across the barren horizon, the drizzle turning into steady rain.

Concerned with the water dripping down my aching back, a tension lacing my temples, I was absorbed in my thoughts and was surprised to hear Simon mumble, 'Yup, here we are, Rector' and then to his horse, 'Nearly home, Bess.' I could see nothing more than a few cottages clustered around an impressively large pond. Simon turned to me, speaking more than he had during our whole journey, 'That pond's cursed. A man drowned there once, crossing the ice. It was Thomas Corder's twenty-fifth birthday, and his mother had to watch him drown.' He faced forward again, his expression lost in the night, as I turned to spy the pond glittering in the moon's shadow.

Then we seemed to leave the village behind. The road began to gain some gradient and a hillock gradually appeared as we travelled up between dark trees. The horse came to a standstill and Simon, slinging the reins around their securing post, thudded heavily to the ground. I turned on my seat and, peering into darkness, made out the shape of a large square building, its many windows flat and black, like the dead water of the pond, staring back at me.

So this was Polstead. I had arrived.

III

Rectory Journal
7th January 1851

I will continue my narrative, describing the days that have passed since my arrival—just four short days, yet I feel I have known Polstead for much longer. I can hardly believe that just one week has passed since I was in the comfortable home of my childhood wondering what would await me here and now I marvel that I was so misguided in my imaginings of a rural idyll. For this part of Suffolk depresses the spirit. From the hour of three in the afternoon the whole valley in which the village is situated becomes a deep well of night and the trees and hills loom over the houses like misshapen Goliaths. Why does the land sag so, as though it cannot bear their weight? I now know there are several ponds of significant size that compound the feeling that we are sinking, like a smaller, and infinitely uglier, version of Venice. The whole village is closer to Hell—except for the Church which stands proudly aspiring heavenwards on a hilltop—than to anywhere I have set eyes on before.

My predecessor, the Rector John Whitmore, was watching out for me from an upstairs window when I arrived at the Rectory. I fancy that he was beginning to think I had changed my mind, and that he would be required to return to duty! He did not seem at all pleased to see me, and was most dismissive when familiarising me with the Rectory, barely taking the time to show me anything. His unfriendly manner was matched by his tidings; he warned me that I must not expect to be welcomed in Polstead. By his account, Suffolk people take time to trust strangers and this community is especially guarded in the welcome it gives to outsiders. Just as I was becoming even more downhearted at this lengthy lecture, he speculated that, given time, acceptance was possible as his own case proved. Cold comfort indeed.

'The move to Kent is most necessary,' he informed me, 'As my wife is an invalid. She has suffered for many years with a disease of the nerves, and keeps to her bedchamber most of the time. I have decided it would be best for her if we are nearer the coast, as the sea air may calm her disposition.'

He went on to tell me that his wife had travelled ahead of him, accompanied by her sister, whilst he had stayed on to bid me welcome. He said this as if expecting gratitude, but I could hardly take over the post without some guidance.

It may be useful here to describe my surroundings, which I will detail as best I can. I only wish I had my dear mother's powers of description, but I will try my best to convey the gloominess of my dwelling.

The Rectory is a large, dark, forbidding building. The library is the most impressive room, and it is here that I sit penning this journal. Two of its sides are flanked by tall bookcases; many of the books are familiar to me from my own studies. It is clear that those who have lived here before me have followed the same theological path. I have added to this collection my brother's medical books from his studies, which I treasure both as a memory of him and as valuable tomes in their own right. There is a small fire in the room, for which I am most grateful, as a cold wind continually howls outside. Two shabby armchairs face each other aside the hearth, with a table between. There is a plentiful supply of good sherry and a tolerable port, so I am well provided for.

It is immediately striking that there is a lamentable lack of daylight inside the house. Oddly, the dining room is situated upstairs although, when the house was built, it was presumably intended as a bedroom. It is not over-large and the window faces the front, but what could have been an interesting view is quite obliterated by an enormous oak, which, bare of its leaves, obscures the sky with its intimidating presence. I doubt that anyone could love such an ugly monstrosity. John Whitmore told me that it is known as the Gospel Oak, and in Pagan times godless rituals and perversions were performed under its boughs. I am sorry to say that he found this amusing, when I would consider it a reason to chop it down. But I digress.

The room allocated as my bedchamber is on the same level as the dining room, with just a small window looking to the side of the house, and no view at all. There is a larger bedroom next door but it seems that Mrs Bright, the housekeeper, considered the smaller room more appropriate for me. It seems churlish to disagree. The heavy furniture is not to my taste, although the bed is sturdy enough. I hope that these negative sentiments towards my lodgings are merely because of my newness to the place and, in truth, I confess to a feeling that I am an impostor living in another man's house, a man older than myself.

Although I cannot see why I would ever need to venture into the kitchen, Whitmore insisted on showing me the back of the house, where Mrs Bright was preparing supper. The evidence thus far is that the epithet of her name is entirely undeserved. She wears a dreary grey housedress, and her white hair is pulled back severely from her pale countenance. I fancy she did not welcome the intrusion, although my guide seemed oblivious to her frosty stare, which appeared to be directed at myself. Here a change came over my guide, and he spoke with some pleasantness. He was almost fulsome in his praise of her skills, which I hope to see evidenced in the fullness of time.

'I promise you, young man, Mrs Bright will look after you—honest food and no unwelcome guests. Isn't that so, Elizabeth?'

She looked down quickly, but not before I saw the indignation in her eyes. Biting her lip she mumbled, 'I will do my best, Rector, as you know.' I silently prayed that he would stop there but the old fool was oblivious to our shared embarrassment, 'More than your best, Elizabeth. I shall be lost without you.' Mrs Bright looked quite mortified, and clearly wished us gone. She scowled into the bowl she was mixing. He fell silent as he led me back up to the dining room to await our meal.

I felt quite worn out by the time we retired to our beds, and was therefore relieved when the next morning he finally departed, as I had begun to wonder if he would leave at all.

I make no secret of the fact that my parents had expressed a preference for me to accept a living nearer home, as I am now their only son. I have promised them faithfully that I will not exceed my contracted term before returning to Cambridgeshire—my mother's sickly constitution requires such promises. But let me state plainly that I am resolved to making the best of this, my first appointment, however much I find the place not to my taste.

This morning I took my first service. I cannot describe my satisfaction at finally utilising the theology I took such pains to learn at Cambridge. Naturally, I preached a simplified version of the scripture that I thought suitable for my uneducated parishioners—even this version of the Fall of Man may have been beyond them as its reception was met with stony silence. In fact, the congregation was not as large as I had been led to expect, and after the service they left with most unseemly haste. I suspect that they congregated within the secular confines of the local hostelry, The Cock, with much more enthusiasm. But I am prepared for a challenge! To be a Rector is to battle constantly against the seductions of this imperfect world, against the lure of impure thoughts and deeds. To call to the souls of men to look heavenward. To contemplate the rewards of an unstained life in the next world, deferring pleasure and glory. I know that flesh is weak, that the spirit wavers. Only strong words and ardent prayer can guard against inevitable sin; as Vaughan wrote, 'flints will give no fire without a steel'. I therefore intend my sermons to be robust and uncompromising, and I feel I have made a good start.

After I had bid good day at the door of the church, a peculiar incident took place that has already taken up a good deal of my thoughts, which I shall recount now, while my memory of it is still fresh.

One parishioner remained in her seat while the others surged forward. Initially I thought that my talk of the Devil and all his works may have been too much for her constitution, and I was somewhat concerned. She sat in total stillness, her head bent down. I feared that she had died, and a funeral service so close to my arrival was not a pleasant prospect. Fortunately, as I approached, she moved her head upwards revealing a mature yet handsome face. Her skin, although pale, was smooth and I could see that she must have been attractive once. Despite her shawl and heavy dress I could the thinness of her shoulders, and she stooped slightly, yet her dark eyes were sharp and intelligent, assessing.

Without waiting for me to speak, she told me through remarkably thin lips that she required some of my time, 'I am Ann Marten, Rector.' She seemed to wait as if expecting this to mean something to me. I gave her my hand, which she held longer than was necessary, and was disturbed to feel her cold dry skin in my grip.

'You do not know the name? Well, good. They have not got to you yet. I would like to speak with you. About something... personal. It must be soon.'

I was surprised at this haste to meet, and tried to find the reason, but she would say no more.

'I will tell everything, Rector. But not here.' She looked sideways as if someone was listening, but we were alone. 'It is important. Will you agree?' When she saw me hesitate she said, 'I have listened to what you said today, about Adam and Eve. I have listened when you spoke of temptation and sin. And I believe it is to you that I must speak.'

At this point she paused, as if gauging my reaction. Her voice dropped to a whisper and she leaned forward until I could smell her sour breath, 'My stepdaughter, Maria, was murdered some twenty years ago, here in this village. You must know that?'

I thought I did recollect something, but had not set any store by the fact.

'She was buried in a local barn for eleven months before she was found. And she was found on account of me. I dreamt of where she lay buried. I want to tell you about… I want to ease my troubled thoughts.' Her eyes sparkled with moisture, though she held her face still.

She did not go into more detail, nor did I press her for fear of causing pain. But I agreed to meet. Her face relaxed when I suggested a time, but she continued to whisper, 'And will you write down all that I tell you, Rector? Will you have some paper ready, to bear witness to my tale?'

In agreeing, I thus discovered the first task of my appointment. As I am newly qualified, I have had no experience of dealing with a murder victim's stepmother, and I am slightly daunted by the prospect. But I shall rise to the task. It is my father's wish that I establish myself as an esteemed member of the clergy and all my other ambitions are now subsumed in pleasing him, as he has been so cruelly deprived of his elder son, who would in all likelihood have proved more worthy of his expectations. I will therefore endeavour to assist Mrs Marten, as befits my calling.

The moon is now waxing full in the sky, and I see from the smouldering embers in the grate that it is time I took my rest. I feel sure that my meeting with Mrs Marten can only be a good thing, for both of us. It may be the opportunity I am seeking, to ease the suffering of a bereaved woman, and to prove myself an able and worthy Rector. Our first meeting is tomorrow.

IV

Rectory Journal
8th January 1851

I was looking out from the dining room window when Mrs Marten arrived. I was not watching for her deliberately—although it was already past the hour of our appointment—but rather observing the steep curve of the land from the Rectory, and wondering why its architect had decided to build in such a depression of the earth, which results in a lack of perspective. Because of this limited view, I did not see Mrs Marten until she suddenly emerged from the hidden top of the path.

She did not proceed down the slope but slumped against the trunk of the monstrous oak, which screened her from view until she moved forward into the cold January light so that I could see her again. The walk must have worn her out. I could see her panting breath—she had over-reached herself. She stepped hesitantly forward and looked up at the Rectory, forcing me back from the window lest she caught me spying on her.

Mrs Marten steadied herself and continued. She passed through the gates, which screeched like rooks as they opened. Fingers of moss and ground ivy have stolen the path and she had to push away clinging ropes of vines to find an opening. The grounds are a mess; John Whitmore obviously let nature rule here, but maybe I will pay a man to keep it under control. No doubt someone will be in need of a shilling for such work. At least the tree hides the windows, which are filthy. I cannot abide uncleanliness. I was taught at boarding school that cleanliness is next to godliness, and my dear mother also lives by this maxim. Windows give a view to the world, and I must tell Mrs Bright to ensure that mine are transparent.

Mrs Marten arrived at the door. The brass knocked dully against the wood and I was surprised to find that in that instant anxiety gripped me. After all, I was expecting her. I heard the door opening and Mrs Bright greeting my guest in her usual brusque and rude manner. I heard her say, 'Can I help you?' as if she did not know who the visitor was, although in this close-knit village everyone must surely know each other.

I heard an equally firm voice reply; 'I have an appointment with the new Rector.'

I slowly made my way downstairs and joined her in the library, where my housekeeper had lit the lamps, which cast flickering shapes over the bookcases. Mrs Marten stood by the unlit fire. She smoothed her skirt and put her hands behind her back, as if to assure me that she had not touched anything. She has an opaque, closed face, which I cannot read. I offered my hand and she reached forward so that at first I thought we would touch, but instead she waved her wrist, dismissing my welcome. I gestured for her to sit and she lowered herself into one of the green velvet chairs beside the hearth.

Between us on the low table was a cup of forgotten tea, a white skin on its surface. A good housekeeper would have taken it away, but Mrs Bright evidently does not consider me worth the bother. The darkening room lacked the light and warmth of a fire, despite my request at breakfast that one should be lit. My guest wore just a thin hemp dress and shawl and although I was in a wool suit, even I could feel the bite in the air.

I have never been good at guessing ages, but Mrs Marten must be a similar age to my mother, but much less well preserved. Undoubtedly handsome in her youth, her face being of a pleasing shape with dark eyes, her sombre countenance bears witness that life has not been kind to her. She held her body straight, yet the sharp corners of her physique show; sharp elbows and shoulders, which are all bone, define edges through her thin dress. Her eyes, however, are bright and clear. She sat still in her chair, her arms nipped to her sides and her lips pursed, waiting for me to settle before she spoke.

As she had requested, I had arranged to have paper and ink ready so that I may record her testimony. I wrote down her words verbatim, as I have perfected a system of shorthand writing to assist me in composing sermons that will now come in most useful if I am to be burdened with more confessionals from other members of my meagre flock. This is what my visitor said.

Ann

It seems strange for me to be here in this room. I see the Rectory often as I pass on my way to Stoke. I see it sneering at the likes of me, reminding us lower people to fear God. I have been inside only once before now. Sitting here now I remember that day as if it were yesterday.

It was April 1828, twenty-three years ago, and Maria's rotted body had just been found in the Red Barn. I can't bring myself to think of how pretty she was before—all I see is how she was when we found her, eleven months buried under the loose earth and straw. Anyway, my husband Thomas and I were here to talk with Whitmore about giving her a decent burial. I still wonder, does she rest easier knowing she had a proper funeral in the end, or does she long to be back in the Red Barn, where she fell? Where her and William Corder used to meet. Where their fates became locked together.

You are new here. You bring a promise of salvation. Not like Rector Whitmore. He smelt of death and I hated to be near him. I will always think of the way he buried Maria; how he couldn't find any good words to say about her even after all she had suffered. As if she had not been punished enough, her sins weighing heavy on her soul. He insisted on a quiet, quick burial, which it would have been but for the bloodthirsty folk who sniffed around, eager for a story. People came from miles around to see where she was buried, and to see the Red Barn where she had been murdered eleven months before. They even stole timber from the Barn for souvenirs. And they called me unnatural! It rages my heart to think of it! It was a mercy when the Barn burnt down.

What a fine room this is, Rector. Just look at all those books. Imagine all those words! I have never read a whole book myself, though I dusted plenty when I was in service in Kelsale. That was the only other time I was in a house this grand. Except for the Corder house, of course. That was very fine, although I doubt it is now with only Mary Corder living there like a ghost. Especially when it was decked out for the harvest celebration. It was the yearly custom that the family would serve us farm workers for a change. The food would be laid out on long tables, one for savouries and one for sweets. Deep pies with thick crusts, piles of potatoes coated in newly churned butter, jugs of freshly brewed ale. I ate until I could barely stand. I remember the last harvest party I went to, the year before Maria died. I had worked hard on the Corder farm. I threw stones from the path of the Suffolk Punch and my hands were always red and sore, but that night I sat in a deep chair, the same crimson colour as my blistered fingers, my belly full with warm food.

But I have prattled on and told you nothing. Are you wondering what it is that I wish to tell you? When Maria was murdered there were things kept hidden and they are still hidden all these years later. That is why I am here; it is why we must speak. But I can hear Mrs Bright preparing your tea. My ears are as sharp as ever they were. When the clock chimes four, Simon Stowe will be at the end of the path to deliver me home.

I am now in my fifty-fifth year, Rector, and my strength is failing. I get a pain in my heart and it is often hard to breathe. Do not frown for me; I am not sad to be so near death. Indeed, I have outlived others who should have survived me. When my stepdaughter died she was half the age I am now. I find that I have a need to rid myself of the secrets I have carried inside me all these years. Maybe you can bring me comfort. Or, if not that, then some peace by listening to my voice. You are young, and, I hope, patient.

But I must be honest with you. It is not faith that makes me seek out the ears of a Rector, although I do believe in the power of the Almighty. I have seen how He punishes those who sin, and I know Him to be a meddler—after all, how else would he spend His time? He must be bored up there, with no one for company but angels, looking down on our trifling lives and thinking now, what shall I do today? But forgive me, Rector, I see that I have shocked you.

I live in a small cottage just up the lane from the big pond. I have lived there for the best part of forty years. There's just the two of us now; Thomas is eighty-two but shows no signs of sickening, and still skins as many moles in a week as others may do in a month. I wonder how it is that he lives on, and think that maybe God has forgotten about him, what with everything that has happened. Even his daughter's death did not seem to worry him and many times I have wondered if he has worked too long with animals and cannot feel as a God fearing man should. He is as blind as those moles that he hangs out to dry. Oh, there is the clock chiming! Simon will be waiting and I haven't even started my tale. So tell me, Rector, will you bear witness to the truth I will tell you about the death of my stepdaughter, Maria Marten? May I come again, and speak with you?

V

I retired last night with a headache, and am dismayed to discover it unabated this morning. In addition to the wincing pain behind my eyes the morning is not welcoming, as the house is not yet warmed and my breath lingers on the air. After such a long abstinence from alcohol (my father forbids it to be in the house) I may have been unwise in exploring the various spirits kindly left by Rector Whitmore. A tawny port got the better of my judgment and no doubt contributed to my fitful sleep.

My university friend Peter Coombes is always keen to discuss the visions which visit us whilst we sleep, and even goes so far as to write his own dreams down in a journal which he keeps about his person. I wonder what he would say about my dream of Mrs Marten last night and, although I cannot readily recall its details, the perturbation of spirit it engendered remains with me. It is now two weeks since our meeting, and today she will visit to continue her tale, which is probably why she invaded my sleep.

The murder of a young woman is a terrible thing and I must remember that a woman's mind, especially when addled with grief, is delicate—this I know from observing my own mother's decline after my brother Henry passed away. His death was hideously protracted and my mother's recovery even more so. I observed her sitting hour upon hour at his bedside, refusing food or rest as though she were punishing herself for his illness— which had indeed been a woman's fault, but one so removed from my mother's goodness as to be of a different kind entirely. Father and I protected her from the true nature of Henry's disease, and she always hoped he would recover. Her gaze was concentrated in one direction only, the face of her son—already a man, but always a boy to her.

As Henry was only my elder by some eleven months we got on tolerably well, with the tensions and jealousies normal to fraternal relationships. Upon embarking on our separate careers we were both fortunate in being located at prestigious establishments in Cambridge. We would sometimes observe that our father, pragmatist that he is, guided one son towards medicine and the other into the Church to ensure the well-being of both his body and his soul. Father had also trained as a doctor and, although this career had provided financial rewards, he regretted his career in general medicine and therefore encouraged Henry to train as a physician. As for Henry, he had talent enough but other aspects of life were as much, if not more, of interest to him. I saw more than I wished of his lustful appetites.

Lusting after the temptations of the flesh may be natural to a Doctor but not to a Rector, so I busied myself with more spiritual matters. Whilst Henry dissected cadavers, I turned to scripture and the redemption of souls. Saving souls is far less straightforward than healing flesh. After all, one can see the life force within a body by the colour of the skin or the rise of the chest, which confirms a doctor's success in keeping his patient alive. Saving souls is far less certain. Who can see inside the mind of another human being?

Hearing Mrs Marten's testimony, and thereby bringing her to a state of peace, can I really know that I have succeeded? Surely only God can know. Human nature is a frail, temporal thing, best mistrusted. And yet, the inhabitants of Polstead are now my patients and I am their physician, entrusted with their most vital and invisible organ—their souls.

And my first patient is Mrs Marten. From watching my mother's grief I concluded that the loss of a child is a crippling thing to the frailer sex, and even though she was merely Maria's stepmother she must have been desolate at her loss. I must take care in my ministry, as her mind may not be sound. There was something in her serious countenance, in the sombre way she spoke, which seemed odd. It may even be that she has a form of dementia which, although I have not witnessed examples at first hand, I understand is devastating, both to the unfortunate sufferers and those charged with their care.

She is after all, not a young woman and evidently not in the best of health. From what she said of her husband he is likely to outlive her, and I myself observed the speed with which he left his pew last Sunday. He seemed sprightly for his years, though reluctant to engage in conversation, and his handshake was briefly administered, his eyes darting to the exit and no doubt thinking of what awaited him at The Cock. His wife, however, seems to have only a tentative grip on life, and with her finite amount of remaining breath it seems she had chosen to speak to me of the murder of her stepdaughter, Maria.

*

I now take up my pen three hours since my meeting with Mrs Marten. I have thought through what took place and I recount it here as faithfully as I am able. It was on the hour when Mrs Bright announced, 'Mrs Marten is waiting in the library, Sir'. (It intrigues me that she says 'Sir' in the same tone that other people would call 'boy' or 'dog'.) Within moments I was in the room. Mrs Marten was standing by the hearth, looking down at my phrenology skull, with her hand cupping its clay ear. I coughed to alert her of my presence before welcoming her, and she jumped in her skin, her hands flinching back from the head as if it had bitten her. She looked shaken and embarrassed, putting her hands quickly down at her sides. As she took her seat she leant heavily on the chair arm but shook away my attempt to help. She was not yet composed when she turned to me, her cheeks flushed and her voice uneven.

'It is time I told you about William Corder.'

I thought for a second, 'William Corder? The name sounds familiar? Did you not say that he and Maria "found each other" in the Red Barn?'

Mrs Marten looked directly into my face, clearly not caring for subtleties.

'William Corder was Maria's lover. He was also hung for her murder. You look shocked! Why, Rector, do you not know that love and hate are bedfellows? Yes, Corder was tried for her murder.'

'He killed her?'

Mrs Marten looked down to her clasped hands, 'He was found guilty, and hung by the neck. The people in the Courtroom were so many that the judge himself had to be lifted over our heads to get to his seat. It was August and the sun was scorching. It was so terribly hot—some women fainted.'

I thought about the heat, and the anguish of watching a man being tried for your stepdaughter's murder. 'It must have been hard to watch.'

'Watch? Why, I did more than watch, Rector. I was the main prosecution witness. Without me he would have been a free man.' She put her hand to her neck, and I saw that her breath was tight. I rang the bell for the housekeeper. When I looked up again, her face was flushed—she seemed angry, although I knew not who with. We waited for the refreshment to arrive. Neither of us spoke, but I could hear her rapid breathing. For my part I sat quietly, hands clenched, my black suit uncomfortably tight across my chest.

When she entered the room with the tray, Mrs Bright set it down and without a word she quit the room, leaving me to pour two glasses of water. I had just lifted the pitcher and was about to perform this duty when Mrs Marten spoke.

'After they hung him, they made a cast of his head—just like your one there. It makes me shiver, to see even a stone head with no body.'

In my distraction I was clumsy, and spilled water onto the carpet, but I ignored it. I re-took my seat.

'And do you know what the Doctors found from the shape of his skull, Rector?'

I shook my head, unable to speak. I had not anticipated the use of phrenology in 1828—the science would have been in its infancy then. And to find it had been used to study a murderer from this very village seemed extraordinary.

'Of course I only know what was told to me from people who could read the newspapers, so I had to rely on their accounts. I had learned some reading back then but I did not have the stomach to look at the lies that had been written. Anyway, I asked Phoebe Stowe to tell me what those Doctors and the like had discovered and it seems he was a bad one, they could tell just by the shape of his head. He was secretive and violent, apparently. But I say it's easy to say such things after a man has been hanged for murder, don't you think so, Rector?'

I thought about what a wonderful thing it was to divine a nature from the bumps on the skull; thought about the uncertainty of the invisible soul and how much I longed for transparency. Suddenly I remembered how Mrs Marten had jumped when I first saw her today, 'When I came in the room, you were touching the phrenology skull. You were thinking of William Corder?'

Mrs Marten lowered her head, a strange smile on her lips. 'I was thinking of his face, yes. Of how he looked when the Judge said 'guilty'. But I haven't told you everything that they did to him. Making a cast of his head wasn't the only thing. They did much worse than that.' She paused, watching me. Measuring her words carefully. 'They took his skin from his back and bound a copy of the trial in it. What could they have been thinking of? How can they judge others for acting in passion when they take a man's skin from his back in cold blood? Passing it around, saying 'Oh look, a Murderer's skin!' What did they hope to gain from it?'

She became quiet and leaned her head back into the velvet, half closing her eyes. Her fingers stroked her cheek repeatedly, as if to soothe some pain she had there. When her voice came again it was a whisper,

'Sometimes I imagine what it must be like to peel a man's skin from his body, to lift the thick leather and expose the red, pink and white, which pulls and tightens under the surface. I've peeled many moles in my time, and I daresay that peeling a man isn't so different. When I cut open the skin I'm always surprised how much blood there is. And a man must have a thousand times more. And women—I know that women bleed a great deal. To take a man's skin, to stretch it taught and bind a book in it. At least gloves are for warmth, but a book is only for show and who would want to read from such a thing? I would like to feel it though. Just once. To see if the softness is still there; William Corder's skin was not roughened by toil, but tender like a child's.'

She had been speaking to herself more than to me, and I could see that she was lost to the past. Her dark eyes were glazed over. I waited for her to remember where she was. Her face was closed to me, her unreadable thoughts creasing her brow. I leaned forward, keen for her to continue, tasting my own interest like a new hunger. I need this. I need this tale. I will bring Mrs Marten her peace.

As if alerted by my need her eyes fixed on me, no longer glassy, but clear and exacting. She too leaned forward. 'I am a haunted woman, Rector. I cannot stop thinking about how they took the skin from his body. How they made that death mask, for strangers' pleasure.'

I felt I must interject. Her ignorance was understandable, but she was ignoring the scientific facts, 'But Mrs Marten, the making of the cast was for your benefit! It was to prove what kind of a man William Corder was—to further the science, which is practiced widely, especially in America. In the future it may be possible to discover a murderer before he has slain anyone.'

I could see that she was unconvinced and sought to bring her some clarity. I stood and fetched the object, taking it to her, kneeling at her feet so she might see. 'This is Professor Fowler's phrenology skull—see the inscription here? It is a quote from the Professor himself,—'For thirty tears I have studied Crania and living heads from all parts of the world, and have found in every instance that there is a perfect correspondence between the conformation of the healthy skull of an individual and his known characteristics. To make my observations available I have prepared a Bust of superior form and marked the divisions or the Organs in accordance with my researches and varied experience.' So you see, the skull shows areas that are more pronounced in those who have in their personality the trait listed on the skull. Look...'

Like a teacher I held the skull and pointed to a bump on the back of the head, near the base, just as Peter had shown me, 'This indicates a love of children. And this,' I touched a place behind the ear, 'reveals combativeness, or a leaning towards violence.'

I finished my little lesson, and saw to my surprise that the woman was suppressing a smile. This was not the reaction I had expected and my voice sounded wounded when I spoke, 'Something amuses you?'

Her face returned to its accustomed severity, but her eyes still mocked me. 'If a person can be understood so easily from their skulls, there would be no need for trials or witnesses. Why, William Corder could have been judged without anyone needing me to speak in the witness box.'

I had returned to my seat, but still nursed my treasured gift from Peter. Still, I persevered, 'Professor Fowler has discovered a highly useful tool for measuring human fragility; far more reliable than the confession box or the pulpit.'

She pondered this before answering, and when she spoke her words were not what I expected. 'Rector, it is your role in life to believe in redemption, and I am glad of it. I hope that you will still have such a belief when you have heard my story. There are many things that you could hear from local gossip about Maria and Corder. But I wish to tell you things that have not been reported. At our next meeting I will tell you something about myself, and perhaps you will understand without the need to feel my skull.'

VI

To Rector James Coyte, Polstead Rectory, Suffolk
From Dr Peter Coombes, Suffolk Asylum,
Melton nr Woodbridge
7th February 1851

Dear James,

And how, I was wondering, is my dear friend faring with his new post? And what should appear on that very morning but your letter. It has taken me some days to discover the information you requested (mainly, I confess, from my error in searching in the wrong place.) As luck would have it I have been able to discover a reference to the exact transcript you require. Did you know how important the case of William Corder was considered? Not only was a mask made of his face after death but also his skeleton was, and may still be, displayed in the West Suffolk Hospital, a short journey from you, I believe.

And you say that your subject was able to discover the body by way of a dream? This is fascinating! As you know the study of dreams is of great interest to me and I should be curious to hear more of this. Has she described the dream to you yet? If so, we could discuss how to interpret the images, thus furthering our mutual knowledge. 'The Great Harmonic' is a most authoritative text on the subject, and I shall send a copy with this letter.

As for me, I find that every day brings an unexpected challenge. Only this morning I was administering to a woman who believes that she is with child, although her child-rearing days are long gone. The poor woman rubs her queerly distended stomach and talks in a soft voice to the baby she believes lodges there. So far water treatment has failed to bring her to her senses, but I will commence bleeding next week—I have seen its benefit in subduing many a tortured soul.

The asylum itself is a large building, as it needs to be for the 208 patients we currently house. I have been surprised at the severity of the wardens here and find that Dr Kirkman tolerates their treatment of the patients with surprising levity. Perhaps I am naïve in assuming that humane treatment would necessitate less brutality, and my ignorance precludes me from voicing my concerns, although I have an increasing wish to speak out.

My lodgings are in Woodbridge, only three miles distance from the asylum, but the town has enough to satisfy me—a few hostelries and a small playhouse. I lodge with a young widow, who keeps her house clean and basic, which is fine with me. Most nights I dine with her and she is an easy companion. So, all in all, I cannot complain of my lot.

I wonder, James, if you would care to visit? You could tell me more of the Corder case—it is fascinating that you have in your parish the mother of the murdered victim (or did you say stepmother? I forget) and that you are ministering to her. Perhaps you have found your calling after all?

Back to the information I found in the asylum library. I will transcribe what Corder's skull revealed—I quote the most pertinent part—

[William Corder's bust revealed] full development of the organs of secretiveness, acquisitiveness, combativeness, and self-esteem with a very circumscribed state of benevolence and reason.

This was diagnosed on 8th August 1828. It is true, as you thought, that the science was in its infancy, and since then it has been practised more widely by both honourable practitioners and charlatans. There are some who question the scientific basis for the study, and I have essays on the subject, which you may like to view when you visit. (You see how cunning I am, to lure my friend here!) Write and tell me when, and I shall meet you from the coach.

Your friend, Peter

Peter's letter has pricked my curiosity still further, and I find that I am becoming increasingly drawn to the Red Barn Murder. As I listened to Mrs Marten's unfolding tale, I confess that I was simply unable to look away. It is, I suspect, like observing a woman in a state of hysteria, or some other form of mania. I must seek advice from Peter on this condition. Perhaps he is aware of such women seeking to tell their lurid tales in order that they may re-capture the ecstasy of the illness—if I visit him he may even be able to show me a case.

But I must also consider that she is my parishioner. She has, I fear, but a short time before she is accountable only to her Maker, and it is my duty to wash her soul as clean as it may be. Thus, I must use whatever skill I possess to decide the best treatment for her tormented spirit. Our next meeting is tomorrow.

As I sit here writing, I am once more alone in the Rectory. Upon discovering that Mrs Bright has left me thus (following an unanswered bell), I took a short tour around the rooms I have not previously entered. The house still does not feel in my ownership. The unoccupied master bedroom retains the musty tang of John Whitmore's cigars. An over-large mahogany bed dominates that room, its solid wooden frame boasting excessive strength; built to carry two people. The room is eerily untouched, as if the past inhabitant may return at any moment; the bed is freshly made and turned down, and there are flowers on the dresser. Mrs Bright does not trouble herself to such a degree on my account.

Nothing prevents me from changing my rather less capacious accommodation for this, but I am reluctant. There is just one picture in the room, depicting the Crucifixion. Our Lord's face is twisted in agony, the thorns digging into his bloody forehead; his eyes are bluer than usual, and are strangely familiar. His body is slim and pale, ribs visible through the transparent skin. He wears only a thin loincloth, which is tied loosely and barely covers him. It would not be my choice for a bedroom. Despite my ability to sermonise about suffering I prefer not to see such images. I could not sleep under it.

Even a more gregarious man would be affected by this house, shrouded as it is by the overgrown oak, and I am sometimes afflicted by mild melancholia. I have sought solace in Whitmore's choice of liquor. Having already experienced the port, today I have chosen to partake of the sherry. Whilst taking my glass from the sideboard I saw my mother's elaborate handwriting on an unopened envelope, propped against the decanter. As I fingered the ivory paper, I caught the scent of lavender and disappointment. The letter was, as always, neatly folded three times.

To Rector James Coyte, The Rectory, Polstead, Suffolk
From Mrs H Coyte, Four Elms, Ely, Cambridgeshire.
7th February

Dear James,

I am writing with some urgency as I have not heard from you, and I am therefore trusting that all is well. Of course it is natural that a young man starting a new life will have little time to enquire after his mother, although a short note would certainly brighten my day and it has been some weeks now since you left us.

You will be sorry to hear that your dear father continues to be in a poor state of health. The Doctors are unable to define his sickness, but he is so lethargic and his appetite is poor, I am quite beside myself with worry. Yesterday he felt better in the morning, and took a walk in the grounds whilst enjoying a cigar to clear his chest. However, even this exercise seemed to exhaust him and by luncheon he was ready to retire to his room again, without even touching his ham or soup. If only Henry was here, I feel sure that he would be able to ascertain the source of this lingering sickness. Still, I must not dwell on such things and will bend my pen to cheerier subjects.

I continue to be much involved in local activities, hoping to do my small part for the less fortunate members of our community. Yesterday I visited a local family, where the man had been laid off on account of the reduced crops, and I took some bread, which Mollie had baked freshly. To be sure, they were quite surprised to see me, as they were probably feeling that the world was not on their side. It seems to me that the new steam machines have much to answer for; they are the cause of many layings off. Although your father will not discuss such matters with me, I have been reading a pamphlet recently and discover that feelings run very high on the new inventions, which can do the work of many men in half the time. Do you have an opinion on this subject, dear son?

You must write and describe Polstead to me, for I am sure that I have never heard of the village although you tell me that a famous murder was committed there some years ago. As you know, I have a keen interest in local history and would be delighted if you felt able to share your thoughts. Although Mollie offers some companionship it is of a basic kind and with your father so out of sorts I often long for a conversation of more depth. When you and Henry were here I took it for granted that talk would enliven our dinner table, but now all is quiet.

Please do not worry about my trifling concerns, but if you could write for the sake of your father I feel sure that it would cheer his spirits. Or even better would be to see your dear face soon! It is in anticipation of this that I end this letter, as always,

Your affectionate and loving, Mother

I am not insensible to the fact that she is offering me the intimacy that she enjoyed with Henry. I could tell her of my doubts about Polstead, of my wish to progress to a better living as soon as possible, maybe even of my secret fears about my suitability for this vocation—but to reveal any of this would be unthinkable. Or I could relate to her my meetings with Mrs Marten. She, presumably, would have some sympathy with the wretched woman, although she would never talk so openly about her own insupportable loss. Mrs Marten must have had the same reaction when Maria died, although she seems a cold woman. Perhaps the death of her stepdaughter hardened her, for what becomes of a mother who loses a child in such circumstances? What happened to the Virgin Mary after she saw her son nailed to the cross? The Bible is strangely silent on this point.

I replied to my Mother's letter with, I am sorry to say, the usual meaningless trivialities. I offered my sincere condolences for Father's continued ill health, and assured her that I would call upon them very soon. Instead, I am determined to visit Peter at Woodbridge to find out if he knows how I should proceed with Mrs Marten.

VII

Ann

As I promised, Rector, I shall now tell you something of myself. Perhaps you cannot imagine me as a young girl, but it seems only yesterday that I could run like a rabbit. I was born in 1795 and was a restless child. Mother said I would cry for hours and not be soothed. Time and training broke my spirit, but I still think of the girl I once was and wonder what happened to her.

I was my parent's first child, and my father doted on me, as men will tend to do with a daughter. My mother made no secret of wanting a son, and I can't remember a time when she wasn't with child or nursing. But she was often unlucky, many times loosing them in the middle months of confinement, and twice the baby was stillborn. But she continued to try, and when I was nine had one son and then, a year later, another. After this she fell pregnant again, but never bore another live child.

Peter and Jacob were spoiled rotten, and Mother would run after them like she was their servant. I didn't blame them for their ill natures and slovenly ways, as they knew no different. Mother had little time for me, and I was grateful to have Father. He, at least, took care to notice me and I always knew that I was his favourite. That numbed the pain of being around the rest of my family who simply saw me as someone to fetch and carry.

You may not believe this, to see me now, but I was a comely girl. I had very dark hair, and clear skin, and there was more flesh on my bones than there is now. I'm not saying I was beautiful, but I wasn't plain either. Although I couldn't write at that time, I was known to have a sharp brain, with a tongue to match, or so some said. As bright as a button, Father would tell me as I helped him count out his wages, or fix the chicken coup to stop foxes breaking in. Mother thought that he gave me ideas above my station, and maybe she was right. I always wanted to know more, to see more. The first chance anyone gave me to better myself I took it, and as soon as I could read my name I wanted to hold a book. It wasn't until later that I learned the danger in dreaming.

When I was thirteen Mother put me into service with a gentleman farmer and his wife. Father had tried to keep me at home, but she said that work would curb my wild spirit. They shouted about it, but in the end she won and I was sent to Kelsale where my tasks included scrubbing the floors and cleaning the kitchen. It was wearisome work. But I was not there more than a year before they let me go, as it was hard times for farmers with the unseasonable weather and the crops failing. It was last in first out, so I came back home. Mother was not pleased—another belly to fill, and no extra money coming in—but Father took me in his arms and nearly wept with joy to have his girl home. He set about finding me work with him and that was how I got to labour on the Corder farm. Because of my small hands I was paid to pull the caught grass from the plough as it moved, and also to dib the soil for seeds. I enjoyed this work better, as once I set to no one bossed me around like they had in service. I was just left to get on with it.

My closeness to Father caused unrest within the house. She would accuse him of thinking more of his own daughter than his wife, and would look at me blackly, as if it was my fault that he had no love left for her. Besides, she had her doltish sons to mollycoddle, so why should she deny him of the one person he truly loved? So Father and I would often be pushed together by Mother's bad temper, and we would seek an escape from the house, choosing instead to walk by the pond or in the woods, where Father would teach me the names of trees and birds.

And so it was that on an especially warm day in May I set out to walk with high spirits, his promise to find me later, if he could get away, still warm in my ears. He had a job to finish on the farm, but in the milder seasons the days started and finished early, so we would spend late afternoon together. It was just after lunch when I left our cottage, and he had already been out of the house since sunrise. It was a true May day, the tepid sun milked down by random clouds that frothed in the sky. Mother was in the kitchen making oatcakes. She had turned one of the ladder chairs on its back and placed a tray over its upturned legs to dry the biscuits on. I reached for one but she slapped me away, leaving me to go without as usual. Peter and Jake would have eaten them all by teatime, so I wouldn't taste their sweetness.

As I left the cottage Mother's eyes cut into my back, and I smiled to know that she could not touch me, for fear of Father and what he would do if she did. But I have some understanding for her now as I can see that I was little help to her and only served my own pleasure. I have felt the same way, watching Maria wander off from the cottage when there was work to be done. It is true that I would not willingly do household chores, although I did learn some things when in service which came in useful after I married. After all, a married woman has no choice but to work in the home.

All wrapped up in myself, I took the track from the cottage to the pond, following the direction of the sun. The path I chose was not a common one—I could see a rash of infant nettles, which would make it impossible to pass in summer, unless accompanied with a bunch of dock leaves to soothe skin stung by the poison. The path led into a wood and the air became cool, in spite of its being the hottest part of the day. I became aware of the mardling trees, and the whisper of the leaves, making my breath quicken with fear of their secrets. My way was no longer clear among the briars and I walked on a soft carpet of new growth, enjoying the thrill of being in a strange and undiscovered place. I was not afraid. I felt powerful and bold, and snapped twigs and thin branches from trees as I went. I soon found myself standing in a pool of light. Looking up, I saw sky where trees had parted to make way for the sun.

Feeling drowsy, I sat down, my back pushed against an ancient elm tree. I lazily skimmed stones across the ground, aiming at the trees opposite. I was pleased to find that my aim was as good as any poacher's. I have always been able to hit a target. As a challenge, I threw at a tree further away with more and more stones so I could hear them hit the bark like thunder claps far away.

A stone was held in my hand, ready to throw. I was aware of a movement, a flicker that I saw from the corner of my eye, something alive. Another person, maybe? But no, it was a small deer, often seen in the woods around Polstead then. This one was very close, and especially pretty, its dark eyes defined by black lashes. It must be young, I thought, as it was not wise enough to be afraid of me. Perhaps I was the first human it had seen. Also, its mother would surely be nearby.

I gazed at the fawn and she at me. She was so beautiful. Red velvet marked out her pretty muzzle, and her long finely boned face, such as many a lady would kill for. Her body was small, balanced on trembling legs, and I guessed she was only a few days old. She saw me and began to move forward, step by tentative step, her muzzle reaching to catch my scent.

I didn't plan to hurl that stone at the deer. It just happened, and my aim was true. I think I meant to shoo it away, back to the safety of its mother. But she fell instantly. She lay on her side and could have been asleep if it had not been for the bloody mark above her eye. I kicked her but there was no movement. She was dead.

I am ashamed of what I did next, and have wondered many times about it, but I was only young. It was not so much what I did but how I felt. Excited. I began to run in circles around the little body, shouting up to the sky. My heart banged in my chest like a horse's hoof on dry land, and I jumped in triumph over the deer—my deer. I don't know how long I did this, but the sky had turned darker when I finally re-traced my steps out of the wood, leaving the mother to approach her dead infant.

In judging my actions, you could blame my nature, or you may even wish to examine the bumps on my skull. I'm not proud of what I did, but when I think back I can summon that excitement again, and would not wish to have never felt it. You may think me unnatural, Rector. All I can say is that I am an honest woman before God, who made us in His image.

When I arrived home I knew straight away that something was wrong. The Doctor appeared on the landing and we crossed on the stairs, which is unlucky. He did not look at me, or speak. There had been a death. I thought it must be Mother, as she was always ailing, and each lost baby seemed to weaken her more. She was often ill.

I pushed the curtain back, and stepped into the bedroom. The cloth divider was raised and I saw Mother's back bent over the bed. Her shoulders were shaking and her hands fisted the bedclothes. The body in the bed was large. Not a boy, but a man. All I saw were my father's shoes still caked from his toil in the field. She turned and saw me standing there, and I saw her face. It was not grief that her eyes spoke of—it was fear. For the second time that day I turned my back on a dead body and ran.

Father's death sealed my fate. Something inside me died with his death. He was not even cold in the ground when my circumstances changed. Mother was still young enough to marry again and still hoped for more babies. A grown daughter in the house would put off any likely suitor; another mouth to feed, another body to clothe. I also sensed some other reason. I was sixteen, and classed as full grown, though I didn't feel it. I now know that she saw me as a rival, but I didn't think of that then. It was not until years later that I understood.

When Mother thought I was not watching, she gave me a scowling look, such as she saved for the chucks when they failed to lay, or for Father when he had drunk too much brew. I knew then that she wanted me gone. Father was the one person who had truly loved me and he had abandoned me.

It was not long before Mother decided that I would be married, and to who. My tears had not yet dried when she began to plan my marriage to Thomas Marten. Love was not considered. I was only sixteen, barely a woman, and did not know what love was anyway; it was many years until I found out. And so, just after my seventeenth birthday, I left home to marry. I should not complain about my marriage. There are worse men than Thomas. He wanted a wife and I needed a husband. I was young when I married him, and he seemed ancient, but now I am the one who is old. To be sure, he will outlive me, just as he did his first wife. He looks set to live forever, and says that killing moles keeps him young, as though taking their lives has boosted his own. But he is welcome to it—I have no desire to see next Harvest. Every day I wake up wondering why my lungs are so stubborn that they keep on going, taking in life. I listen to my wheezing chest, as it moves up and down, and know that my body has outlived my heart, which died years ago.

I became Maria's stepmother on October ninth in the year 1812, when I married her widowed father. He was forty-two, which was older than my father was when he died. Thomas Marten was a tall and thin man. A mole catcher by trade, with long bony fingers ideally suited to delving into the flesh of small creatures. His face was gaunt, with long bones protruding from under his deep-set eyes. His hair was wispy and of such a pale colour that it did not deserve a name. It grew long on his neck, and wanted cutting, but he was not a man to care for such things. I had hoped for more in life than marriage to an elderly man who caught moles for a living, respected though the occupation is. But my hopes were the foolish dreams of a child and not based on my prospects.

On my wedding day I was still clinging to childish fancies, and felt angry with Mother and with my life that was to come. I dressed slowly, in a costume, which was like play-acting, sewn up in another's clothes as I was. This was a game I enjoyed as a child, but I was not enjoying it now. The dress was borrowed from May Humphries, whose mother was friendly with mine. I've never liked May and of all the dresses I could have worn hers would be my last choice, even if it looked well on me, which it didn't. Mother gave a dozen eggs for the loan of the dress, which didn't fit and held me tightly across the chest making it difficult to breathe. Everything changed that day; a bride for one day but a wife until death took either him or me from this earth.

I had hoped for a better man, Rector. Thomas Marten had two grown daughters, and they would be my burden now although I was little more than a child myself. I remember looking into the glass and wondering how I had come to this. I thought of myself as full of promise, before that day. Mother fussed around, and I wished she would stop, that everything could stop. She peered at me through the borrowed veil of heavy lace, which smelt of mothballs, as I stood ready for the journey to the church. She said she wished Father had lived to see this day, and smiled with glistening eyes, reminding me that I too should smile, although my eyes were dry like bone. Fortunately, the veil hid me, which was a blessing. For my part, I was glad that Father could not see me on this day, which began the second part of my life.

All girls dream of marriage but I had never thought beyond the dress and the church. I didn't dare wonder about lying down with a man, and would have gone red at seeing one without his shirt. I had seen my own brothers in the bath many nights, so I knew how men were made. But a complete stranger is a different thing. To be truthful, I had always imagined I would love the man I married. But these were just childish dreams.

So, I left Father's house—I still thought of it as his—and after the vows I went with Thomas Marten to his house. The cottage, smaller than my father's, was cold, and in need of a good clean. There was only silence inside and two strangers to fill the emptiness, and I didn't know what to say. His two daughters were at a neighbour's so that we could spend our wedding night alone. Even Thomas, who had been married before, was clumsy as he led me upstairs. Once in the bedroom he began to undress quickly. It was not yet evening, still too light for modesty. Even at home I could only undress in the dark.

I felt caged and afraid, my clammy hands unable and unwilling to undo the buttoning. I didn't know where to look. The dress, too tight already, held me like ropes in that low, airless room. He stood in just his long white shirt, and I saw his thin shins and knobbled knees beneath the cotton. At the open neck a few straggly bits of hair protruded, and his shoulders jutted out at angles. Then, to my horror, he lifted the shirt, and in one motion, stood in front of me, naked. I was not prepared for what I saw. Although I had seen my brothers bathe they were young and lean. And never like this.

Thomas Marten, his thin bones loosely covered with white flesh, his belly loose and round, was stood with his member grown swollen and hard. In the instant I thought of tales from friends, the talk of chambermaids, the smutty stories my father liked, and saw at once that it all came to this. And then I realised what it was that he meant to do to me. He jumped into the bed and under the coarse blanket. Waiting, no words. My heart rattled in its cage, and I thought that he must be able to hear it. Oh, how I wished that I was a bird and could fly out of the window! Blood rushed to my head. My sight darkened, as though I had been hooded, and then the room went black.

When I came to, it was morning. I was still wearing my wedding dress but the skirt was hitched up to my thighs and there was an unfamiliar dampness between my legs. Thomas had already left the house, leaving me alone on the floor where I had fallen.

I had promised to love and to cherish from this day forward, and from that day my life was different. Marriage made me respectable but old; my wings were clipped and the cage small. Running a house aged my hands. I became invisible. Thomas would sit opposite me in the evenings and not see me. He would look towards me and stare straight through. His kisses were like the movements of the moles he caught—blind, an act of habit or ritual rather than real affection or need.

Years later, in a letter to another, I wrote down my feelings. I remember my words exactly—If he cannot see me, then what am I? Clear, glass-like? I am light feather and spider's web. I am hollow boned and float on the air without trace. What power I have! I am an invisible woman, disappearing in the cracks and lines of every day. I could enter someone's home; touch their life, unseen except for the shadow that would be cast in my wake. Only the imprint in the air, disturbed by a heavier spirit.—Yes, I have learnt to write, Rector. And to read, too, although I own just one book. A book of poetry that was once gifted to me. My eyes ache now when I try to read the print. But still, I love to hold it in my hands and smell the leather cover. It smells of soft skin.

VIII

Rectory Journal
1st March 1851

I have now been Rector here for two months, and I have met most souls in the parish, or those that wish to be met at least. There are but twenty houses in the vicinity, so becoming acquainted with them was not a huge task, except the handful who have dissented to the Chapel or do not attend at all.

Down the lane, which leads to the heart of the village, live Simon and Rachel Stowe, with their son Daniel and daughters Becky and Meg. As well as being the local blacksmith he is willing to act as carrier, and he and Bess have taken me on short journeys around the area to Stoke and Hadleigh. These trips have seen no thawing in Simon's frosty demeanour, but I have grown accustomed to his silence and find him straightforward enough. His wife, Rachel, is also quiet, but this is more from shyness than bad humour, and she ensures that the children behave in their pew on Sundays, for which I am grateful.

Further into the village, to the right, is Marten's lane along which live Mrs Marten and her husband Thomas. Up further is the larger home of May Humphries and Mary, her niece. Then, in a dark small cottage, Mrs Bright keeps solitary, hidden away. These three families have been neighbours for years, and must know a great deal of each other's business. Ann Marten moved there when she was just seventeen, and May Humphries married in the same year so they have been acquainted for some considerable time, although I have not seen any signs of friendliness.

Away from the lane, past the large pond, the way steepens to the village green. The grand Corder house oversees the pond, where Mary Corder lives alone, never venturing beyond its timbered walls. She is one person I have yet to meet, as she has not yet attended Church, and when I called at her house she did not answer the door, although I was certain there was movement from the hallway.

Up in the heart of the village lives Mrs Catchpole, with her husband and son, who both work the land. She is the only musician hereabouts, and attempts the piano in St Mary's with sufficient skill for a rural village, where no one else can play.

Then, in a pretty cottage on its own, are the wool-merchant Jeremiah Humphries, his wife, Sarah, and their young son, Joshua. I have passed by it many times and noted how neatly she maintains the land around, and how welcoming the entrance.

Upon Polstead Green, are a Primitive Methodist Chapel, the Blacksmiths and the Public Hostelry. The Cock's landlord is Isaac Pryke, a gregarious young man who is not often seen at church, and his family. The Prykes are a local family, and Isaac's father used to work the land before he lost his sight. He lives away from the heart of the village, and has not been to a service since I arrived.

St Mary's church stands alongside Polstead Hall, a white mansion overlooking a ninety-acre deer park. Chas Tyrell is the principal landowner in the area, and he and his wife are often in London, but when in Polstead they attend the service. Mrs Tyrell is benefactor of a school for poor girls, established in Stoke, but in Polstead itself we have a school whose master, James Howe, lives in one of the larger cottages just beyond the deer park.

The effect of being in such an insular community is to feel stifled and alone at the same time. It is like being in a strange land where the language is familiar but not fluent. It is as though there are things within this community, which are closely guarded, and most natives– excepting the village gossip—pause before answering certain questions.

It is strange, therefore, that Mrs Marten is unburdening herself with such bluntness. When I saw her today, for our fourth meeting I decided to ask about her prophetic dreams. Peter had advised me in his letter to get sufficient detail, so that analysis would be possible. She did not seem surprised at my request, and the words tumbled out of her like a relief. But what I heard has left me feeling disturbed.

Ann

'Yes, Rector, it is time that I told you about the dream. Always the same one. It came to me three times, at night, during the spring of 1828, when Maria had been missing for eleven months. It came when I was alone inside myself in total darkness. Trapped on a hard board, heavy blankets pinning me down. Blind as a mole, though those three visions come clearer than salvation. Does everyone dream like that? Or is it just the haunted? Those of us who are bereft. Maybe the dreams were the visitations of ghosts, souls who could not rest. My dreams terrified me. I still remember everything, even now, after all these years. Without those dreams the story would have been different. It came to me softly at first, whispering and teasing, visions of Maria in her scarlet dress with her hair all undone, her eyes as black as coals. And him. I never saw his face, not in the dream, but I knew it was him. On the wall I saw in shadow a man's form. In shadow, I saw that he was holding her by the throat, pulling something tight around her neck, and then I saw him bearing up a knife. Lunging, stabbing again and again into her. His silence as he cut her down to the dusty floor, the blood all around. And always that taste in my mouth, making me gag, smothering me until I woke gasping for breath. I dreaded that dream, feared to go to sleep. And I hated those that said it wasn't real, that I made it up.'

The change in Mrs Marten's voice alerted me, and I looked up from my seat. Her cheeks were flushed with emotion. She was frowning at her lap, looking angry. I had been writing her words down in this journal, so until then I had not seen her extreme agitation. I decided to say what had only just occurred to me,

'Mrs Marten, may I make a comment? Recent studies have shown that dreaming of a deceased person occurs frequently to those who have been bereaved.'

She continued to stare at me, the flush still in her cheeks. I softened my tone and stopped writing, 'When you had your dreams you had been without Maria for nearly than a year, wondering and worrying about her. These feelings will naturally have affected your thoughts and this resulted in your dreams. It is, apparently, a common phenomenon.' I had hoped to bring her some comfort, but I stopped talking when I saw the return of her twisted smile. She seemed to be mocking me again, but when her voice came it was just a whisper.

'That's as may be, Rector,' she said slowly, after some thought. 'But Maria came to me in that dream and told me exactly where her body had lain for eleven months. That she must be dug up and given decent burial.' She regarded me with those penetrating eyes. 'Is that a frequent phenomenon?'

'No, I grant that it is not. But this was surely mere coincidence.'

I sat back in my chair and put down my pen. The woman was clearly more disturbed than I at first realised. She was confusing her grief for a vision or something similar. I could see that she was tormented, and I sought to ease her pain. I thought of her lack of learning, that the only knowledge she must hold is village folk law and that preached from the pulpit. I sought that language now, 'It is true that there are many prophecies described in the Bible as dreams, but I doubt that yours resulted from divine intervention. My Doctor friend, who has more knowledge than I of such things, often states that dreams are symptoms of a troubled mind.'

Mrs Marten was frowning and looked unconvinced. I decided to give some more information, diluting the science to a level at which she could understand. 'There is some new research about dreams from a fellow named Andrew Davis, and I have read with interest some of his case studies.' I reached to the floor and retrieved my copy of The Great Harmonica, published last year, and thumbed the pages until I found the relevant part, 'Listen—*Even in prophetic warnings, the soul does its work almost invariably... perceiving those events which laws of cause and effect are certain to develop.* So you see, it is not surprising that you should experience such visitations. Of course, it would have been unsettling to so accurately predict the location of Maria's body, but this was, as I have said, merely coincidence.'

Having been silent for some minutes, Mrs Marten laid her head back into the chair and moved her hands onto her lap, 'I will think on what you have said, Rector. I am comforted that you set so little store by my dreaming. But would you rest easy after such nightly horrors? I will tell you exactly what came to me those three nights.' She paused and took a shallow breath, closed her eyes and recited, 'I am walking up Barn-field Hill, and my feet are bare...'

She was lost in her recollection, rocking herself to and fro, as the ghastly tale unfolded. Then she suddenly opened her eyes, and cried out, 'But you've stopped writing, Rector! You promised to take down my testimony! What will become of me if you do not write it all down?'

She became quite agitated, clasping her hand to her throat as if she might throttle her own life out of her.

'Please forgive me, Mrs Marten,' I hastened to assure her, 'but I am in want of more ink. I wonder, should we pause for some refreshment?' Although my pen was indeed dry, my hand was shaking, and I was grateful for the excuse to stop writing. As I rang the bell, I noted my own irregular heartbeat.

'Ah, Mrs Bright! I wonder if you could make some tea for Mrs Marten and myself.'

'Very good, Sir' She was gone as quickly as she arrived, and I was once more alone with my guest. I re-filled my pen and turning again to her, asked a question which had jumped into my mind.

'Did you recount the dream you have just told me at Corder's trial?'

'Why of course, Rector. It was my dream that proved his guilt. Whatever your Doctor friend or your clever books say, I know that dreams like the one I've just told you always have to mean something, or what is the purpose of them? Mine was to see that Maria was finally given decent burial and that Corder was found guilty.'

I did not answer her, but busied myself blotting my papers. It is true that many God-fearing people recount tales of visions and prophetic dreams. I have never experienced one myself, yet I have come to believe that there are a few things in this world that cannot be explained by rational means. Henry would have scoffed at the very notion that dreams have the power of prophecy, but then he was a man of science, not the spirit.

The opening door made us both jump. Mrs Bright re-entered and, pursing her lips in a thin line, poured out two cups of tea for Mrs Marten and myself and then eyed the upturned book at my feet. Mrs Marten snatched her cup up, and I saw that she was as dry as my nib. I chastised myself inwardly for not offering my guest this refreshment—my mind had been quite taken up with her horrible story. She drank greedily and I had to steal myself from wincing at the sound of her slurping. Her mouth was not yet empty of the biscuit she had helped herself to when she began to speak.

'I had to tell about my dream in the Court. They made me, see. I was on oath to speak the truth, so it would be against my immortal soul to keep it back. They asked me how I knew where Maria lay buried, how it was I could send Thomas to find the dead body of his own daughter.' She drained her cup with a final greedy slurp, and then smiled up at me with a countenance more at ease than at any time during our interview. 'You look shocked, Rector! But there's more to come. Much more!'

IX

The Rectory Journal
10th March 1851

On waking, my first thought was that I was at last to have
some new society; today I was to meet Rector Charles Walpole
from the neighbouring parish of Layham. This was a visit that
had been arranged by John Whitmore, who, I felt sure, would
have impressed upon Rector Walpole that I would be in need
of some guidance in the pursuit of my duties at Polstead.
Although anticipating a dull meeting (reminiscent of seminars
at Cambridge, no doubt) I was glad of respite from the troubling
meetings with Mrs Marten and my subsequent ruminations.

I had been invited to lunch at midday, and was looking
forward to the three-mile walk, which would introduce me to the
surrounding area. Although it was still quite early I decided to set
off at ten and make the journey more leisurely. I hoped the walk
would lift my spirits, as I have been having bleak thoughts about
Polstead. I am resolved to be positive—a short period here must
surely lead to a more comfortable living in a prosperous town. If
I could achieve some success during my tenure at Polstead, some
significant milestone in my ministry, I may even secure one of the
more favourable livings in Newmarket or Felixstowe. Although

a man of the cloth, I am not insensible to ambition and since my meetings with Mrs Marten it has occurred to me that if I could shed further light on the Red Barn murder my name may come to the ear of the Bishop.

Thus went my thoughts as I set out on my walk to Layham. The weather was cold, but this did not deter me, as I needed liberation more than warmth. The Rectory can be most oppressive, and I was glad of a reason to leave if only for a few hours. Pulling my long coat close and steeling myself against the biting wind, I walked head down along the lane that leads into Polstead and thence to Layham.

I had not yet warmed myself through, although I had gained the village green, when my name was called and, on turning, my heart sank when I saw a group of four women, one of whom was Mrs Marten. (It seems that she is everywhere now.) The other three, I have only met after Sunday service, included the excessively talkative Mrs May Humphries, who had dominated my attention with her incessant prattle, on more than one occasion. She was stood with her sombre niece, Mary Teager, a young woman of plain and modest countenance, and her daughter-in-law, Sarah Humphries, singularly pretty with striking yellow hair. Beneath her cloak a child of about two was keeping warm.

I had caught them in idle conversation, and they soon engaged me in similar small talk. I will not describe tedious details, only to say that the discourse of countrywomen is far from stimulating. May Humphries was asking me if I had heard of Polstead before taking my post here, and when I said that I knew the name of the village she declared, 'Why who hasn't, Rector? Sure, we're famous now,' and then she launched into telling me of the notorious murder of Maria Marten, and spoke freely of the case, even as Mrs Marten stood mute as a scolded bride,

'Oh yes, the Red Barn murder certainly made Polstead famous, that's for sure! Why people came from America even, asking to see the Barn—course, that burnt down years ago, but some still

came just to see where it stood. Some people have no sensitivity!'
She declared, while Mary nodded her head and Sarah giggled into
her shawl. She, at least, could see the irony in the statement. What
choice had I but to be polite? I merely noted what a distressing
thing it was for all concerned but the woman interrupted me,
not needing any further encouragement, 'Oh, yes it was Rector.
Especially for Ann here, and also for poor Mary Corder. Why,
it wasn't her fault that her son was a murderer now, was it? And
Maria, well, she did have something of a reputation. You'll know
that she had three children, all by different men, I suppose?'

She could see by my face that I didn't know, and I was
embarrassed to see Sarah considering me frankly. I hope she
does not suppose me green—being shocked at immorality is not
the same as naïvety, and Maria must have been something of a
whore, even if she was not paid for her favours.

'Why when she was nineteen she had a daughter by Thomas
Corder. They called her Matilda and she was a bonny thing. But
then Thomas decided he wanted no more to do with Maria, not
with Mrs Corder's threatening to cut him off from the farm, and
then Matilda died suddenly. After that some folks tried to say it
was Maria's own doing, but I wouldn't believe it.'

I could hardly believe what I was hearing; was she saying that
some thought Maria was a murderess? I looked at Mrs Marten,
but her head was bowed so I could not see her face. So Maria
was lovers with two Corder men. And then I recalled Thomas
Corder's name from my conversation with Simon Stowe, as I
entered Polstead, and asked, 'Wasn't Thomas Corder the man
who drowned crossing the frozen pond?'

'Aye, Rector, that's him. It was his twenty-fifth birthday and the
ice split beneath him. Mary Corder watched it happen—there's no
wonder she's gone queer with all she's had to bear. But that was
years after he finished with Maria. After Thomas wanted no more
to do with Maria she took up with Mr Peter Matthews, who was
related to the owners of the Old Hall, and visited often. They met

at the Cherry Fair one year and after a few months of courting in Ipswich and London she fell pregnant. He sired Thomas Henry, who was such a lovely boy, wasn't he, Ann? We haven't seen him round here for years now.'

Quick movement interrupted the talk as Sarah's child pulled away from her hold and ran to his Grandmother, who bent down and put her arms around him. Sarah, free of her charge, stood taller and smiled at me—it was like the sun coming out. Once Joshua was settled Mrs Humphries turned to me again.

'Anyway, after Little Tom was born Mr Matthews wanted nothing of Maria. Then she got with William Corder and afore long she was with child again.' Mrs Marten coughed, and I saw that her eyes were sharp and fixed on May Humphries, as if in warning but she did not heed it,

''Course, we didn't know that Maria and William had had a son together, as he died suddenly too and was buried in a field afore anyone saw him, but it all came out in the trial. Although you knew, didn't you, Ann? It was very strange, how that boy was kept so hidden afore he died. And no-one could say what he died of.'

This information was new to my ears, and I half-glanced at Mrs Marten, but she would not meet my eye and indeed seemed to be withdrawing into her black cloak. Silence reigned, and we all seemed to be waiting for Mrs Marten to say something. When her voice came it was as sharp and thin as a knife, 'You don't want to be listening to any rumours like that, Rector. Maria was many things, but she would not harm her own flesh and blood.'

Without missing a beat Mrs Humphries was all concern, 'Poor Ann. She was just like a daughter to you, wasn't she? And to think, William Corder had left her body to rot for nearly a year. It's praise to God himself that our Ann here dreamt of the body, or that scoundrel would have run free, wouldn't he Ann? Not that Maria was any better than she should have been. She certainly had her share of callers in her short time on this earth!'

I asked if any of Maria's lovers had intended to marry her and Mrs Humphries laughed into her shawl, 'Lord bless you, Rector, Maria was not the sort of girl that a man marries!' If I can interpret this reply, it seems to be that most men would have been unlikely to desire anything more than sport from Maria. Not that she seemed to mind, from what May Humphries said. I am wary about accepting such an account as the Truth as I observed that she was thoroughly enjoying the telling of this information, even at the expense of her friend, who was much discomfited. However, I have met such women as Maria, in my time at Cambridge—they are a type who are most entertaining but who would never be considered by gentlemen as suitable wives. I have seen them in the lower class taverns, advertising themselves in gaudy shades of red. Such women carry disease like rats.

My awareness of Mrs Marten's extreme discomfort prohibited me from asking directly about these men whom Maria had ensnared. As May Humphries began to tell me about William Corder, Mrs Marten had a short but violent coughing fit. Mary immediately went to her aid but the poor woman was quite unwell. May Humphries at least had the grace to look perturbed, handed Joshua back to his mother and offering her hand out to her old friend, but it was pushed away. Seeing that she had caused offence, the gossip was now full of soft words, but it was Mary who seemed the most genuinely concerned. The pair insisted on walking her back to her cottage, each trying to take an arm had the proud patient not resisted. I was most relieved when they gave me a brief nod and escorted her home, from whence she should never have strayed on a cruel day like this.

Even I was submitting to the sharp wind, and Sarah Humphries's young child, no doubt bored and hungry, began to grizzle from inside his mother's pretty blue wrappings. We were left alone now and as she gave me a sweet smile, I felt some surprise and pleasure that such a rustic place houses a fine woman, and she spoke easily with me despite the scene we had just witnessed, 'You said you are for Layham? I shall walk with you some of the journey—my house is that way.'

So we continued to walk from the green, along the side of the pond where a group of boys were testing its thin covering of ice with a stick. I thought of Thomas Corder's tragic death, and hoped those boys would not be so foolish, and said so to my companion. She nodded, holding her son's hand tighter, 'Such a terrible thing for a mother to see. Mrs Corder has had an unlucky life.'

I concurred, thinking of my own mother briefly. Then Sarah stopped and indicated, 'She was watching from a window in her house, there.' The Corder house is an impressive building, certainly eclipsing all its neighbouring houses in both style and dimension. It is timbered, as I imagine most sixteenth century farmhouses are, and is brown and cream in colour, unlike the red of many Suffolk cottages. It wears its importance without ostentation. My thoughts flew back to my own childhood home, with its over-grand entrance and great swathes of fabric around its windows, and I concluded that the Corders were possessed of simple good taste. (I write with some regret, as my mother is not so blessed. She was fortunate in her choice of husband as she herself was not from a wealthy family. Newly acquired fortune can often result in flamboyance and this is certainly true of my mother's preference for display.)

The position of the Corder house is such that the view from the front rooms over the large pond must be impressive, although a constant reminder to Mrs Corder of the accident. As we walked adjacent to it Sarah leaned towards me, 'She lives there all alone now. Within a space of four years she lost her husband and all four sons. William was the last, and she was by herself when she went to see him hanged. I'm not sure I could have borne it. How does someone cope with such loss?' She shook her blonde hair, sadly and then looked to her son, as if to recollect her own good fortune, and her smile returned.

I observed that it is a human truth that some families are dealt a larger portion of grief than others, and that property or wealth is no protection against the will of God. We walked silently for a few paces before Sarah announced that this was where she must take a different turn. As we bade each other good day I thought how this small walk with her had been the most enjoyable event of my time in Polstead yet.

And so I continued to stride briskly to Layham, musing on what I had been told. I do wonder at a young woman in a small village bearing three children to different men to whom she was not married, and then being murdered by one of them. The incorrigible May Humphries even suggested that Maria might have dispatched two of their innocent lives with her own hand—but then Mrs Marten had urged me to ignore such any rumours. That such a thing is spoken of so loosely makes me shudder! One has a natural inclination to pass judgment on the whole village—what principles, if any, do they live by? Can they not distinguish right from wrong? In regard of Maria's behaviour, why did the Church not intervene? What had been the opinion of my predecessor, John Whitmore? After all, I have known of two women in Cambridge who were locked away for immoral behaviour, whose conduct was not of such a low degree. Why was Maria not held to account? Thus musing, I resolving to discover if Rector Walpole knew anything of the case. I approached his parish as the church bell tolled twelve o'clock. My timing was exact.

X

Rector Walpole's parish is certainly more prosperous than Polstead, and I must own to feeling immediately at ease. I lengthened my stride, approving the carefully tended cottages, which were much finer than those in my poor parish. Even on this cold day, the sun was making its presence known behind the snow-heavy clouds, and the scene twinkled pleasantly.

The Rectory itself is in a prominent position and, despite its plain outlook, is an elegant building, surrounded by a neat and simple garden boasting a gathering of early snowdrops and a row of winter cabbages. It was clear to me that a neat feminine hand had tended the plants, and placed the decorative wreath on the door. These touches are singularly missing in my own accommodation. I had previously assumed that Rector Walpole was unmarried, no wife having been mentioned in our brief correspondence.

After knocking at the door I heard quick steps within, and I was confronted by a woman in her middle years wearing a smart navy and white smock. She welcomed me with a simple smile, standing aside to let me pass. Momentarily confused, given my recent pondering on Rector Walpole's marital state, I was struck dumb until her request for my hat and coat gave me to understand that she was the housekeeper. What a contrast to the wretched Mrs Bright! Following her through the hall, I noticed how much more appealing his house was, and as we entered the morning room I could see that the personality of the Rector was firmly marked on the place, and even before I saw the man I had an impression of him. Books lay scattered around the lumpy crimson settle, and on the rug a pair of slippers lay where they had been discarded. The room was rich in colour, with an abundance of pictures crammed together on the walls. It seemed clean but was pleasantly untidy.

Rector Walpole came thudding down the stairs, whistling as he did so. He strode into the morning room and immediately stopped whistling, his mouth stretched into a wide smile. He greeted me most cheerily, taking my cold hand in both his own and wishing me a warm welcome. But he was old! Of course, I should have guessed this, but in my mind I pictured a younger man. He must be at least sixty-five, and yet his movements are quick.

Before I could even return his greeting he offered me a glass of constitutional claret, which was most agreeable after my cold walk. I am delighted to report that it was of excellent vintage.

I was directed to one of two deep-sided chairs, upon the other of which Rector Walpole seated himself. He invited me to call him Charles, despite the obvious difference in our ages. Once seated, I found I was enveloped in heavy damask, more relaxed than I have felt for weeks.

'So James, you did not come by horse on such a day as this? You must be fond of walking?'

'No, I cannot say I am. But I am even less fond of riding horseback, and my usual carrier is hard at work as a smithy today. In fact when I was a student in Cambridge I chose lodgings near to the lecture halls, and did not delight as others did in the exploration of Cambridgeshire.'

'Then we are of the same mind!'

As he said this he patted his ample stomach. Charles Walpole may be old, but his face reveals that he is happy with his lot in life. He is portly in a comfortable, pleasing way, suggesting a healthy appetite and generous larder. He has a pale complexion except for a circle of red on each cheek, and a similar one on the tip of his nose (no doubt an indication of his indulgence in fine wine.) Despite his years he has a mass of brown hair and a full beard to match, which he stroked as he talked, as others may stroke a cat or dog. He is a short man, and his trousers were too long in the leg, making him appear even stockier, but this rather added to his character. I concluded that he is a man who would intimidate no one and be liked by many.

He told me that he has been the Rector of Layham for some forty-three years, it being his first post, and he has never seen the need to move on. (The thought of remaining at Polstead for forty months, let alone years, makes me uneasy.) Despite this lack of ambition, Charles appears to retain great enthusiasm for his vocation. He was born in East Anglia and has no desire to travel further afield; his concerns are an orderly parish and he evidently gives no thought to personal importance. He prides himself on being a steady presence, and I suspect he is much loved by his parishioners.

As we became acquainted, the housemaid moved swiftly in and out of the room, placing bread and a large steaming pie on the far side of the table. My stomach groaned as I saw the risen crust. I had eaten nothing since breakfast.

I was pleased that we were to eat in this room, rather than retiring to what I assume would have been a formal dining room. It was warm in the morning room, and I felt thoroughly relaxed. Charles told his housemaid, as she placed a decanter of wine between the two settings, that she had done a splendid job. Then he turned to me and remarked that he felt himself truly blessed to have the best of all women care for him now that he was a widower. He declared that he was famished, and he was not mistaken in assuming that I must be also after the distance I had walked.

We moved to the table and took our places, Charles saying Grace before pouring two large glasses of deep burgundy wine and dishing out the chicken and ham pie. His enjoyment of the food was obvious as he tucked into the pie, chewing quickly whilst piling his fork. Between mouthfuls he urged me to tell of my religious training and suggested that an injection of new theological thought might be just be what the local area needs. He is under no illusions about his own influence, and is content to be an old-fashioned parson. He told me that he enjoys helping to further the ambition of others and I took this to mean that he will offer support in my endeavours to improve my situation.

'And did you enjoy your time in Cambridge?'

'Well, Charles, in truth my pleasure was adversely affected by the presence there of my elder brother Henry. We did not share lodgings but student circles are somewhat restricted, as you may recall, and my brother was known to be a charismatic fellow.'

'And you do not feel yourself to be so?'

'I confess to lacking that attribution. Henry was popular—and not just with his fellow students. Women became coy in his presence, and would watch him walk across a room with interested glances. Naturally, my vocation precluded any indulgence of female attention but for him, as a trainee physician...well, you may imagine.'

Charles laughed. 'And did you not have any female acquaintances yourself, James?'

'Indeed, no. Although a consequence of Henry's philandering was that women spurned by him would sometimes seek solace in my company. Perhaps I was the nearest they would get to Henry. I believe they regarded me as a bookish type of man who would not jeopardise either their reputations or their hearts.'

'So you did not relish this role as second fiddle?'

I smiled and shook my head, not speaking my remembrances of the woman who had intrigued me. Catherine was a small, slim creature and not exotic enough to secure any serious attention from Henry, but I liked her unassuming presence and found talking with her reassuring. I flatter myself that a time came when she saw me on my own merits, and she began to seek me out, often insisting on attention that I would not have willingly imposed upon her. Henry noticed her attentions and his ridicule, combined with her increasing forwardness, made me withdraw, and eventually she stopped frequenting the places were we had met. This was shortly before Henry became unwell, and the rapid progress of his illness resulted in us both leaving Cambridge: me for a short time, Henry forever.

I told Charles of Henry's untimely death and his merry face took on an unaccustomed solemnity. 'My dear boy, forgive me. I would not have taken the subject so lightly had I known. When did Our Lord take him?'

'He died last February. After the funeral I returned to complete my studies but was unable to shift the sense of heaviness which had settled on my shoulders in the proceeding months.' I thought of how I had only seen Catherine once more, and how terrible the meeting had been. After that I did not discover what became of her. It had been strange being back there alone. In some ways the removal of Henry's shadow was liberating. But also, the deceased are beyond reproach and my brother was frozen in time at twenty-seven, forever beautiful and bright. That is my own age now, and I feel neither.

'And how have your parents coped with their loss?'

I considered this, leaning back in my chair, 'My father has withdrawn into his private world, and my mother occupies herself with charitable work. But enough of this talk—it is making us melancholy.' I did not want to tell Charles of my mother's good deeds, afraid that his admiration would render me a hypocrite. If my mother put such energy into her own family things may be different now, and my father may be recovered.

Whilst helping himself to another ample portion of pie, Charles asked me how the people of Polstead were treating me. Perhaps I imagined it, but I think I detected in his smile an understanding of how rustic Suffolk people can be. Thawed by the fire, made unusually garrulous by his pleasant company and the free-flowing wine, I went on to recount the strange visits of Mrs Marten.

'Ah yes. Such a terrible business—Maria was a fine young woman.' He must have seen my surprise and continued 'Oh, I knew her when she was just a girl. She worked here for about six years, and started in my first year; she was seven years old and only a slip of a thing. But, my goodness, she was strong as a Suffolk Punch. As she got older she became a general housemaid to Iris—our housekeeper at the time—and the short distance allowed her to return home on Sundays.' He paused, selecting a piece of chicken from his plate, then added, 'Of course, my dear wife was alive then, and Faith—my daughter—not yet married, so the atmosphere was—how shall I put it?—more conducive to having a bright young girl growing into womanhood around. In fact, Faith—let me show you her sketch…' (He reached to the sideboard and handed me a sketch, 'She drew this self-portrait when she was seventeen.' The careful picture showed a disappointingly plain young woman, podgy faced like her father. And this, from her own hand.) 'Faith was most fond of Maria, and would hand down her dresses and other female accoutrements when she had finished with them. Oh yes, Maria soon developed a taste for the finer things in life, even then. But there was no malice in the child despite what some would have you believe. Mainly women, I think, who may have other reasons to be jealous.

Maria was very pretty and turned many heads.' I remembered May Humphries telling me of how she had taken up with several men, and her implicit suggestions about Maria's dubious virtue.

'Of course, her story may have reached a happy conclusion if she had just settled down and married. But she always aimed too high, choosing men above her station. Poor Maria! So pretty, but not the sort a man of standing marries. She was just thirteen when we let her go. My wife ascertained her—what shall I say—levity of behaviour even then. It seems that even at that tender age she was acting inappropriately with a young man in our employ. Such a situation is not seemly, particularly in a Rectory, although I did feel it a shame for Maria. My wife was well pleased with her work and she was a companion for Faith—Suffolk does not offer much society for the young, James, as you will discover. Still, there was nothing else to be done. And then her mother, Grace, passed away so it was best for everyone that she should return home to her father's cottage and care for her younger sister.'

A thought seemed to occur to Charles at this point and, after wiping his generous mouth with his napkin, he spoke again. 'About Maria's wantonness. You may think that we were neglectful to allow such a situation to arise when she was in our care, but I can assure you, the fair sex are very private over such things. I knew nothing of it until my wife, God rest her, told me. I think—although I never spoke with her on the subject—that Faith knew of her behaviour but then, young women will have their secrets, will they not? Faith was most upset to learn of Maria's death, and would have returned home to attend the funeral had she not just discovered that she herself was with child. She lives in Norfolk, so the distance was not insignificant. Mundesley. Do you know it?'

Of course I knew the town but, not wishing to dissuade him from his topic, shook my head. Charles fingered his moustache and continued, 'It's a fine town, if a little desolate, and it is near the Broads, which rather detracts from its charm. Faith married a naval officer—very well provided for, you know. But I digress. Can I interest you in another glass of claret?' I shook my head. I wanted to maintain my clarity now that he was talking about the Red Barn murder. I urged him to continue.

'Now, you asked about her stepmother. I can't say I know Ann Marten personally. She married Thomas Marten just after Maria stopped working for us, so I never had any occasion to make her acquaintance. I had met Thomas a few times and found him to be a most agreeable fellow. He was humble, in the best sense, if you understand me, and I have always found that to be a most endearing quality.

'But it was John Whitmore who recommended Maria to my household. He was obviously familiar with the whole family. Have you not asked him about the Marten family? What is it exactly that you wish to know? Surely the facts of poor Maria's murder are well enough documented?'

As I looked at the kindly man, I had a longing to ask for some advice, which I felt sure would be given without prejudice, unlike that offered by my own father. He had only either lectured or judged. This was, of course, before he succumbed to the silence that has immersed him ever since Henry's death. I felt that I could bare my soul to this man, that I could tell him of Mrs Marten's prophetic dreams, and even mention my unsettled reaction to Sarah's pretty face. But once spoken, such words cannot be unsaid. I did not trust my judgment after indulging in more glasses of wine than I am used to. I therefore fought back the urge to confide in him and kept my own counsel, as is my way.

When, four hours later, I rather reluctantly took my leave, the weather had turned very cold and snow was beginning to fall. I walked briskly back towards Polstead. On nearing the dark shadow of my own dwelling I confess to some resentment. I would have welcomed a prettier view or a lighter atmosphere or even a more cheerful person than the dour Mrs Bright to welcome me home.

Once inside, so inhospitable is its chilly interior that one's breath hangs on the air like smoke, I was greeted with total silence except the howling of the wind that gusts under doors and up the staircase. Still in my coat, I came here, to the library. I adjusted the paper on the desk and began to write the letter that occupied my thoughts on my return journey from Layham. For I feel the need to know more about the Red Barn murder than I do.

From James Coyte of the Rectory, Church Lane, Polstead.
To Rector John Whitmore, Long Marsh, Herne Bay, Kent.
10th February 1851

Sir,

I hope that this letter finds you well and that you are enjoying your retirement in the South East of England. I do not have the pleasure of knowing Kent myself, but understand it to be a most pleasing county and well suited for relaxation and good health. I trust that your wife is benefiting from the sea air, as you anticipated, and is recovering.

For myself, I am finding Polstead an interesting village, although I cannot claim to know my parishioners well, yet. I am trusting that this is because of their natural reserve and not, I hope, a reflection of any lack of interest on my part. There is a singular exception to this reticence, however, in the form of Mrs Ann Marten. She has requested some of my time in order that she might dwell on events of her past. Without wanting to disclose the nature of these conversations I must own to wishing that I knew more of the murder of Maria Marten, and believe you to be a reliable source of information about this. If I may, therefore, impose on your time and good nature, I would be most grateful if you would set down for me the facts of the case.

Yours in Gratitude, James Coyte, Reverend.

I sealed the letter and placed it on the silver tray, on the sideboard, to indicate its readiness for Mrs Bright to post tomorrow.

Sitting back, and aware once more of the numbness in my toes, I poured a small glass of Rector Whitmore's port. Knowing that the Church would provide me with lodgings, I have never bothered to acquire any but the most necessary of possessions and often feel myself a visitor in someone else's home. Perhaps I will invest in a few sticks of furniture to stamp my authority on this place, although I pray that I will not remain here for long. A feeling of disharmony with one's environment is unnerving. On an evening like this, alone in a place in which one does not feel at home, the merits of taking a wife are manifest. A woman like, for instance, Sarah Humphries, would certainly make time pass most pleasantly. Even Jesus sought female company in Mary Magdalene, and the Bible praises—indeed eulogises—the institution of marriage. Yet, was I so inclined to take on a wife, there are few suitable women in Polstead. Sarah herself is unfortunately already mated, and May Humphries' niece, Mary, although eminently suitable, is not to my taste.

As the room darkens around me I feel I have arrived at a destination only to discover that I had anticipated arriving elsewhere. As I replenish my glass I hear scurrying feet overhead, no doubt belonging to rats who believe the house to be empty. Perhaps I should read, rather than write in this journal, as introspection is causing me to feel maudlin but the standard texts of theology lining the three bookshelves, do not inspire. Perhaps this journal will be my gift to Polstead when I leave. I shall think of a title—The Memoirs of a Village Rector, starting with an Account of the Most Notorious Murder of Maria Marten. Or, perhaps, a more weighty text exploring the complexities of confession, as a means of delivering the soul from torment. Yes, I prefer that—more scientific, more substantial.

Father would approve my keen intellect, demonstrating knowledge of secular matters as well as the religious. Not that he has ever questioned my intelligence; he has never, however, given me quite the same encouragement that he bestowed on Henry. His opinion of the talents of his elder child was exalted, as were his hopes that Henry would become an eminent surgeon. My brother's untimely death has prevented him from discovering whether Henry was truly capable of fulfilling these expectations. I myself would never enlighten him of Henry's true nature, vouchsafed to me at Cambridge: his philandering, drinking and other pursuits I cannot in all decency describe. Henry rejected religion and I wonder how my father, whose faith is as steadfast as my own, would react if he knew that Henry died an atheist. If a man has no religion he has nothing, in my view.

But enough of this introspection. I will replenish my nib and turn to my bequest to this village. I will commence my self-appointed task to set down the account of a soul in torment about the Notorious Murder of Maria Marten. It will be my version, however. The James Version.

XI

Ann

Yes, Rector, I am recovered from yesterday—though the cold air does not suit me and I have been coughing a lot. I have a hurt in the space where my heart used to be, a shooting pain along my arm, under the thin skin, like I've been stabbed. I feel a weight across my chest like someone's pressing down on me, suffocating. But, in spite of these pains, almost daily now, I carry on about my normal business. And I wouldn't miss our meeting. It is too important to me.

I imagine you have some thoughts on what you heard yesterday from that gossip May, and I shall have to put you straight on some things. But I must confess that some of what she said is true. And of course I have already told you of my dreams. But let me tell you of what happened after the dreams, and how I got Thomas to dig in the Red Barn.

After my third dream, I told my husband that I knew Maria was dead. I told him to go to the Red Barn, and where to dig. My dream had become clearer and I had seen everything in shadow. May God strike me down if that is not the truth.

But Thomas had to be coaxed into going there. Being a man of this world and not afeared of the next, he put my dreaming down to morbid idle fancy. It was mid April when he finally gave in. I told him over his supper that the previous night I had dreamt for the third time of Maria and that she was in the Red Barn. I told him that this time I knew the exact location. He slapped his hand on the kitchen table and shouted at me. He would sometimes make much of putting me in my place, calling me gullible and even simple—though I am not. He is twenty-five years my elder and he would make something of it, when it suited. Happen he should have thought of that afore he wedded me.

Anyway, a woman learns ways to make a man listen, as you yourself will one day discover. So I said no more for a while, and began to wash the pots.

You have only met my husband a few times, at church, and if you hoped for a longer talk with him you would need to visit The Cock. Thomas is more there then at our home. He lives as he always has, being a man of simple tastes and habits. It may surprise you to know that he is literate and yet, despite being able to read—which not many can hereabouts—he is content to catch moles for a living. If you can call it that, for what he brought home barely fed the mouths around the table, when Maria, Anne and Little Tom were with us.

After we wed I pestered him to teach me to read and write, but he would have none of it. But, I do have some learning now, no thanks to him. Thomas was not ambitious for himself or his family, and was not even shamed by having a harlot for a daughter, which most decent men would be. Left to him, Maria's body would still be rotting in the Red Barn and William Corder would be living a free life with another woman. When I think of that I am glad I made Thomas look for her, though it was no easy task.

Maria had been gone for nearly a year—eleven months to be exact. Nobody missed her, because we thought she had left Polstead with Corder, that they were to be married in Ipswich and would return when the dust had settled. But, nearly a year had gone by with no news of her except what Corder told us when he came back here to mind the farm. Oh, and he gave me a few letters, but not in Maria's hand as he said she had hurt her wrist. And there was something else—I asked him once if he and Maria would be having any more children. You see, Rector, Maria had given birth just six weeks before she went missing—the poor baby boy didn't last, and didn't even get a Christian burial. When I asked Corder this it was September and I had not heard from Maria since May. As we thought they were married it was natural to ask him if she was with child yet. His reply was odd, and made goose bumps rise on my arms. I remember how he looked at me, bending forward, narrowing his blue eyes, and saying slowly, 'There will be no more children for her.' He looked at me in such a strange way, that it made me blush, and then tried to joke with me, his mouth pretending to be jovial as he said, 'She's had her lot, as far as that's concerned. She'll have to be content with Peter Matthew's bastard, since the two she bore of Corder blood didn't last.' I was struck dumb by his callousness. To refer to Tom as a bastard, when no sweeter child ever lived. And then to talk of poor Matilda, his brother's daughter, who died so young, and his own son who was not even named, so coldly made me flinch.

It was then that I started to suspect all was not as it should be, but I said nothing until after the dreams.

Even when I started to doubt Corder's innocence I could do nothing on my own so I kept quiet. For six long months I heard nothing from Corder, and then it was April and Maria had been gone nearly a year. I knew that I had to convince Thomas that Maria being missing for so long meant that she was dead.

When Thomas arrived home from his work that evening, tired and muddy as usual, I hung his jacket to dry before brushing the dirt off it. It was a warm night so I had not lit the fire. The top half of the stable door was ajar, letting in the evening sun. As usual he was half starved, and much pleased to hear that I had prepared some bacon, along with some fresh bread. I poured his drink and we sat up at the table. I had no appetite, so I just had a bit of bread with some of the cooking fat and a drop of small beer. Thomas was not minded to talk much so I told him how I had been remembering the day in September when I had met William Corder on the village green. I reminded him that it was now eleven months since Maria had left Polstead, and seven since last we'd seen Corder. My husband gave me a weary look, and I saw that now was the time to tell him. I took a deep breath; 'Last night I had another dream that our Maria was buried in the Red Barn.'

I remember how the evening sunshine threw light on his face Thomas looked towards the door, forcing him to close his eyes against the brightness. He sighed and asked, 'And what do you suppose I should do about it?' I looked at his lined face, his rheumy eyes and stooped posture. I felt he was not my husband at all, but another woman's, and I was just witnessing the painful scene. My voice was so steady and cold it seemed to come from another person entirely. It was this other person who told him to dig in the Red Barn.

He did not seem surprised at my suggestion, as I had asked twice before, after my previous dreams, and this time he nodded slowly, his eyes to the ground. We didn't talk further, but Thomas went to see William Pryke that night—he was Mrs Corder's bailiff, and had the keys to the Red Barn which was locked up that time of year, storing straw for the summer. They agreed to go to the Barn that coming Sunday.

The next Sunday was the 19th of April 1828. When we got back from church, Thomas removed his best shirt and put on his workday one. As he was doing this, in walked William Pryke. I greeted him but he barely acknowledged me. Instead, he turned to Thomas, saying something like, 'I'm not sure about this, Tom. It seems an odd thing to me.'

I knew that he was thinking on my dreams and maybe wondering if I was a witch, as some already said. I kept my eyes steady and looked at Thomas straight, so he knew he would have no peace if he changed his mind. He looked from me and back to Pryke, then handed him a mole spike—they're about a foot long, with a sharp, rounded end. He said that the sooner they started the sooner they'd finish, so they left me to my own thoughts and went off to the Red Barn.

I would not have wished to go with them, but hardly wanted to be alone either, given what I was sure they would find, so I went and sat outside on the doorstep watching Tom make mud pies with clay from the warm earth. He asked if I wanted to play too, but I smiled and said I was content to watch and could he make the biggest mud pile in Suffolk, did he think? He said that he would try, and dug his podgy hands into the earth. He was three and a half then, and getting bigger by the day. He never asked about his mother and I think I can say in all honesty that he didn't miss her. After all, I had always been more of a mother to him so her absence was no loss.

I waited for what seemed an eternity but was in truth just over an hour, and then I heard Thomas's footsteps, slower and heavier than usual. My whole body started to shiver. I heard him enter the cottage, and following behind were the steps of William Pryke. I remember turning to Pryke, feeling sick at his incessant chatter. He said he had gone into the Red Barn first, Thomas behind. This was only proper. There was a covering of straw on the ground and Pryke described how they had raked it away to find some great stones and loose soil right at the place where I'd told them to dig.

He stopped at this point and closed his eyes tight before opening them wide, 'Oh, Mrs Marten,' he wailed, 'I poked the end of me spike into the earth and felt it come up against something hard, yet soft also, if you get my meaning. And then I lifted it out of the straw and, God's honest truth, there was black flesh dripping off its end.'

He had looked at me, sort of pleading, as though I could give some reassurance. I will always remember that look. But I simply nodded my head, and sat down, pulling Tom onto my lap, putting his ear against my chest although he couldn't understand what was being said anyway. Pryke was shaking his head mournfully, his head cupped in his large open palms. He said how her flesh had all but rotted away, leaving just bones and shreds of her clothes. A spike had been put through her hip, pinning her to the earth.

I looked to my husband and saw with disgust that he was weeping. This was the second time I had seen a man cry and both times sickened me. His face was dirty from the digging, and the tears made lines down his pitted cheeks, like rain on a dirty window, and he was holding a red and white spotted kerchief tightly in his hand. I had forgotten about that kerchief, but now I remembered placing it around Maria's neck myself, and tying the knot at the soft place at her throat.

Thomas then told me, between sobs, that he had lunged his mole spade in the same place and the blade had hit against something solid. He had stabbed into his daughter's fleshless hipbone. He has never got this out of his mind. I think he felt as if he had murdered his own child, although she was beyond all pain by then. Tom, seeing his Grandpa crying, started to wail and went to him, climbing on his knee. The poor mite didn't know what to make of it all.

Pryke was repeating the same sentences over and over: 'What a terrible thing!' and 'Who would have thought?'

I would have thought. I could have said, but who would have believed me? Even Maria, with her high dreams and low ways, could not have dreamed of such a destiny. I knew it, though. I saw it the first moment I set eyes on my stepdaughter. She was ill fated, just as the gypsy had foretold. And now here was her father all silent and sorry. But he did nothing to stop her loose ways while she was still young enough to learn better, and now it was too late. 'Well,' I thought, 'let the shame be borne by those who allowed her to carry on as she did. Her death was inevitable. I do not blame her murderer as much as them who stood by and did nothing when she was growing.'

Both men were exhausted and the unseasonable heat had added to their toil. They sat slumped in their chairs, as though waiting for someone else to make sense of the situation, which must be me, as I knew what had to be done. I asked Pryke if he had locked the barn but he shook his head, so I took charge. 'You've got to go back and lock the door. Then go fetch Rector Whitmore, for he'll know what to do.' Pryke saw the sense in this and,quickly summoned his energy to do as I bid. I was left with Thomas, who had stopped shaking but his face was still wet with his tears, his cheek pressed against his grandson's neck. I told him to go back to the barn, to wait for Pryke and Whitmore. He should stand vigil over Maria 'til she was brought up.

XII

Rectory Journal
20th March 1851

As I sat this morning perusing the various files left by my predecessor, I heard the crunching of gravel and, looking up, saw Simon Stowe the blacksmith approaching. I stood in readiness, as we had agreed that he would today take me to Hadleigh from whence I will travel on to Woodbridge. Slung over his left shoulder was a brace of pheasants, held fast by his gloved hand, their necks swinging as he strode past the front entrance toward the back of the house. I went to the hall and listened to the dull murmur of voices from the kitchen. The exchange was brief and I only just got back to my desk before I heard him walking round to the front door where he rang the bell and waited for Mrs Bright to open it. What a charade. If my suspicion is correct, he was bringing birds he had poached to sell to her.

I collected my small bag and Whitmore's folder of files, which I had decided to take for the journey. Fortunately, there was no rain today as I joined Simon on the wagon and we began the reverse journey that we had taken almost three months ago. Simon sat slumped over the reins, his body huddled in his overlarge coat, and his head dropped forward into his hands. When he glanced at me I saw he was frowning, and that his eyes looked sore. I expected that we would continue our journey in silence, but as we left Polstead Simon spoke. 'I'll be pushing Bess today, Rector. I don't like to be away too long at present.'

I asked the obvious question. 'It's my boy. He's sick, see. Some may say it was my fault.' I asked what ailed his son. He had been injured when shoeing a horse, Simon explained, a heavy Suffolk Punch with an angry temperament. As the boy was trying to fasten a new shoe the horse kicked out and at the boy's chest. 'I fetched Doctor Badwell and he told us that Daniel's got some broke bones, and we're to see him rest so they can mend. But the skin was cut good and proper, so we've got to keep that dry and bound. Rachel's out of her mind with worry—I told her I'd be as quick as I could.'

He whipped his horse, and we cantered down the narrow lanes overhung with elms, and swiftly made our way.

Once at Hadleigh I boarded the stagecoach and took out Rector Whitmore's folder. It was thin, with no writing on the cover indicating a subject. I opened it, my fingers leaving marks in the dust. The first item was a cutting from a newspaper, browned with age and creased down the middle. In the top right hand corner was written, in faded hand:

Sunday Times, April 27th 1828.
The village is an exceedingly obscure one, and does not contain more than from 20 to 30 houses. The residence of the prisoner's mother (Mrs Corder) is, perhaps, the best building in the place.

The wheels went over something in the road, causing a jarring in the carriage and I looked up. The driver cursed, but soon steadied us, and I returned to my place, drinking in the description:

The barn where the body was deposited, and where it is the opinion the murder was committed, lies about half a mile to the left of the village. With the exception of two small cottages (one of the Marten's) distant about 100 yards, there are no buildings for a quarter of a mile around.

Carefully lifting the article I saw another piece of paper, folded in three. It was a letter on a headed sheet, written in large dark ink, only slightly faded.

West Suffolk Hospital, Bury St Edmunds
20th April 1842

Dear Rector Whitmore,

In response to your recent enquiry regarding the skeleton of William Corder, murderer. I can confirm that the skeleton (minus its head) is currently used to educate and instruct nurses training at the hospital. It is therefore not possible to assent to your request to return it to Polstead in order that you may perform a Christian burial. I understand that this will disappoint you, but the skeleton was entrusted to us following the execution and we are legally at liberty to keep it in our possession.

Yours Faithfully, Robert Hurst (MD)

I re-read the letter. It was nearly ten years old. Turning to the flat landscape, I wondered where the skeleton was now. I was listening to hooves on stone, thinking of William Corder's headless corpse. When I felt calmer, I returned to the folder on my lap and looked at the next article, a section torn from a newspaper, which read;

From the hour when his fate was pronounced, the confidence which Corder had exhibited previous to, and during the trial, forsook him. Tremblingly he was led from the bar to his cell, when, stretching himself on a table, he was observed to groan deeply. Since his trial he has shown little of that apathy and levity, which before he had so markedly done. Before the trial he had buoyed himself up with unfounded hopes of an acquittal, and such was the confidence of

such an event taking place, that preparation was actually made
for him when that time should arrive. Corder, prior to his leaving
the gaol to the scaffold, developed his guilt to the fullest extent; he
acknowledged that he committed the murder, that he shot her with
a pistol, that she died instantly; but to the last he denied having
stabbed her with the sword as imagined.

By the time I arrived at Woodbridge it was dusk and I had a headache. My eyes hurt, and the loss of daylight was a welcome relief. Standing off the platform, I felt the queasy sensation that I was still in motion despite my stationary feet. A hand on my shoulder grounded me—with his other hand Peter gripped mine, 'Welcome, my friend! And how was your journey?' His enthusiasm ebbed as I explained that my head was aching and that I felt I should lie down, but he assured me that he had just the thing to sort that out. 'But first, James, we should eat. There's a coaching inn just across the way.'

Peter looked tired, his friendly face dulled by dark circles under his usually bright eyes. After exchanging the usual pleasantries Peter wasted no time in asking about Mrs Marten, and as I spoke he leaned forward to catch every word above the din, 'I think she's unstable. When she described her dreams to me she spoke of blood running down the walls and a man in shadow stabbing a young woman. It was all so morbid. She's also told me of a time, when she was young, that she stoned a fawn to death.'

Peter nodded, speaking quickly 'She sounds like she's suffering from hysteria. It preys on females of delicate conditions, and can be triggered by loss or grief. I shall show you some examples tomorrow at the asylum.'

When we had each digested a bowl of broth and a huffer, we left The Crown, and then Peter took me to his lodgings, where his landlady had made up a small room for me. She had retired before we arrived, but a candle was left burning in the front room. I looked around the dim surroundings, taking in the outlines of a table and two chairs, and Peter directed me to one asking in a soft voice, 'Has your headache gone yet?' When I shook my head he disappeared, returning with a glass vial. Sitting at the table he carefully filled the dropper, depositing a tear into each thimble of milk which he had readied. The clear liquid melted into the white. It looked like a child's drink. 'It's laudanum, James. Marvellous for treating headaches, insomnia…all kind of ailments. We have a plentiful supply at the asylum, and use it on most of the patients. It's a remarkable remedy.' I copied Peter in downing my milk in one gulp, tasting the medicinal edge to the drink. Peter smiled, 'Your headache will be gone in no time.'

After we bade each other goodnight I found myself in a small box room. To my pleasant relief not only had my headache abated but I felt deliciously relaxed and warmed. Thus composed, I slept well—far better than usual, and woke with a clear head when the watery light penetrated the thin curtains.

The journey was just three miles and we embarked on the walk in companionable silence, contemplating our own thoughts as we entered the wooded hill, which precursed our destination. Suddenly, upon emerging from the wood, I saw it below us in the valley. My heart leapt in my chest—there stood the asylum. It was a Georgian building, with huge barred windows and massive red-bricked walls. The gradient of the hill enforced a swift descent and we were soon stood outside the main entrance. Here Peter stopped and allowed me a moment to survey the surrounding scene. In the stillness I could hear screams and a cracking noise, like a whip, echoing around the buildings.

On seeing my face he nodded sagely, 'Some of the wardens are not as enlightened as we, and Dr Kirkman prefers not to chastise them for their brutality.'

He took the heavy ring of keys from his pocket, and I saw that they were attached by a chain around his waist. It dawned on me then that his patients were also prisoners. The door was massive and heavy, and once open I realised how effective it was as a sound barrier. Once inside there was a persistent sound of moaning, which was coming from both directions. We turned right, and walked towards the dreadful chorus like doomed sailors following the Siren's calls. The corridor was dark, the windows high and barred, our feet echoing our progress as we walked to the next door.

Another key was selected from the ring, Peter pausing to look grimly my way, 'This is the women's ward.'

As the door opened I felt like I was being led into the seventh circle of Hell. It was not the sound, although that was terrible, but the smell. The smell was of soiled garments, the stench of sewage. The room was long and each side held twenty or so low cots, most with a huddled figure rocking beneath bedclothes or laying asleep on the bed. Some of the huddled figures were silent but most moved slowly to the chorus of a moan, the sound of wounded animals. My eyes took in the grey of the blankets, the black iron of the beds and the dirty white of the long nightshirts worn by the many women. Most did not even look up as the door opened, their hopelessness too complete to care.

I felt Peter tense beside me and to my surprise saw that his characteristic smile was gone. He leant to me but did not whisper, as if the women had lost the ability to hear along with their sanity, 'We must not be friendly. It creates over-dependence, and jeopardises the treatment. The women must be treated fairly but firmly.' Like children I thought, but did not say. I could see that some of the women were little more than girls, but most were older and it was strange to see their loose hair, unwashed and uncombed, lying tousled on the beds. None of the women had their hair pinned up, and the effect along with the nightdresses was unsettling—they were and were not like children. Some of these women would be wives and mothers, and here they lay, with bare legs and ankles on display, their shifts gaping at the neck and their bodies loose, without the structure of a corset or dress. For an unmarried man the sight was strange and terrible.

Halfway down the corridor I saw a quick movement to the side, and was shocked by one woman who flung herself in front of me, her bare arms gripping my knees and her head pressed to my thigh.

'Oh, oh, oh,' she repeated. I recoiled, trying to free my leg, as Peter knelt down beside the woman, speaking firmly.

'No, Maisie. Back to bed now. Let go!' But she was not listening, and held tighter to my leg, shaking her head, a senseless stream of words coming out which I could not comprehend bar the odd word—she was saying sorry to someone, but I could not decipher who and was more concerned with being released.

I had not previously noticed any staff around, but in response to Maisie's outburst two wardens ran forward from the corner were they had been talking. One stood as if to stop any other patient becoming involved, while the other pushed Peter aside and with her brawny grip, grabbed Maisie from behind and bended her over. The other matron then grabbed her head roughly, sausage-like fingers pulling on the unfortunate woman's hair.

'It's the cold room for you!' she shouted, smiling maliciously at her colleague as Maisie began screaming, trying to free herself from the iron grip of the two burly women.

'No, please. Please, Sir.' She was begging for help from Peter, from me, but we just stood and watched her being man handled down the corridor. And then I noticed that the moaning had stopped, and that all the women were laying still, listening and watching Maisie be led away. We could hear her screams until the door slammed shut behind them. Later Peter told me that Maisie had been admitted after procuring an abortion. The man who made her pregnant was a gentleman, and abandoned her when he discovered she was with child, but on hearing she had been to a local witch and had it removed he informed the authorities. The tale made my soul quake in remembrance.

My visit was brief, but included an audience with the Medical Superintendent, Dr Kirkman, whose office was paneled oak and very dark. The main piece of furniture in the room was a massive oak desk, behind which Dr Kirkman sat. Even seated it was apparent that he was a small man, and most of his face was obscured by a bushy grey beard. His hand, when offered in welcome, was small as a woman's. No sooner had we been introduced than he launched into his enquiry.

'So, Rector Coyte, Peter here tells me that you have a special interest in the female malady, hysteria.'

I looked at Peter, who nodded in agreement, and began to explain, 'James, I took the liberty of advising Dr Kirkman that you are ministering to the troubled mind of Mrs Ann Marten...'

His speech was halted by an interjection from his superior, whose diminutive form belied his commanding presence. He came forward, and what he lacked in stature he made up for in the sheer weight of his personality. He confidently placed a hand on my arm and guided me to a chair.

'So tell me about the case. You need not bother with background—I have been in East Anglia all my life and was a boy when William Corder was hanged for the murder of Maria Marten. And you are giving comfort to the unfortunate girl's mother?'

I glanced at Peter, who was perched on the desk, keen interest lighting his face. Dr Kirkman settled himself in his chair by an overloaded bookshelf, lit a pipe and commenced dragging on it luxuriantly. This was why I had come—I began to share my story.

'Well, Dr Kirkman, Mrs Marten is now in her fifty fifth year. She is a sick woman, and believes that she will meet Saint Peter at the gates of Heaven before the year is out. Although I have little experience, I understand that those near death wish spiritual guidance and a cleansing of the soul. This is to be expected. But it is the content of our sessions that is disturbing me.'

The Medical Superintendent leant towards me, his sharp eyes fixed on mine. 'How so? Please do not be afraid to be specific—we hear most things here.'

Judging from the scenes of mental torment that I had seen on my tour I did not doubt the assertion. I repeated Mrs Marten's story about the discovery of her daughter-in-law's body and the fact that it was her dreams eleven months after the murder that had sent William Corder to the gallows.

Dr Kirkman listened and nodded. I spoke of our meetings, of Mrs Marten's wish that I write everything down. Finally we sat in silence until he said, 'I hope you have enjoyed your visit, Rector. It has been a pleasure to meet you.' To my disappointment he stood, looked at his fob watch, and began to leave the room. My surprise must have been evident. Halfway to the door he turned, took his pipe from his mouth and eyeing me beadily he asked his protégé, 'Well, Peter. What is your diagnosis?'

Peter looked up like a delighted puppy, 'Hysteria, I should say. I have spoken with James about cathartic intervention, so I think his meetings will serve…'

It was pitiful to see my friend so eager in receiving approval from his arrogant mentor, who was laughing softly whilst re-lighting his pipe. He held it aloft, dramatically timing the degradation, 'Dear boy, have you learnt so little? The woman described is not hysterical. She is not mad. Her dreams are the sign of a guilty mind, her visions a form of wish fulfilment. It is evident to me that she wanted her step-daughter dead.'

And with that he was gone.

XIII

Rectory Journal
25th March 1851

And so, returned from my visit to Woodbridge, I approached my meeting with Mrs Marten today as a Doctor would approach a patient. I was firm and clear, I welcomed her but assessed her with a clinical eye. Henceforth, I shall make her an object of study as I wish to understand more of her story, and her motivations.

Snow had settled on the window ledge, and the Gospel Oak balanced white flakes on the milky air. For an ailing woman it must have been a hard walk to the Rectory. When she appeared on the path she was indeed walking slowly, and snow was balled around the hem of her skirt. The world looked empty and clean, all white except for her dark figure approaching.

Mrs Bright took her cloak and put a mat in front of the chair for the snow to melt cleanly. The fire cackled up the chimney, and we sat in our usual places. I could hear her stifled breathing as I dipped my quill, laying paper on a small table by my chair. When I looked up I saw that Mrs Marten was staring at the phrenology skull; she often sneaks looks at it when she thinks I am not watching.

I thought about what Dr Kirkman would say if he saw her now. If he is correct, that she is not mad or hysterical but sane, then how is it that her thoughts are so disturbed? And how did her dream of Maria's murder come to be so true? What force was at work upon her then? Is she so haunted by the past because, as the Doctor said, she wanted her stepdaughter dead? I am also beginning to suspect that William Corder may have been more to her than she has thus far revealed

I must be careful, though. I must be mindful of her fragility, although my mouth was wet with appetite for more news of Maria, whom I am coming to see as a woman like one I have known before. But I must be patient; and so I listened.

Ann

I did not tell my husband that I was coming here today. He has no interest in my comings and goings, so long as food is on the table and there is ale in the larder. Eating and supping are his occupations, and between these he spends his days catching the moles that hang in the cottage all year. I have grown accustomed to having them indoors, which is on account of poachers. A farmer will pay well enough to be rid of the little pests, which ruin crops with their burrowing, and everyone knows that a poorly paid molecatcher is a curse on the land, as who could prove it if new mole runs appeared on a certain farmer's fields just after he refused to pay the catcher? One good thing about this cold weather is that they don't stink. It's hellish in summer, when the heat rots them. It used to turn my stomach, but you get used to anything with time.

Thomas lives his life and I mine, and if we come together to share a bit of pig and potatoes, then all well and good, but we have no more to say to each other. So he doesn't know that I have been coming here, to speak with you about secret things. He doesn't know that I have started to dream about Maria and the Red Barn again and, most of all, of William hanging from the gallows.

In my dream he has his eyes open, and they are staring straight at me, as if I am the one who tied the noose around his neck. There was such a crowd to watch him hang. People came from miles to see his body jerk on the end of the rope, and to cheer. When his weight fell his neck didn't break like it should, and he had a long strangled death. There was a smell of fear; I was stood near the front and had to cover my face. But in my dreams I do not look away. In my dreams I have been there again many times.

But I was telling you about Thomas, and I should not complain. My marriage has not been too hard; he has not been too cruel or too cold toward me. He had his needs in the beginning, which I bore out of duty, but he stopped bothering me years ago now. We live together in silence, which is not unfriendly, and rub along well enough. Our wedlock has not been what I dreamed of but then life is like that and it wasn't a bad thing to learn that lesson young.

Before I married I thought mole catching was a trade like any other. Just a way to make a living, the same as a smithy or a baker. I know now that this was wrong. The Trade makes men different, or maybe different men join the Trade, and it is a singular, solitary life. When Maria was still alive he would walk for miles, although he doesn't go so far nowadays. He would trek around the edges of fields and woods, right out to the far corner of Corder's land, as it was Mr John Corder who employed him, William's father, and the farmland stretched out for miles. Out Thomas would go with his walking stick, pressing the earth before him, looking for the main run of those black velvet creatures that paid for the roof over our heads. He would set his traps up either end of their main run, and keep to the same route, checking for caught prey and setting new snares.

Whereas other men worked the land in gangs, or had the company of an apprentice, Thomas worked alone as he plodded his path, picking the dead vermin from the traps, then bringing them home to skin and sell at Bury. We would journey once a month there, to a warehouse that used to buy the scrubbed skins to make into smart waistcoats and jackets for Gentlemen, or else into gloves for Ladies. At the warehouse they were stained, not just black but white, red or a delicate cream. Unnatural colours to make the rodents more appealing. I liked the white ones best, as I have always wanted spotless hands. I suppose it comes from working, and having red knuckles, scarred from boiling water and rough from hard toil. Also, I have a scar across my wrist, which is unsightly, and I keep it covered up when I can. A knife slipped and cut me once, and the scar has never disappeared as it should.

I don't know if you've been to Bury, Rector? I used to like the trip there to sell the skins, and I was sorry when the factory closed down, but it had to as moleskin went out of style, and there was hardly any call for it anymore. Still, the railway men like the toughness of moleskin trousers and Thomas himself has a moleskin waistcoat, which has lasted years without even a hole. The pelts of the moles are tough as nails, as well I know from cutting their innards out, as you need a sharp knife and a strong elbow to get through. Of course it takes a lot of moles to make just one glove, so we often had a whole line strung across the cottage, from under a pail on the top shelf of the larder right across to the door handle at the entrance. You get into the habit of ducking as you walk around, except for Little Tom of course, who would just walk under the stubby tails of the black animals. I should think he's taller than any of us now, but I don't know for sure. It's been six years since I last saw him, and I doubt I'll ever see him in this world again.

I think that the solitary nature of the work may have turned Thomas's mind inwards, as he never had much need of talk or society, which was fine for him but no pleasure for a young wife. I was lonely in the early days, before I hardened to it, and I suppose that Maria was some comfort, being a closer age to me than her younger sister Anne was, and she at least had colourful stories to tell. We lived together, but her life was so different from mine, as Thomas let his daughter carry on in a way that he would never have stood for in a wife.

She was eighteen when she took up with Thomas Corder and he was taken in by Maria's ways for a time. He was her first conquest, and she would have married him if he'd have had her. She was nineteen when she felt pregnant, and by the time the baby was born Thomas Corder had already tired of Maria.

She went into labour early and her father went to fetch old Ma Garner who lived at the corner cottage, as she was midwife to women in their confinements, and knew all the tricks. (She also got rid of some babies before their time if paid enough, but often the girl died, so she didn't get much business that way.) When she arrived Ma Garner took control, and I was glad, as I had never seen a child born. Mother would not have me in the room when she birthed my brothers, so I had no teaching on childbirth.

Ma Garner took it in turns with me to walk Maria up and down the room, only a short walk but it took long enough what with the groaning. When the pains came she breathed in deep, like she was sucking her teeth, and she looked grey. We had a bowl, and water with rags. Maria started to be sick and Ma said this was a good sign; as well she might for she didn't have to clean it up! The pains came quicker after that and then Maria went a bit mad, cursing the Corder family and swearing like an old sailor. She said some cruel things to me too, about me being barren, and that she wished it was me in agony. Ma told me that this was to be expected, and not to set any store by what was said, but some things cut deep and I didn't forget her cruelty. Then, she went quiet and Ma said, 'Get the stool', which I quickly did, and Maria squatted over it. I could not see much on account of Maria's long skirt, but Ma had her hands ready and caught the slippery babe as it slid out.

She birthed a baby girl, whom she named Matilda, but she died when she had been just three months in this world. Rector Whitmore buried her in September 1822—her grave's marked by a little cross, though I shouldn't think anyone tends it since both Thomas Corder and Maria are dead. You heard about him drowning in the pond, on his birthday? There's certainly a lot of ill luck around Polstead.

Anyway, after Thomas Corder, Maria took up with Mr Matthews. We all knew of it, as her bed wasn't slept in on many occasions, and she'd come home with bags of fine ribbon brought all the way from Ipswich, where she told us they'd dined in a good hotel. I knew they'd done more than drink there, as she always came home freshly bathed and smelling of good soap. Sometimes she'd steal the cake of soap from the hotel. I know, as I'd smell it on her for weeks later, after she'd washed, although she was careful to never let me see as I might have called it thievery or else asked to try some. Not that I had need of fine soap, for I didn't have a gentleman to call on me!

Mr Peter Matthews was a Gentleman, and as such he didn't do any work but just swanned around pleasing himself all day. His cousin lived at the Old Hall, so he often visited, although his home was in London. He had a fine grey horse and we got accustomed to seeing him ride past, doffing his cap at us in a most friendly manner, but other than that I had nothing to do with him. He was brightly dressed; all trussed up like a peacock. I have never much cared to see a man dressed in scarlet and purple—it gives me indigestion. He was handsome enough, though, with unusual yellow hair, like a girl's. Little Tom was blessed in looking like his father, rather than taking his mother's dark looks. But I'm galloping ahead again. You may wonder why a gent like Mr Matthews should take up with a common slut like Maria, but I suggest you use your imagination. At first I was worried about the scandal it would bring on our family name and I would say to Thomas, 'Do you think it wise to let Maria carry on like this? Yesterday at the shop I heard May Humphries talking and she said unkind things.'

But Thomas would reply, 'Mrs Humphries should mind her own business. Leave the girl be, Ann, she's all right I tell you!' I would try to say that maybe he should speak with Maria about it, but Thomas would scoff, 'She is full-grown and has a clever head on her shoulders. She knows her own mind!'

On that point he was right enough, for never has a girl known her mind better than that one, even if it was her undoing. Anyway, before long her belly started to swell and I heard her being sick in the privy shed. But was she put out? Not on your life! Even while she was still pale from sickness she had this secret smile, like she knew something we didn't, and I reckon she thought Mr Matthews would marry her. I'm not saying she got pregnant on purpose, but she sure as Hell wasn't concerned that a little one was in her belly! She soon came to her senses though.

As the baby inside her grew, Mr Matthews called on her less, though he still sent her presents, as he was a generous man. She soon realised that he would not marry her, but he wouldn't see her starve, and promised her money. So, she came back from London and Ipswich and stayed under our roof. Another mouth to feed and a baby on the way that was not mine but my stepdaughter's. Some in the village were brazen enough to ask, 'Any news for yourself, Ann? 'Tis a pity that the girl should fall so easy when she's not married, and you remain barren.'

As you know, Rector, in some families a mother would pass off her daughter's baby as her own to avoid scandal, and maybe that would have been for the best, but I still hoped to have my own child. Maria didn't care about gossip, so the whole village knew the truth about her. She wasn't even concerned that Peter Matthews wouldn't marry her, as he promised to give her five pounds every quarter for the baby, whether it was a boy or girl, and that was as much as she could earn working in the fields, so she was happy. Course, there were no more trips to Ipswich and she stopped smelling of fancy soap, but she gave herself licence to lie around the house all day and never thought to earn her keep now that she had money. So I scrubbed and baked and sluiced and skivvied while she sat rubbing her stretched stomach and dreaming of a better life.

The child came late, despite Maria's impatience. It was nearly Christmas in 1824 when her waters broke, but this labour was quicker. It was a boy! Ma Garner handed him to me so that she could attend to Maria. I looked in his face, and he squinted back, seeing me even before his own mother. I loved him in the instant, as I always have, and wished he were mine.

Maria was too tired to want to hold the babe, so I took him down to Thomas who was stood by the unlit fire waiting for news. I couldn't speak, I was too overcome, but Thomas looked at the baby and smiled, breaking my heart as I knew that he was thinking how he wanted a son of his own. The boy stayed in with us that night, as he did for a long while after, as Maria needed rest. I would take him to her when he needed a feed, but I did everything else for him. He was called Thomas Henry, after his Grandpa but we always called him Tom.

After Peter Matthews finished with her he didn't come to Polstead much and kept to his own home in London, or so the notes would say which accompanied the money for Tom. So, Maria had her eyes open for another match. Now William Corder, he was not for everyday use. I doubt that he knew how to wax his own shoes! Maybe that made him seem more handsome than he was. And William Corder was Maria's third lover.

It's a strange thing, but Maria having her eye on William made him seem more comely to me, though I don't know why that should be. Anyway, he seemed an exotic creature, and could have been my downfall if I was not blessed with such a sharp brain. And I was certainly his downfall, wasn't I?

*

Mrs Marten put her hand to her chest, as if in pain, and stopped talking. I looked at the clock on the mantelpiece and saw that two hours had passed. I had not noticed the time, too busy with recording her tale in this journal. My head was aching with questions, but I can see that she was exhausted. Her eyes drooped, and she looked pale.

'Mrs Marten, next time we meet I must come to you. It is only proper.' I meant because she is ill, but did not say it. Instead I blamed the weather.

I saw her to the door and, watching her footprints cross the snowy path, I felt the cold air bracing my face, bringing relief from the headache which was descending. As I stood on the gravel, taking deep icy breaths, I felt watching eyes on me and, turning, saw Mrs Bright looking out from the top window, her face pinched and her mouth snapped tight. She was watching Mrs Marten leave with undistilled hatred on her face.

XIV

It is the fate of all those who are new to their tasks to be subject to the instruction of their superiors, and I am evidently no exception. As today is the final Sunday in March it is an important day in the Religious calendar, being Mothering Sunday, but there was an extra significance today, as a religious census was also taking place. As Rector I was tasked with counting and registering the congregation at St Mary's. No doubt influenced by this fact, my superior—the Bishop at Bury St Edmunds—asked Rector Walpole to 'assist' me with the service here in Polstead. I was not pleased by this news as I had viewed today as something of a milestone, and see the Bishop's interference as rather undermining. What message does it send to my parishioners? I shall pause to pour a glass of water for my laudanum to ease my disquiet...

Now, to relay the events with composure. To his credit, Charles Walpole graciously told me prior to the service that I would act as his assistant. I was grateful to Charles that he allowed me even a minor part. I cannot be censured for baulking at being instructed by such an old fellow as Charles, surely? He is a good man, but hardly up to date with the latest teachings.

The one advantage of the Bishop meddling was that less preparation for the service was required from me. But I cannot help a feeling of indignation that on this, the most important Sunday since my arrival in Polstead, and when the church was unusually full, it was Charles, not I, taking the service. Most of Polstead attended, many of whom would otherwise still be in bed or propping up the bar in The Cock.

Before the service got underway, I surveyed the congregation from the top of the knave, half-hidden within the shadows, as they entered and found their places. St Mary's is an ancient building, as old as any other in the neighbourhood; its walls are dark flint, and built to sustain the blows of time. Within its dark embrace there is no colour, except from the stained glass windows. There are inscriptions on the windows for people who have bought eternal life by having their names etched on the glass.

Charles was standing by the altar, dressed in the same red surplice as myself, the same white collar at his throat, greeting the arrivals. Together we waited for them to settle. Many had already taken their seats in the pews but a small huddle of women stood by the entrance. Clearing my throat loudly, I indicated to the gathering that we were about to begin. Mrs Catchpole, who had been chopping away at the tuneless piano as people arrived, stopped abruptly. The sudden lack of noise silenced the group, which was bigger than usual, and included Simon's wife, Rachel, talking with the sour faced Mrs Bright. I saw them look to Sarah Humphries, who was sitting with her husband in a pew, thus revealing that she had been the topic of conversation.

On hearing the voice of Rector Walpole the small group sat down. He paused and the gathering hushed each other, turning up their faces to his welcoming smile. When his voice rose above the murmuring it was warm and even, and seemed to soothe the crowd instantly.

'We are gathered together on this special day when we give thanks for our mothers. Some of the single women normally amongst us, particularly those in domestic service, are not here today as according to tradition they have been given leave to visit their families with their master's blessing. My own cook, Janice, has returned to Lavenham for the day but I am glad to say that before leaving she was able to prepare an excellent simnel cake, rich in fruit and covered in marzipan. These cakes have for many years been eaten on Mothering Sunday, a tradition which I am glad to say persists.'

The audience laughed, looking to each other in acknowledgement and anticipation, no doubt thinking of the cake awaiting them at home.

'The gift a mother gives is life,' he told his audience, 'just as Mary gave life to Jesus, thus making God mortal. Today we give thanks and praise for this, for we are all of woman born.' I could see Sarah Humphries holding her struggling boy tight, telling him to be silent. I saw her yellow hair fall and touch his cheek as she looked down. Charles was talking of mothers whom I did not recognise, kind women full of love. My mother had love for only one child, and I have never felt her lips on my cheek.

'On Mothering Sunday, which occurs on the fourth Sunday in Lent, it is customary for children to give small presents to their mothers. When my daughter Faith was a girl, she would wake up early to collect violets to make a small posy to present to her mother in gratitude. For it is mothers who sustain and nurture children from the moment that they enter the world, just as Our Lady nurtured and sustained Our Lord, suffering with him as he died on the cross.' I could see the congregation had warmed to Charles; I saw that they liked his personal references to his family and his cook. For my tastes his style was provincial and cloying.

'Now, Mothering Sunday, or Mid Lent Sunday as it is also known, traditionally commemorates the banquet given by Joseph to his brethren which is the subject of our first lesson. The traditional Gospel reading is the Feeding of the Five Thousand.

Now you may well ask why it is that Mothering Sunday has two readings, neither of which mentions mothers or apparently makes any reference to mothering?'

My attention drifted again. I watched Sarah. Her son was now sat quietly, and I could see that he wore a fancy lace cape; the pair made a pretty picture. She was dressed in an ice blue shawl, which looked to be made of a fine thread, and had placed a matching blue shawl around her son. Her husband, the wool merchant, sat beside her. It is unusual to see Jeremiah Humphries in church, but then his mother boasts that he is away a lot on business. I saw how he looked to his wife, as if she was an angel come to earth. He looked at the fine shawl on her shoulders, brought back from some fashionable trading town. She looked up at him, her eye speaking a foreign language to me. She is without doubt a beautiful young woman. And Jeremiah is in her shade. He seems rough, and even his pressed shirt cannot take away the impression of a large, ungraceful figure with a stooped back. He has a large oval face with a stubbled beard and thick jaw. Because of his comparative wealth he may have been the best catch in Polstead but Sarah is worthy of a better man than a wool merchant. I felt almost sorry for him, as his clumsy reddened hand closed on her smooth white one. In a second she had pulled away, not seeing the sullen look on his face.

At that moment the congregation stood for a hymn. Some of those around were slow and slouched forward, leaning on the pew in front. I have discovered that the hymns that work the best are those well-known, loud ones, if they are to be sung rather than mumbled. The Polstead parishioners are a stubborn bunch and most will not even do the courtesy of miming when they choose not to sing. Likewise, they are not hampered by any desire to pretend interest if they deem a sermon boring. But I had to acknowledge that Charles had won their attention.

'And hence we return to the theme of mothers, for one of the symbols of the Church is that of the Virgin Mother. Salvation comes from God alone but, because we receive our faith through the teachings of the Church, the Church is our mother. Because she is our mother she is also our teacher in the faith. In Galatians it is said that 'Jerusalem which is above is free, which is the mother of us all' and 'Our Mother' is also described as the spotless spouse of the Lamb. It is she whom Christ loved and for whom he delivered himself up so that he might sanctify her. It is she whom he unites to himself by an unbreakable alliance, and whom he constantly nourishes and cherishes. In the name of the Father and of the Son and of the Holy Spirit.'

As everyone stood to leave, Mrs Marten kept to her pew. She could not struggle along with the mob and would no doubt wait until the church was empty. I joined Charles by the door, where we spoke and shook hands with the congregation. I am still uneasy about this part, it makes me nervous, and I find it a struggle to remember names and exchange pleasantries with these people. Still, the regulars approached with more familiarity, and this included May Humphries, with her husband lagging behind.

'A good sermon, Rector. Of course, I always think that Mother's Day marks the coming of spring, and that the hymns should match, don't you agree? Ah well, maybe next week. Sarah, come and speak with us, show me how Joshua looks in his handsome hat. Is he not the prettiest boy, Rector?'

I nodded a greeting to Sarah, who was holding Joshua close and smiling like the Virgin Mother herself. Pressed to her side, as if jealous of his own son, was Jeremiah Humphries. He offered me his hand and May crowed, 'And here is my son, Rector. This is Jeremiah. His business is at Lavenham, so it's not often he can attend our services. I have been so blessed, Rector, in my son. And in my new daughter, of course.' She patted her wet eye with the corner of her handkerchief, and Sarah twisted her mouth as if to stop from laughing. 'And see, Rector, what a fine shawl this soft wool makes. Why, Jeremiah always thinks to bring home something for Joshua, isn't that so, my dear? If ever you need the finest wool you must speak to my son, Rector, and he will give you the best price.' It is a shame to see a grown man blush like a boy. Jeremiah shuffled his feet, but still I saw he was flattered. I recognised the vanity I had often seen in Henry when our mother boasted of his talents.

By now, most of the villagers had left, but some were waiting for a few words so I wished Mrs Humphries a pleasant day and bade Sarah farewell, then went to speak with the rest of them

I saw Mrs Marten slowly rise from her pew. The church was now empty apart from Mrs Catchpole, who was putting on her coat. She did not have any music to carry, as her playing was by ear and she had never learnt to read the notes. Without a word she scurried off, leaving me alone with Ann Marten. I noticed how much colder the building seemed without anyone else in it, for despite what May Humphries had said about the arrival of spring, there was frost on the ground this morning. It was then that I saw something catch the light. Mrs Marten saw it at the same time, and she was closer. It was Sarah's blue silk shawl, fallen from where she had been, fluttering on the floor like a lost bird. I snatched it up and ran its length through my hands. I could smell juniper, and it was soft against my fingers. How could she lose such a fine thing and not know? I heard footsteps behind me and, expecting Sarah's husband, turned my head. It was Mrs Marten.

'What's that you've got there, Rector?' But she was smiling in a knowing way, smug with secret knowledge.

'It's a shawl belonging to Sarah Humphries. She must have forgotten it'

'Indeed. She must have.' She said it with irony, as if she thought something different, then held out her hand, with a crafty look in her eye. 'Give it to me, then. I shall see she gets it safely.'

As she stepped forward I pulled the scarf back greedily. I could not allow her to return the shawl to Sarah—she must not tire herself. I will return the pretty garment to Sarah myself. But I will wait until tomorrow, when she will be less busy.

As I stood amid the emptied pews I reflected on the day. I thought of Charles' sermon, of his devotion to the Church. Whilst I dislike the familiarity of his preaching, there was a moment as I listened to his gentle yet forceful tone when I saw my own faith reflected back at me and saw it was sullied; it is not pure. Although he is Rector with simple theology, Charles believes every word he speaks. I am ashamed to admit that a feeling like envy rose in my chest.

A thought gripped me; is this why the congregation seems distracted when I speak? But what nonsense! An intellectual cannot be expected to have the same depth of faith as a rural man. If the congregation fails to give me its full attention, this results from their lack of education, and if they were listening with more interest today, that is no surprise. I thought of Rector Whitmore, concluding he probably had a similar style, and they are more used to such Sermons.

It was clearer to me than ever what I must do in order to be accepted by these simple people, yet I was also clearer in my mind than ever that my deliverance from Polstead to a living in a more congenial location could not come soon enough. I must make my mark quickly. If not, I could be stuck in this backwater for some years yet and that terrified me. I felt the distant throbbing of my headache returning. And then, as if she had appeared from the shadows, was Mrs Marten, who I hope will be my means from this place to a better one. It will be in penning The James Version, and thereby allowing her soul to be eased of its burden, that the Bishop will be forced to recognise my worth.

And so, rather than bidding Mrs Marten a good day we resumed our seats in the empty church. Everyone else was with their families and children but us two outcasts sat together. She told me more of her story, easing her troubled spirit, and I listened and scribed, gathering words for my own salvation.

XV

Ann

It was the final Wednesday in July, 1826, and the heat was stifling. The Polstead Blacks are sweeter than ever at that time of year and people from the neighbouring villages were visiting to taste and buy some, as well as to share in the festivities of our yearly Cherry Fair. Do you know our Polstead Blacks, Rector? The fattest, sweetest cherries in all of England.

As usual I had entered two jams, one cherry and one apple, and was eager to see how I had fared in competition against other women. (There is a delicious pride to be found in winning, and I am known as a good cook.) I walked Maria and her sister to the stand, where I saw my jam, dark as blood and rich with the bittersweet taste of virgin fruit. Then I saw it—a yellow rosette! Puffed up with pleasure, my heart pounding, hands shaking, I reached for the card pinned to it and saw the number one in firm hand. I had won first place! I wanted to know what the judges had said about my jam and, as I could not read much then, I looked around for Thomas, who had wandered away. Maria saw me and sauntered over, lazily curling her dark hair around a finger. I saw that she was wearing a new bonnet, but chose to ignore this and instead of commenting on where she had got such a fine item, asked, 'Did you see where your father went, Maria?'

She shrugged, and then, seeing that an audience had gathered, a mischievous light appeared in her eye. 'Did you win, Ann? Let me see what your prize is!' I eagerly pushed the card into her outstretched hand and felt my cheeks warm as she read in a loud voice, 'First prize! For her excellent cherry jam Mrs. Marten has won… Oh Ann!'

And then a cruel look overtook her features, and her dark eyes narrowed. She started laughing, tears rolling down her face. I felt hot shame as Maria made an exhibition of me. I quietly ordered her to tell me what was on the card, then pleaded with her to be silent, but she would not. What with her carrying on and everyone looking, I felt tight around my chest and my head hurt, and so angry I could hardly speak. I slapped her, hard, across the face.

She stopped laughing instantly. A hurt, and then cruel, look overtook her dark features. 'If you were an educated lady,' she taunted, slowly and loudly, 'you could read it for yourself. You have won a stinking, bloody, rump of mutton!' At that she threw the card at my feet and turned on her heel, leaving the audience gaping at me for a reaction. Shamed and fuming, I snatched the card from the ground and scuttled quickly through the laughing crowds, in the opposite direction to Maria, my face burning. No prize is worth this, I thought, cursing Maria a thousand times.

There was one attraction at the fair getting more attention than any other. A white horse was tethered to a sycamore tree and nearby a Romany caravan stood unhitched. The wagon was brightly coloured with the flame of reddle or bulls blood, and also green, and I wondered how the gypsy had got such a bright colour. The wagon was small and rounded, like a massive beer barrel chopped in two, with an entrance at the far side, over which a sign showed a veiled gypsy, who I knew to be Hannah Fandango.

I had heard talk in the village that she would be coming to the fair. She was talked about a lot at that time, and I came to know more of her before the year was out.

She was reading fortunes inside the wagon, and I watched as Phoebe Stowe emerged, to be pounced on by a group of women who asked eagerly, 'What was it like?' and 'What did she say?' Phoebe was lost into the huddle of women, and I couldn't hear her answer and was loath to step forward. Still stewing from my fight with Maria I didn't want to talk with anyone, but was curious to hear what was said so I sat nearby under a large tree. I leant back into its shade and welcomed respite from the sun. As I waited I saw Mrs Mary Corder leave the wagon, and by the look on her face she was much aggrieved by what fortune had in store for her. She ignored the questions of the throng, pushing away the inquiring hands on her arm, saying, 'It was all stuff and nonsense,' and 'the Gypsy is a fake.' She would have done better to have that opinion before she entered the wagon and paid for the privilege!

But Mrs Corder was wasting her breath, as her protests did nothing to discourage the crowd, who seemed even hungrier to know the secrets of the Romany. Still, fear made them hang back and no one else entered the wagon until Maria arrived. When I saw her I shrank back into the shadow, but she didn't notice me and I rested in my hiding place, watching her from my hidden corner. Always a lover of attention, she declared to the crowd, 'I shall see what my fortune holds, and I will tell you all when I come out.'

Having gained the audience she always desired, Maria slowly climbed the three steps to the wagon, and then—like an actor on stage—pulled back the green curtains before being swallowed by the darkness. Several minutes passed, during which many in the crowd moved on. Curious to hear what fate had in store for my stepdaughter, I waited. Feeling the warmth of the day wearying me, I closed my eyes.

I must have nodded off as when I opened them the crowd had gone and all was still around the Romany wagon. The green curtain was open to show that the gypsy was free, so I had missed Maria. A sudden desire to enter the wagon and hear my fortune surprised me.

Lifting the green fabric, I peered into darkness. Rather than the gloom that I had expected, the room was very cosy, with lots of coloured scarves hanging across the ceiling and around the sides. From the entrance I took in Hannah Fandango sitting on the floor to my left. She did not look up. Her generous skirts covered her so completely that I couldn't tell if she was on a cushion or a stool. In front of her was a round object, which looked like a drum or some other such instrument and onto it she placed cards, face up, carefully creating a pattern. I had not moved from the threshold, and finally she spoke. Her voice was even, yet had a strange lilt, belonging to a different country. 'Please enter.' I look around to check it was me that she meant. I nearly turned and fled. Instead, I hitched my skirt up and clambered inside.

I felt big and clumsy in this neat wagon, and it took my eyes a moment to become accustomed to the darkness. The small, dark gypsy sat opposite me. Her skin was the colour of turned earth, and her eyes like jet. She was indeed beautiful and strange, her dark hair wrapped with a crimson scarf, and she wore a long sleeved pink dress, which gathered around her legs, and below the hem I could see a naked dark foot, with a silver ring on one toe. I had heard of Hannah as she had a small cottage just a mile from Polstead, but she was seldom there, and most of what I had heard was probably malicious gossip. I knew that Hannah's mother was from some far off land, and had dark skin. Her father was a sea Captain, and had money enough to send her to boarding school in London. But this was the first time I had actually seen her. I too sat on the floor and waited for what seemed like a long time. I told myself that others had been here and left smiling, choosing to forget Mrs Corder's angry, fearful words.

The strange woman, who was about Maria's age, placed cards into the shape of a cross in front of us. I steeled myself, thinking I had made a mistake in coming. Rector Whitmore always said such activities belonged to the devil and led to damnation. Nervously, I forced a smile but got none in return. Without looking up she took the middle card, showing a woman riding a horse. I was shocked to see the woman had no clothes on, though her hair was arranged to protect her modesty. Such immoral images on a pack of cards! Hannah took in my reaction with her inquisitive eyes and asked, 'Why have you come?'

Taken aback, I felt my face slacken as I searched for an answer, 'I saw others coming in. I thought it would be...interesting.' I heard my voice, as weak as water, trailing off. Though she must have seen my panic she repeated the question in the same deliberate tone, this time checking me with black, sparkling eyes. I frowned and held my voice as steady as I was able, answered honestly, 'I don't know.'

She did not press further and offered me a pile of brightly coloured cards. Well, I understood this part well enough as I had often played cards, so I felt relief as I jumbled the pictures up a few times and then placed the pack back in the woman's dark hand, surprised at how pink her palm was against my white one. She took the pack with such seriousness that it made me shiver, and then spread them like a lady's fan above the cross.

'Pick four,' she ordered, fierce as you like, and I did, taking the cards from different places in the fan and handing them back to her. She was so quick as she looked at the cards, placing one on each end of the cross's four points. Then, staring straight at me, she said, 'Who is the man?'

I blushed in shame, although God knows I had no reason, and I looked at my lap. 'Oh, he must be my husband, Thomas.' Why did I blush? She looked across at me, nodding slowly, as if she had heard more than I had said, and then her eyes bore straight into me.

'He is not who you seek.' Her voice was unnatural, foreign sounding.

I didn't know what to say to this, and then I saw that it wasn't a question anyway. As if I was a stupid child who was wearing her patience, she jabbed her finger at me and then pointed to the naked woman on the horse. 'She is the one. It is no man. You just imagine that he represents the answer, but he is the instrument, not the tool. Look.' She pointed at the second card I had picked, which had a picture of the sun, its rays shining down on a small hut. 'You want a home, but not the home you have. You do not see that it is in you and not in others. You see another as the problem or the solution but this is not so. There is grave danger for you if you do not see this. I see three bodies across your path. You can choose a different road, and find what you are looking for within. If not, blood will flow in the river and three times you will weep in grief.'

She regarded me with such a cold stare that I felt ashamed. I saw that she was waiting for a reply, but how could I answer when I didn't understand the question? It wasn't just that she was half foreign. I didn't understand the meaning. I felt desperate to leave, like I would scream if I stayed a second longer, so I asked her how much I should pay her, but she held up her hand, 'No money will cross hands between us.' I got the impression that she was not doing this out of kindness, and I couldn't bear to be with her any longer. I felt I had been suffocating and I gulped down the fresh air when I quit the confines of that caravan.

When I arrived back at the cottage Maria was already there. I could hear her singing upstairs. As the door banged shut, she stopped and called, 'Is that you, Ann?' Without waiting for a reply she jumped down the stairs and appeared in front of me, her dark eyes glinting with unpleasant mischief, 'Where's the mutton, then?' I turned away, placed my hat under the stairs, and told her that her father would pick it up tomorrow, but she wasn't listening anyway.

It was plain that she had something to tell me and I had barely finished speaking when she began to crow over her better news. 'Ann, I have been told great things. I went to a fortune teller and had my cards read! She knew so much about me, Ann, it was amazing. Anyway, I'm to meet a rich man and he will be my true love! She said that although I am not destined to live a long life, I would break three hearts. What do you think to that?'

I looked at her rosy cheeks and sparkling eyes and, remembering her taunts from earlier in the day, felt spite rise in my mouth like bile. 'What nonsense! And are you happy to be told you will be loved, even though you will die young? You may have some learning, but you haven't the sense to see when you've being duped. And how much did you pay to be told that? Give me half the amount and I'll say whatever you please. Silly girl!' Her crestfallen face made me feel guilty for just a moment until I saw how quickly she shrugged off what I had said and turned on her heel. Maria was not a girl to disbelieve anything that suited her. Oh no, she knew her own mind, that one. Still, I felt needled that she had tidings of a great love to come from the same charlatan who had scorned me. But that was afore I knew how our fortunes would turn, and how Hannah Fandango would signify for both of us.

XVI

From Reverend Whitmore, Herne Bay, Kent
To James Coyte, The Rectory, Polstead, Suffolk.
30th March 1851

Dear Rector Coyte,

I am writing after receiving your letter, which I must admit gave me cause for disquiet. As I advised you when we met, Polstead is a small, rural community and the people are of a different countenance from those you may be more familiar with.

Before I left my post, which—as I may have told you—I held for many years, I took the precaution of advising my parishioners that, although you are still young, and with much to learn, you are capable of making a valuable contribution to their spiritual health. (I hope, in this, I was not wrong). Although they will naturally feel the loss of a Rector who had served them for so many years, I felt sure that they will eventually withhold all prejudice and greet you with open hearts.

It is not always easy to succeed an established Rector, and I do not think I flatter myself in saying that I had a firm and respected influence on the village. My dear young man, with the best will in the world, these things take time! Indeed, time is one thing with which you are blessed, unlike myself, although I do fancy that the Kentish air is already adding to my expectancy of long life.

Now, James—if I may take the liberty of addressing you thus, aware as I am that you are of an age to still require some paternal guidance—to the more concerning matter of Ann Marten. I find myself pausing whilst writing, and I will choose my words with care, but please comprehend their meaning. The murder of Maria Marten was a tragic event in the life of the village. As you know, I was Rector at the time of the murder and was therefore familiar with all those concerned in the grisly tale, including the unfortunate victim and her headstrong lover, who acted so cruelly in taking her young life. In fact, I was the person brought to her when her body was first discovered by her father—not a pleasant sight, and one I strive to forget. You may wish that you are never called upon in similar circumstances.

Maria was not a regular presence in the church, and she was attracted too frequently to the corrupting influence of Ipswich and even London. You may be aware that she had three children out of wedlock, two of whom I baptised that their souls may be cleansed of her sin. Sadly, the daughter died when young but her son, Thomas Henry, grew to be a fine young man, if a little nervous. In my view the woman to whom you refer proved a most excellent surrogate mother to him, when his own was too fickle for the task. I have attempted to tell him the same, as he has taken against her in his manhood having got some foolish notion in his head that she in some way failed his mother. Never the less, Ann Marten is a reserved and respectable woman, without whom the murder may have gone undiscovered and the murderer untried.

I would advise you strongly against any rumours you may hear concerning her relationship with William Corder; this is just idle gossip and without foundation. Ann Marten is a married, God-fearing woman and Corder was a scoundrel. There, now have I made myself clear enough? Although I could say more, I am reluctant to vex my spirits further. I trust that you will desist from this curious and—if I may be so bold—morbid inquiry. It may be that I was too hasty in leaving you to your duties—I am considering a return to give more direct guidance. I shall write and say when to expect me.

I feel sure that you will soon settle into the gentler spirit of Polstead and, with God's help, perform adequate ministry to the simple souls that inhabit thereabouts. In this endeavour I intend to assist you, with wise advice and stern counsel.

You enquired as to my enjoyment of retirement, which I am coming to terms with, although idleness has never been something I subscribe to. But this move was necessary on account of my wife. Doctor Badwell had advised a change of air, although I am unable to discern any change in her temperament and fear that the Doctor underestimated the gravity of her condition, which is of a nervous nature and not swayed by the quality of the air. Added to this, is the nuisance of hiring a reliable housekeeper; I find that I cannot replace Mrs Bright and would have you pass on my regards to her.

Yours, John Whitmore MA

He cannot mean to visit me—the journey would be too long. What could make him wish to return? The idea is absurd and deeply unpleasant—I must dismiss it from my thoughts, lest it heralds another unwelcome headache. I sit writing this at the breakfast table, as I wish to catalogue my reaction to his letter. It is not my habit to write whilst eating but, in truth, the kipper which Mrs Bright set down in front of me was not appetising, so distraction was necessary. The fish gazed at me with its one visible eye, and I could only attempt to eat it after placing a napkin over the offending organ, like an executioner placing a bag over the condemned man, but even so I could only force a few mouthfuls. I did not ask for kippers, nor did Mrs Bright ask if I would wish to have such a smelly offering. I can still taste the brown flesh disintegrate in my mouth as I breathe in its smoky rancid smell.

When Mrs Bright brought in the letter she was holding it close, as if wishing to ask after the author, and I saw that she was reluctant to hand it over.

Her routine never varies, and I am in the habit of following its time constraints without question, just as I consume her almost inedible food.

At least I do not feel obliged to engage in polite conversation, which I would hate, and this is a blessing. I have never been at ease with petty topics and prefer weightier discussions, especially if accompanied by a glass of port. This may be why intimate relations with the fair sex have always eluded me. I have observed men with less to offer than I succeed in attracting women easily enough, but I do not know how to begin to engage their interest.

At Cambridge I often joined Henry punting down the River Cam with several ladies. With the exception of Catherine, I do not recall specific women, and my memory retains them as silvery forms against the water, with ubiquitous porcelain features and thin rainbow coloured dresses. I would take my place at the back of the punt, from where I watched them fawning over Henry, vying with each other for his attention. I saw, even if I did not totally comprehend, the draw he held for them, for he was animated and cordial, holding a bottle of champagne in one hand, gesticulating with the other as the punt approached a low bridge, laughingly pretending to be unaware that his boater would surely be knocked off, before ducking at the last minute and bowing to his rapt audience.

I struggled to find anything to say to these butterfly girls, who moved around daintily in clothes of silk and fine wool. To a man used to the fens and the unpromising women who lived there, such beauty was a revelation. They seemed unreal, and the only subjects I could speak of to them were bookish and secular (I have never considered the study of religion as an exploration into the mystical or spiritual, but as a practical understanding of the word of God.) Any conversation I initiated felt heavy and incongruent amid the effervescent atmosphere created by Henry and his harem.

There were serious girls amongst the group but they seemed to be the colour of fog compared to the bright creatures that swarmed to my brother like moths to a flame. The foggish women generally expressed an interest in academic study and lamented their exclusion from the halls of learning. These blue-stocking types considered themselves above the butterfly girls, who did not concern themselves with politics but occupied their time in pursuit of fun and frivolity and, eventually, a husband. This lesson into the minds of the fair sex taught me that there are two kinds of women, and that those whose personalities are most in opposition to my own are the ones whom I desire—in short, the butterflies.

The young women in Polstead further confirm my theory that women fall into two types. For example, take my impromptu meeting on the village green. The spinster Mary Teager, a pleasant and modest woman, has the same fog countenance as the bluestocking girls in Cambridge. How unfortunate for her that she is so outshone by her pretty cousin, Sarah, and how often it is that beautiful butterfly women have dowdy companions. One can only assume that this is charity on her part.

Sarah Humphries is indeed a pretty jewel and, having seen her husband about the village, I feel she could have done better. Her husband is respectable enough, and clearly loves her, but he is a bumbling fool with an indulgent mother. He has only attended one church service since my arrival, and that was on Mothering Sunday when even the village dog will make an appearance! Thus I have only spoken with him once, but I recognise the type. For such a man the acquisition of a pretty wife is like owning a fine piece of art; he cannot understand her, they are not on the same level. He may look up to her, but how lonely is the pedestal on which she sits? As a wool merchant I imagine that he has moderate wealth, which does at least go some way explain Sarah's choice, for he is a hardy character who could not be described as refined. Judging by his red face, any profits he makes are spent in the tavern. To a man like that, women are like horses or cattle, and yet it is always such men who have fine wives, holding their hands and looking so proud. If only the Bible was able to give the reason for that truth!

Although one must not speak ill of the dead, Henry would often treat women as accessories—this one for a trip to the theatre, that one for a night dancing, another still to introduce to our parents when they visited us. Whilst I scorn such treatment, the women, for their part, did not seem to mind that they only got one aspect of their lover. They were unconventional in their lack of desire to possess a man totally, content to enjoy what was offered, evidently sensing Henry to be a superior creature and grateful for the meagre offerings he gave them.

I doubt any woman would accept such treatment from me. For my sins, I am the marrying kind, the kind a woman may settle on in the assurance of security and comfort. Why has Sarah not chosen a reliable, intelligent husband but instead fallen for a clod-hopping wool merchant? Does she not know that the world offers many prizes, greater than the one she has chosen? She could have married someone more steady, who would always have been grateful for her benevolence and would have cherished her like a fine jewel, always knowing her worth and thanking God for the gift of such a rarity. But enough of this—I feel the return of my melancholia.

As I push my plate away I see Whitmore's letter again, and think hotly of his dismissive and patronising tone, implying that I am treading in deep waters by ministering to Mrs Marten. The man lacks the sense to see that I am attempting to salvage a lost soul in need of guidance, before her arrival at the gates of Heaven. And what is this of her relationship with William Corder? It is clear that she despises him for murdering Maria. Surely it would be unnatural not to, although the Bible does teach forgiveness. I must discover if she is at peace with her feelings for him. In any case, her visits to the Rectory are to continue and I feel that it would be of benefit to have an impartial source of information about the events that are unfolding in her narrative. After all, at her age, she cannot be considered a reliable witness. As Rector Whitmore is unwilling to oblige, I will have to seek my answers elsewhere, from a more forthcoming source. As to Ann Marten, well she will continue her story tomorrow when I visit her at her home.

XVII

Ann

So Rector, despite the teasing sun promising spring, winter hangs around. I am not well, and find it harder to get around as I used to. Thomas goes out most days, walking his route with Coops, his bad tempered terrier, poking the sandy earth to see if any traps have sprung. As usual he was already downstairs when I awoke today, and as soon as I heard the door bang shut, I pulled myself from the bed and put on my warmest dress which, rough though it is, has a comforting weight.

I am feeling my age today. When I came down this morning I moved carefully on the short but steep staircase, placing my hands against the rough damp wall for support. Pulling back the heavy curtain I tried to see this small room, as you must now see it. How fortunate you must think yourself, with your clean clothes and warm home. But that is your reward; the profits of your labour. I don't envy your task; to bring Polstead folk to the feet of God will require more effort than you may imagine, with your youth and smooth face. You are ambitious—anyone can see that. Your are always dressed with care and scented with sweet oils, a man who wants more from life than your current lot—I have met another like you before. And such ambition always leads to a fall, in my experience.

Are you cold? I could warm the stove, though I wouldn't normally put on the heat until Thomas is due. At least you can now see how I have suffered—you can imagine what it was like when Maria and her sister were here.

It is a long time since a young man has visited. I remember William Corder coming to court Maria, sitting in that same chair, leaning forward to warm himself by the fire. It seems like an age ago and yet it seems like yesterday. You are a bigger man than either William or Thomas.

I find words are coming to me easily today. I can speak freely. Perhaps that is because you have come here, where the memories are always near. Let me tell you some more of my tale. Let me tell you about Maria.

I never really knew Maria, which may seem like a strange thing for a stepmother to say, but she was a strange girl and, after all, not my own daughter. Our ages were not far apart so I didn't try to be a mother to her, although I always watched out for her as well as I was able.

I had heard of Maria even before I married Thomas. She had a bad reputation, even then. I had heard she was wilful and, although I've never liked loose talk, most gossip has truth at its heart.

At seventeen I took on the duties of both wife and mother and I'm not sure I had the stomach for the job, though none could say I didn't care for Maria and her sister, Anne, as best as I could. Before the wedding I didn't think that it would be such a task. I had bigger fish to fry, you might say, with a new husband to look after and I didn't think beyond that, at the time. Maria was just twelve then, and she was used to being spoilt. Her mother had died a year previous, and Thomas had no care to discipline the wilful child. Anne was as unalike her as a goose is to a cat.

Maria was a headstrong girl, with a carefree nature, and thought of as a beauty, even when she was a girl. Though her looks had an unbroken, wild quality, not to everyone's taste. Anne was plainer, simpler and therefore easier to handle and I often forgot that she was even there. She quickly took to me with a quiet affection, which I indulged and took pleasure in, as it called to my motherly instincts. I had hoped to have children of my own, not ones bred by another woman, but it's funny how life turns out, and beggars can't be choosers.

It's difficult to describe Maria, though I know I must if you are to understand me. She was like a creature of the woods. Like a deer, maybe. Comely and soft, yet wild. Her eyes were the colour of polished chestnuts. Her skin was a tawny colour, like melting honey, which I know is unfashionable, but it suited her. Soft and velvety, it was, as if you could mark it just by touching, like wet sand. Her mouth and nose were those of a child and she was rather doll-like. In truth, she had a delicate quality, which made her seem breakable. Which, of course, she was.

I remember one time seeing her through the window. I was bent over the kitchen sink, scrubbing hard at Thomas's shirtsleeves, which were covered in blood. As usual, she seemed wrapped up in her own world, her attention all on some ailing rabbit limping across the lane like it had a dose of disease. I went to bang on the window to stop her touching it, but her attention had moved from the rabbit to the sky. She held her arms wide, like she was going to give it a hug, and then she began to spin herself around, quicker and quicker, her feet tapping the earth as if dancing a jig. I stopped my toil for a moment to watch this strange game. She was swaying like a drunkard. I could hear her short laughing breath, arms swinging, as she finally fell on the ground, lying, star-like, allowing the earth to carry her on its back. As I watched I thought how spoilt and lazy she was, and I returned to my scrubbing wishing that I had such time to waste!

As she left her childhood behind she did not settle down, as I had expected she would. After all, that's what happened to me after my marriage. Thomas would not think to push Maria into marriage when she was younger, and after Little Tom was born there was hardly a queue of offers. Although she had plenty of men who lurked around, they weren't after marriage. She had an easy virtue, which blackened the family name.

Maria was sometimes surly and disrespectful towards me and Thomas didn't chastise her—he preferred to turn a blind eye and made excuses for her on account of her mother dying so young. As if that would cut ice with me, whose father died when I was just sixteen!

The summer of 1826 sticks in my mind as being a bad year between us, and it was also the year before she died. Had I known it was her last summer on this earth I may have been more forgiving of her, but who among us can predict the future—apart from the gypsy Hannah Fandango, possibly

Maria had just started courting William Corder, and I remember the first evening he took her to the Red Barn. It must have been a Sunday, as Thomas was home, and it wouldn't stop raining. Rain was falling from heaven in crystal pendants, shattering on the small panes separating us from the outside world. From my chair here, by the window, I could see only the smallest corner of it, and it reminded me of a bloodless face, almost obliterated by a relentless stream of tears.

Pitch-black clouds pregnant with thunder soon darkened the view. The airless cottage stifled me, and I couldn't breathe. I was captive here. I was thirty-one years old.

That day we were all prisoners. We paced like cats in this small room, aware of each other's restlessness, weary of each other's faces. We tasted each other like soured milk, Thomas slouched in his battered seat, resigned to not catching moles that day. At least they had a reprieve from the teeth of his snares.

Maria sighed, 'Blast this cotton! That's twice it's caught. I knew I shouldn't listen to you, Ann! No cotton at that price was going to be any good.' She stopped her mouth with a pin and I watched her quick hands, her needle stabbing in and out of the unmarked fabric. We were such an unlikely trio, and I turned my back on the father and daughter. She was not my blood, and he was not my heart.

It took all my resolve to sit still, and I counted raindrops, searching for a chink of light, but it looked like the weather would only get worse before getting better, as is often the way. So I waited. As I cleaned the grate, as I stoked the fire, as I fed Tom, as I scrubbed the floor. I was counting time, which hung heavy like chains.

But then something happened to me. It was as though the world had stopped, and all except me were frozen in time. I was ignored, and their indifference freed me. I was invisible, a mere scrap of air.

I opened the back door, just the bottom half. No one moved or spoke; so I knew it was true; they did not see me, I was clear as glass. Taking a deep breath, holding it like I was under water, I stepped outside.

Once I was free I closed the door, pressed my back against it. The timber planks digging into my spine, which I thought was odd, since I was only made of air. Or maybe water? Slowly, lingering in the touch of the wet warmth, I walked further into the rain. I felt I could walk forever in a warm cloak of cleansing water.

The rain was fierce and I was awash with it, unsure where my body began and the wall of water stopped. My dress stuck to me like a second skin. My own mouse-brown hair drank the rain, a quicker version of the treatment I would lavish on Maria later when I washed her hair in the water from the bucket she had placed earlier to catch the rain. Although she was courting a gentleman she had no servants to plait her hair with fine trinkets, or soften her face with powder sent from Paris, or rouge to put a blush on her cheeks. She only had me. Always me to help her prepare for her meetings with men. And I was enough. For then, anyway, while she was still beautiful.

I turned back to the cottage, both hands gripping the rim of the heavy bucket of rainwater. It would be easy to drop it, to tell Maria I could not wash her hair that day. But I decided against it. Despite myself, I wanted to help her to look her best for William.

I lost a slip of time because the next thing I heard was her voice calling, as if from far away, through the rain thundering around my ears, 'Ann!' Then again, 'Ann!'

Reluctantly I followed the voice. I was no longer invisible but a plain woman standing in the rain. Maria was a beautiful girl about to get ready for her meeting with William Corder, and she needed my help. She had boasted about William, but I had not spoken with him yet and knew only that he was the Squire's son, recently returned from London.

And so, Rector, I helped her. Can you picture us, sat here in this very room? Maria by the cackling, spitting fire in the hearth in her red under slip. She sat straight, her head tilted back into my dry hands as I rinsed her hair with the rainwater. My nails were short and torn, and sometimes I caught them on the dark rope of hair, and she flinched. Despite my clumsiness she never told me to stop, as she knew she couldn't do it so well on her own. The only sound was the spitting fire and Maria's rapid breathing. She was always nervous before he came and would ask over and over, 'Do I look well, Ann? Do you have some berry for my cheeks?'

Taking a piece of starched muslin I swaddled her dark tresses, rubbing roughly against her scalp. By the way her jaw was set and her teeth were pressed together, I could tell that she was enduring the pain for his sake. I plaited her hair with a blue ribbon, which he had bought her, and she looked very fine. She was tense with nerves, and when I nearly dropped the ribbon she snapped, 'For God's sake, watch it! The floor is so sooty.'

She had three dresses, but you would think she had more, as she was skillful in adding a ribbon or pleat, lowering a hem or lengthening the sleeves to give a different look. That day she had pinned a narrow strip of blue velvet around the edge of the skirt and the neckline of her best dress, which she had lowered to show off her chest. The velvet was forget-me-not blue and it matched the ribbon in her hair. Once dressed she could almost pass for a lady.

Then William arrived and took her by the arm, off to some adventure. He did not come in, but stood by the gate, a silhouette in a dark suit, smoking a cigarette. What tales he must have to tell, what secrets! And Maria was to hear them all. While I was left sitting, and waiting for her return. Watching the rain, which would not stop. A storm was brewing.

XVIII

Rectory Journal
6th April 1851

It is indeed a strange way in which the Lord works! Only a few days ago I sat here pondering on the way of the world, lamenting my lack of objective information about Maria Marten, wondering who might assist me in my endeavour. Yet now, just a short time later, I have happened upon the very person.

To explain: in recent weeks I have fallen into the habit of walking abroad in the afternoons, when I have completed my other duties. The air does me good, and I am becoming familiar with the hidden paths of Polstead. I was feeling melancholy today, dwelling on the sorrow of Rachel and Simon Stowe whose son, Daniel, is not expected to survive the week since gangrene set into his wound. Today I decided to walk a distance further from my usual route as I wished to find the place where the notorious Red Barn had once stood. I had some notion that it was near to the Martens' cottage, which I visited yesterday, and noted several fields thereabouts. I hoped instinct would guide me to the right spot. And so it was that whilst walking along a line of trees bordering a field, I came upon Sarah Humphries

I would not have spoken so freely to her had our paths not crossed. When we encountered each other, we were both, I think, taken aback, as we had each supposed ourselves alone. It was she who spoke first, and her words were matched by a smile like sunshine, 'Good afternoon, Rector. What a beautiful day!'

I agreed that it was, and was relieved that she continued to talk whilst picking some of the pink flowers clustered around us. 'This willow herb is tasty with a few cold potatoes. Have you ever tried it? Here, have one. Just the leaf, not the flower. Well?' she watched my face while I tried it, wincing at the cloying sweetness, 'You don't like the taste of honey? It is weaker if you boil it up into tea.' She looked up, the creases around her eyes betraying good humour. I think she thought it amusing to see me munch on a leaf, and in truth the idea of her boiling the leaves amused me; she did not look like she belonged in a kitchen.

'Are you laughing at me, Rector?' She brushed down her skirt as she stood, the brim of her hat touching my chin.

'Laughing at you, Mrs Humphries? Why, no. I was marvelling at your knowledge.'

'Ah well, I have not always been a wool merchant's wife, you know,' she said, 'and although I have Nancy to help with the chores, I like to work in the kitchen when I can. Making willow-herb tea is an innocent pleasure, is it not?'

I agreed, watching her touch the leaves and bend to the buds as we passed. She touched one delicate white flower (she told me the name which I cannot recall), her hand as pale as the petals, her long fingers (that would look so fine in silk gloves), caressing its bowed head as if it would rise up to her. Everything she touched seemed miraculous. She notices things that I take for granted, and even the naming of wild flowers felt to me like a small adventure.

'What a joy, to be free on a day such as this. Don't look so sternly! I merely mean that Joshua is with his nursemaid for a few short hours, and I may take some peace. Is that your purpose in being here?' Her jovial mocking brought me out of myself. I responded in kind, feeling my speech to be more lively than usual. I have never conversed naturally with women, unlike Henry. Perhaps a man of my calling should not have noticed the sunshine colour of her hair but it reminded me of Catherine's, the woman who had once claimed to love me but then pushed herself onto me and tried to ruin me with her slander.

Theological study taught me about female beauty. Through depictions of the scripture in art, I learnt to admire the aesthetic quality of women. I would wander through the Cambridge art galleries for hours, drawn to religious works of art, especially those depicting the Madonna. Catherine came with me once, before her fall from grace. But she was a woman who deceived; Sarah is an angel in comparison. And now, without the child balanced on her hip, she moved with freedom, revealing a fine delicate figure.

We walked around the boundary of the field, her trailing hand caressing the dog roses, which grow wild in the bushes, smoothing the silk petals through her fingers. But then she cried out, having caught her finger on a thorn. Holding the injured hand to her mouth, she sucked the blood squeezing through the tear.

'Ouch! Just look how it bleeds from one small snag!'

I passed her my folded handkerchief, and she pressed her finger against it, the white linen turning red.

'I'll make sure to return it, and it will be as spotless as a lamb.' She resumed her walk, and I followed close behind. 'So tell me. You have been here long enough now. What do you think of our village?' Her relaxed confidence put me at my ease, and for the first time since I came to Polstead I felt I could be truthful.

'I confess I find it a little strange. It is so small, and everyone knows each other. I still feel an outsider.'

Sarah raised her eyebrows and gestured with her hand dismissively, 'Oh tush! You must not consider it so heavily. It is just the way in villages. Why, I myself have only been here two years, since I married Jeremiah, and I was not welcomed at first either.'

I looked at her, unable to believe that she could be unwelcome in any place, 'Oh yes, Rector, it's true. A new face must always be accepted before being welcomed. But I have found my place now, as you will, too, no doubt. And haven't I, at least, made you welcome?'

My voice failed me and I remained silent, looking ahead as we walked. She was teasing me, but I found I liked it.

'Do you walk here often?' I asked.

'Not as often as I should like. But that makes these times all the more precious. When the nursemaid, or someone else, takes Joshua I enjoy the peace up here. My arms sometimes ache with lifting him, so it is a joy to have only myself to carry for a while! And what about you, Rector? Where do you walk?'

I hesitated only momentarily, before thinking that this may be my opportunity to find understanding, 'I have been trying to find the place where the Red Barn stood.'

Sarah laughed. 'Well, you'll not find it here! You're some two fields out. I'll walk you there myself—come.'

And, before waiting for my agreement, she turned and led the way up the hill and across two fields. We walked in companionable silence, towards a place on the brow of the hill where the earth dipped heavily, and no grass grew.

Although the Barn itself no longer stands, the ground that once held its heavy frame was sunken, as though the memory of its burden still remained. The earth on the parameter was rich, ready to welcome the crops of the next harvest and provide the farmer with a good livelihood; but the rectangular area in the centre, like an island, is desolate and barren. If there had ever been flowers they were there no longer. There can be no doubt but that we stood in a sinister place.

Together we stood in silence until she shivered. 'This place gives me goose bumps, to think that this is where Maria was murdered. Why do you look at me like that?' I had been surprised by her intimate tone. Her soft voice felt so calming to me that I spoke my mind, 'It was just how you said her name. As if she was your friend.'

'Yes, that may seem strange. Had she lived, she would have been an old woman by now. But I think of her kindly. After all, her only crime was to love too much, and she was killed for it.'

I was shocked at this remark. 'She was not an upright woman, Mrs Humphries. Remember that she bore three children out of wedlock.'

She nodded. 'But surely there are worse sins? I think to not love at all is one. But you are smiling at me as if I am a simple child! Then I shall say no more.' She playfully turned her back, throwing the bloody handkerchief in the air and then snatching it back. She was close to me, the mood easy and light.

I would guess that Sarah is no more than twenty. Anything she knows of the Red Barn murder must be from local gossip, or from her mother-in-law. I should like to know what she has heard. But it did not seem right to ask her about evil deeds; I was already mindful of having overstepped myself in letting her guide me to the site where the Red Barn had stood yet I could not resist asking the question which had posed in my mind all afternoon, 'May I ask you, Mrs Humphries, what else you know of the case?'

'You may, Rector Coyte. If you call me Sarah.'

'Sarah.'

'Well, I know why the Red Barn has its name. Do you?'

I had not thought of it before, and considered the questions. I ventured that it was likely to be named after the shedding of red blood under its timbers. Sarah shook her head, pleased at my ignorance, 'That's what many suppose, but it's always had it's name from the way the sun sets behind it, casting a red hue all around. It is a strange coincidence, though. As if a murder was always going to take place here.'

Sarah shivered. She was not dressed for the changing weather and the sky had now clouded over. Her dress was thin, the colour of melting butter and it looked well on her, her hair being just a shade lighter. In any fashionable town her face would be her currency, attracting men of note. If fate had decreed that she be born into a higher station in life she should have had sapphires to match her eyes. I also suspect that, in a fashionable town, Sarah would be unlikely to spend any time with me. Thinking thus, my natural sense of inadequacy stopped me from prolonging our meeting.

I looked around and decided I did not wish to dwell any longer in that place, but Sarah seemed fascinated by it, and was wandering into the centre, looking down at the dark earth, 'This must have been where she was found.' Darkness fell on her angelic features; dusk had begun to settle around us. I joined her, feeling the temperature drop suddenly. 'It's getting late.' I said, 'Will your husband be wondering where you are?' 'Oh, Jeremiah is away in Lavenham... But I don't mind.' She paled, and looked into the sky to see the sun falling beneath the horizon. 'I should be getting back", she murmured, but I could see that she was reluctant to leave. I did not stop to wonder why, but led the way back to the village, calling over my shoulder that we must leave as night was overtaking us. As I turned I saw that Sarah was bathed in the red light of the setting sun.

XIX

Rectory Journal
7th April 1851

On waking I had a foreboding that this morning would bring bleak news, and I arrived downstairs to find that a message had been left. Mrs Bright relayed the information curtly, but even she looked troubled. Daniel Stowe died in the night.

Daniel had never recovered from his accident with the Suffolk Punch. The kick to his chest had broken a rib. Although he had rested since then, and Simon killing their best hen so that he could have chicken stock soup, the boy was pale and weak. The wound did not heal and, just two days ago, a fever started and Doctor Badwell told them that gangrene had set in.

I am no stranger to death, but the heavy hearts in that cottage were enough to sadden any soul. I can only imagine what Simon and Rachel are feeling. The Lord has his reasons, even if we cannot always understand. Still, I have been thinking recently how the world seems more unfair than it used to. I can understand if there is a reason for tragedy; although he was my brother, I must acknowledge that Henry died a sinner. He may have been less responsible than those harlots that shamelessly pursued him, forcing their diseased bodies at him, but he was weak and gave way to lust. As for my Mother, she has suffered greatly the loss of her favourite son, but maybe God is teaching her a lesson in the risk of covetousness, of loving one son so excessively without Christian temperance. Maria was punished for her wanton behaviour, and William for his evil deed so in the case of the Red Barn, God's hand is just. Mrs Marten is also a sufferer, her mind tortured by grief, and if this is her penance then what was her sin? The world is harsh, but fair, so I have no doubt that her inability to forget the past is rooted in some past deed. Dr Kirkman dismissed the other alternative—that she is mad, and I now acknowledge that she is of sound mind. She bears no resemblance to the hysterics Peter introduced me to. Also, from what Peter had said about phrenology, that it is now considered as an unreliable science, the diagnosis about William being evil must be questioned. Can Maria be responsible for her own death? Was she more sinning than sinned against? I find that, even in the midst of a strong argument that God is just, my own thoughts turn back on themselves and I am less certain about things. Young Daniel's death has unsettled me.

Despite the role of Rector giving me access to the private lives of my parishioners, I remain unaccustomed to displays of emotions—even when Henry died my parents did not cry, although my mother wore the glassy look of shock for many months. To see a man in tears, as Simon was when I arrived, is a new and shaming experience. I suspect that my own father does not know how to cry but keeps all his grief congealed within his silent heart, restraining his feelings with stiff suits and masculine pride. One day the emotion may erupt, like a volcano, and after that nothing will ebb the flow, but for now it remains within.

In this way I resemble my father. Like him, I did not shed any tears at Henry's death, although losing a sibling is less of a blow than losing a son. In truth, I had a mixed reaction to Henry's death and acted in a way that was appropriate, if not wholly felt. But today, faced with the dead boy's father, I saw a depth of emotion unknown to me. I watched the crushed man, breathing hard with the effort of maintaining control, and thought, what must it be like to love someone so deeply?

I stayed with the Stowes for two hours and in that time much was said and much was silent. Daniel is not the first child they have buried. I marvel at Simon's ability to feel such grief when he has lost two other children. But this loss must be more painful; those others had been infants and not expected to survive. Daniel had been their eldest boy and, although only nine years old, was as strong as a man. Apparently, he was a natural with the animals, and Simon hoped he would take over as blacksmith in the fullness of time. Instead of which, next Tuesday the boy will be delivered to the earth, ashes to ashes and dust to dust.

When his wife was out of the room Simon confided that he feared he would not get through the funeral without breaking down. He had to be strong for Rachel who, as a mother, was allowed to show her feelings. But he was expected to be manly; and even Rachel did not realise how broken he was inside. He said that he wished that Rector Whitmore were still here, as he had known Daniel. Whilst I understood this sentiment, the comment did add to my feelings of inadequacy. It also meant that, in order for me to prepare the funeral service, Simon had the painful task of telling me about his son.

I searched for something comforting to say, but what I came up with sounded trite, 'I'm sure this must be very difficult for you,' I said, and wanted to swallow the words back again. Simon, too deep in his grief to notice took me by surprise by asking, 'Have you ever had a child?'

I stated, 'I remain unmarried, as yet.'

The man seemed to consider me, as though looking at some strange animal that was interesting but of little consequence. 'There is no loss as great as this. Rachel has not eaten since Danny became ill... She does not sleep at night. But she is lucky. Neighbours call with words of comfort, and bowls of broth. I am expected to carry on as normal when my world has turned upside down.' His head fell into his hands and fresh tears fell onto his calloused fingers. When he spoke again, his voice was like a taut string. 'Yesterday, when we knew it was just a matter of time, I undercharged a man for shoeing three of his best Suffolks. He didn't even have the grace to tell me so. It's not the money, although it was no small amount, but; he has known me for most of my life and Daniel since he was a baby. Everyone's out for themselves. Nobody listens. God didn't listen as we sat round the bed begging for our son to live. I offered my own measly life in exchange. So tell me, what's it all for? What is God thinking about?'

I felt inexperienced and clumsy, my only recourse being to the sermons and teachings from theological college. I realised that I know nothing of life, and that I desperately want to. No, more than that. I need to. I am tired of only living in the shallows, when others swim in the depths of human experience, just as Henry did. My brother died young but at least he had lived first. I am resolved to experience things from now on.

And so, although not easy, my meeting with Simon gave me courage. After I left, I took a short walk to collect my thoughts, and then came back here to the Rectory. I had not been back long when Mrs Bright came to find me. Surprised, I looked at the clock to check if it was lunchtime already, but it was not yet eleven. With a blank, unreadable expression she informed me that Mary Teager was wondering if she might have a word. Of course, Miss Teager is a regular member of my congregation and I have had some conversations with her, but she has never visited the Rectory. I had asked Mrs Bright to show her in and when Mary entered I was surprised to see that she was blushing, and that the colour added some attractiveness to her otherwise unremarkable features. After my visit to the Stowes' cottage, and my continuing disquiet over the prospect of the child's funeral, to see such an unthreatening woman was like a healing balm. I directed her to a seat, saying 'Miss Teager, what a pleasant surprise. Would you like a drink? Some lemonade, perhaps?'

I do not know what made me offer such a childish drink, far too sweet for my own taste, but she accepted it and Mrs Bright was discharged to the kitchen to make it. Miss Teager sat in the lumpen chair, her arms pinned to her sides as if she was unsure how to place herself. I noticed that she sat forward on the seat, so that her feet remained flat on the floor, as though she were an obedient pupil in an assembly. Enjoying the young woman's unassuming manners, I took my time in finding out the purpose for her visit—after all, I have not had much society since arriving in Polstead. To my disappointment it was not for a reason of great interest; she simply wanted to volunteer to help with the flower arrangements for the funeral.

She looked up at me with clear, solemn eyes. There was no cunning there, no wish to deceive or seduce. I noticed her purity like one observes an unusual bird or flower, listening to her simple logic, 'There can be nothing worse than losing a little one. I just want to help, if I can.'

The sentence was hushed, and after speaking she bowed her head slightly as if she feared that she had divulged too much. I think I may have smiled at that, pleased that I could make this naïve soul feel worthwhile, and told her, 'What a noble gesture, Miss Teager. Of course your help will be much appreciated, although I do not have much responsibility in relation to the church flowers. Mrs Catchpole takes the lion's share of work where such matters are concerned. I suggest you speak to her.'

She nodded. Of course she knew this, and it then struck me that the flower arrangement was not her only reason for visiting. The lemonade arrived, although she hardly touched it. When she held the glass to her dry lips, her hand was trembling. I observed with interest that she was extremely nervous.

Sifting through my brain for a suitable topic of conversation, (as I had no wish to discuss the finer points of flower arranging), I asked if she was a native of Polstead.

'Oh no, I was already fourteen when I came to live here, with my mother. We moved in with my Aunt after my father died. Before that we lived in Hadleigh.'

'And how do you find Polstead after the charms of a bigger town?'

She seemed shaken by the question, as if unsure how to answer. Two frown lines appeared on her shallow brow, 'Well, of course I am very indebted to my Aunt for keeping me, especially since my dear mother joined my father last spring. But I do miss Hadleigh—I was happy there.'

She looked up quickly, perhaps fearing that she would be thought ungrateful. She added hurriedly, 'Of course Polstead is a nice village and I have been fortunate to find good family to care for me.' I could see that she was convincing herself and at that moment the loneliness which I have felt since my own arrival was reflected back in her face. I saw her situation clearly. She is a plain woman of a straightforward countenance, no longer young, and dependant on a gossipy old Aunt for her keep. I find her predicament interesting as one might if an abandoned nest was discovered to have a single baby bird left in it; it is a shame, but what can one do?

But then I thought of what my mother would say about Mary Teager. She would be declared A Sensible Girl. Perhaps a little down at heel for her tastes, though this would be implied rather than stated. On balance she would be Eminently Suitable. I made a decision—why should I not have some female company? There is nothing irregular about two unmarried people finding companionship. Besides, have I not resolved to seize opportunities, in whatever disguise they may appear?

'Miss Teager, I have been invited to a music recital at the Rectory in Layham. A young pianist from the parish will be home from his studies and Rector Walpole has invited a small audience on the afternoon of Easter Monday. I wonder if you would care to be my guest?'

The blush that accompanied the surprised, shy acceptance of my hasty offer gratified me. And so it is done. What began as a bad day has turned out to be quite a significant one.

XX

Ann

To hear some people talk of the murder, Rector, you would think that Maria was simply a harlot and Corder as black as coal. But the truth is never that simple, is it?

They wrote whatever they pleased in the newspapers. There were even plays written about it, and I heard that in London people waited for half a day to see actors playing him and Maria, and me! I should like to have seen that actress—I wonder if she was pretty. I'm sure that whoever took William's part was handsome. Phoebe Stowe read the newspapers to me where they called him 'dashing' or 'cruel-looking' or 'fiendish' or 'handsome' and I wonder how a man can be all of these things at the same time?

In truth, Rector, he was neither handsome nor cruel. He gave an idea of comeliness more by his clothes and his way with words than by the shape of his face, which was an uncommon one. He had a bigger head than most, and a solid square jaw line, which jutted out when he was angry or heated. The bones of his face gave him an innocent wide-eyed look and he reminded me of a gentle yet strong animal. He had a gentlemanly manner and always wore his best shirts, not just on Sundays. So, all in all, he held himself well and was generally seen as a good catch around the village, although he was known to be a bit spoilt and not too steady, but then what woman would care about that when there's wealth to be had?

And it wasn't just the women in Polstead who thought him a catch, for he had a whole cackle of women eager to win him when he advertised for a wife. But that was later, after Maria died. We will come to that. First, let me tell about how I came to know him.

It was May 1826, and I remember that most distinctly, as it was exactly a year before Maria died. Just twelve months before her death the world was a different place. And I have reason for remembering that meeting clearly, as it was the day before my life changed. If things had worked as they should—but who can to say how the world should turn? You would answer that God knows the way of the world. But he was no friend to me then, and I shall tell you why.

It happened in a holy place, too. In the churchyard. I remember approaching St Mary's, climbing the final part of the grass bank which levels out at the top. I was holding a bunch of bluebells, admiring the solemn droop of their heads. There were many more around me, scattered across the hill, unpicked and blowing softly in the warm air. I felt light of heart. The chores were done and Maria was looking after little Tom for a change.

When I think back, I imagine myself smiling, as I had a great secret. The best that a woman can have. For I was carrying a baby, and this month I had missed my course. Please spare your blushes, Rector. I should hope to be more frank than this before my tale is told.

All day I silently prayed for the baby. I did not let chores trouble me, or the thought that the house would be crowded, what with Maria back home most nights, and Tom too big to share her narrow bed. Her sister, Anne, bless her, took up little enough room but still there was none to spare. But my baby would be welcome, if I had to sleep in the field to make room. It was all I ever wanted you see, Rector. It was all I prayed for.

So I remember that day. My heart was gently alive from the walk, and I slowed down as I climbed the shallow steps to the church. I felt content; the churchyard was one of my favourite places and I could find peace there. A rare, precious feeling, which I never find now.

Closing the wooden gate to the church grounds, I took a moment to turn and look back on Polstead as you can see most of the houses from that spot, but not my own. I was thinking of the child who would one day stand with me there, and I put my palm on my flat stomach. For a woman carrying a child there will always be dread mixed with the hope, and I had already lost three babies, so I had reason enough to fear. But that time it felt different. I carried this difference in my heart like a secret wish. That little bundle of hope deep within. I was so sure that nothing could harm it. I promised to keep it safe. Oh, I remember that feeling so clearly, as if it was yesterday.

Father's resting place is on the opposite side of the church to the gate, so I walked across the graves, feeling the long rough grass brush my shins—old Whitmore never kept the graveyard neat. It was a warm day and I was barelegged under my long skirt. I walked the edge where the graveyard meets Corder's field, as I wanted to see the lambs. I am fond of sheep; so gentle and such good mothers. As it was May, several of the ewes had babies and I watched them suckling, their little tails wagging as they balanced unsteadily on slender legs while their mothers nuzzled and nudged them to find a dug. I stood for some time watching, thinking of my own child.

When I came to Father's grave I could see that it needed weeding, and the recent arrival of spring had speeded the growth of grass across the small stone cross. I frowned at this, as I used to take it as a serious matter to tend the grave, and would not have others say I disrespected my father's burial place. I wonder who will tend my grave when I am gone? But then, I don't care about such things anymore.

Kneeling on the ground I grabbed the tough grass with fists, working fast to neaten the edges. Some lime had built up on the stone and Father's name would soon be hidden. Cursing myself for not having a hanky I lifted my skirts to purchase a hold on my petticoat, which I spat on and used to clean the stone. Not very ladylike, Rector, but I'm sure you've seen others do worse. So there I was, gripping the stone with one hand and rubbing with the other, squatting over the remains of the dead.

I was still in this pose when I heard footsteps behind me on the gravel path. I took them to be Whitmore, who was always skulking about, and continued my work until I was satisfied, and then I sat on my heels to see the fruits of my labour. Father's name was clear for all to see and the area neat. Satisfied, I smoothed my skirt and leaned back; squatting for so long caused my back to ache.

Turning, I was shocked to see that the footsteps had not belonged to Whitmore at all, but to William Corder, who was watching me closely. I knew him, of course. He was the Squire's son and had returned from London just half a year before. I also knew that he had been courting Maria in the Red Barn for a good month, but before that day we had never spoken.

I coloured with shame. I tried to neaten myself up, harnessing a loose lock of hair behind my ear, wondering how long he has been standing there watching. I thought of him as above my station then, so I said 'Good afternoon, Sir.'

He did not reply straight away, but looked at me as if from some faraway place. Then he seemed to shake himself and I could see him searching his memory for a name to fit my face.

'Mrs Marten, Sir. Ann Marten.' I could have said that I was Maria's stepmother, but something stopped me. Perhaps I wanted to be known for myself, rather than in relation to her for a change.

He seemed to recognise the name and pulled the back of his hand across his forehead and removed his hat in greeting, 'Of course. Mrs Marten, how do you do?'

I just nodded. What could I say to a Gentleman? But then he did a strange thing. He came and sat beside me, right there on the grass, to see what I had been doing. He read Father's name out loud, and the dates, and then used his own hand to smooth down the grass. It was nice to hear his voice reading the words, as although I knew what the stone said I couldn't read then, although I learnt soon after that.

One thing I remember was his hands. I had never seen hands like his, smooth and white with carefully shaped fingernails. Hands more used to gloves than to a hoe. Unmarked and pure. Like your own, if I may say so, Rector. To a working woman like myself such things are rare as jewels. I could see that his waistcoat, deep red in colour, must have come from London, with its fancy stitching. I imagined how soft it must be if I could only reach out and rub the cloth between my cracked hands. He was so relaxed that I soon felt at ease too, and before long he was telling me about his last visit to Ipswich, where he bought some more cattle from the Market. I had only been to Ipswich once, just before my wedding, to get the licence and also to buy a new bed as it was thought unfitting for me to use the one that Thomas's first wife died in. My mother thought a new bed would bring good luck, though it didn't bring me any joy and happen she should have saved her money. But there it is. Anyway, I remembered Ipswich as a bustling place, and I had been a bit scared of the strange noise. I saw one man pulling a woman into the corner of a building and I didn't understand why at the time, as I was green before my wedding night and didn't understand about men's lust. I had not enjoyed my visit to Ipswich, but listening to William I felt that I had not been to the same town.

He told me of fine shops were women sewed thread the colours of the rainbow, and of places were you can eat any fish that swims in the sea, or taste a fruit that had come all the way from America! He told me of another world, of hostelries where servants run you a bath before you change for dinner—'course, I knew of this well enough for I'd run baths when in service, but no-one had ever told me how it felt to be on the other end of such things. William told me of another way of living, and just being with him made that world seem nearer and more real. Sitting next to him made me feel like a Lady, and those thoughts crept into my soul, and whispered what I was missing.

I thought of Maria then, with her shopping trips to London and her fancy soaps and hats. I wondered if all of this could be mine; talking to William it all felt so possible.

It could have ended there. I could have gone back to the cottage, to my life and work, had something not woken inside. Some longing that I had felt as a child, but packed away on my wedding day, thinking never to taste it again. But things seldom unfold as they should, and chance wove a different path for us all to follow. I went back again, Rector. Not to visit a grave or to tend flowers. I will own it now. I went back to see him. To be seen. Not to be invisible, like I was at home. And he was there. He was waiting.

XXI

I am back from my afternoon with Mary Teager. My handwriting is loosened by wine, and sprawls in an ungainly way, but I will endeavour nonetheless to describe events whilst they remain fresh.

From the beginning—

After the Easter Service I returned home to change and have a light meal. The Easter services have taken a great deal out of me, and I felt quite exhausted but, as always on Easter Monday, elated too. After the grief of Good Friday, with its nightlong vigil, it is only today that my spirits rose again. St Mary's was full and the children eager to receive the sweet treats and painted eggs set aside for them at home. This pagan tradition irks, but even I raised a smile as Joshua clasped his mother's hand asking for 'eggie'. All in all, the morning passed successfully and I allowed myself a few congratulatory thoughts as I finished my luncheon.

Later, as I approached May Humphries' house, I was gratified to see a dark head bob back from the window; Mary was looking out for me. Sure enough, my knock was answered swiftly. I could see that Mary had made a great effort to look attractive, and guessed that she was wearing her best dress. It was a pale green and, although rather dated by town standards, was not unbecoming. Her brown hair was loose and had been curled. (This took my thoughts back to when I was a boy watching my nanny tying her hair with strips of linen until it was in tight knots against her scalp. She would sleep like that, in her low bed next to my cot, and in the morning would unravel the ribbons, singing, her long blonde hair falling in rippling curls all down her back. Even as a boy I understood that these were preparations for meetings with a special gentleman. Over the next weeks, her mood became distracted, and she was sick in the mornings. Soon her dresses were too tight around her stomach and my parents dismissed her.)

And so I appreciated the diligence with which Mary must have prepared herself for our assignation, and am pleasantly warmed to think that I was the special gentleman for whom she had performed these rituals.

She stood in the low doorway, blushing fiercely, her eyes downcast as she arranged a shawl about her shoulders. She evidently wished to be away, and fidgeted with her hair, uneasily looking back over her shoulder, as she moved out of the door. We had not left the threshold before May Humphries' voice called from an upstairs room, 'Was that the door, Mary? Is he here then?'

Mary's shoulders stiffened, and she seemed to be studying her shoes as her Aunt appeared over her left shoulder. 'Good Afternoon Rector! So you're taking my niece out then? Well, she's in safe hands, you being a man of the cloth!'

She seemed to find this amusing, and I saw the entertainment she took from taunting her niece. I replied civilly, 'Good Afternoon, Mrs Humphries. We shall be attending Rector Walpole's for a musical gathering. I did think to procure the trap, but was reluctant to trouble Simon so soon after his son's death. Besides, it is a pleasant afternoon for a walk. Do you agree?' I directed this question at Mary.

She nodded eagerly. 'Oh yes! I enjoy walking.'

Mrs Humphries tutted and turned her niece by the shoulders, seizing the ribbons of her hat and re-tying them tightly. 'Just mind you don't muddy your dress. It is such fine fabric.' This, I think, was for my benefit. She watched us leave from the gate at the end of the path, no doubt hoping that others would also see her spinster niece walking out with the new Rector.

Until we were out of sight we were both silent, but once the corner was turned Mary spoke. 'My Aunt can be rather overbearing.' Looking at her rosy face, and hearing the suppressed anger in her voice, I understood something of what it must mean to be dependent upon another's charity, especially when that person is someone whose manner is not in sympathy with your own. It is clear that Miss Teager is of a more refined nature than her Aunt, and comes from a more elevated position in society, yet the loss of her parents and the lack of a husband has reduced her circumstances. Her general demeanour is modest and her manner of speech reveals some education. I felt pleased with myself; not only would I have some agreeable company on what might otherwise be a tedious afternoon, but I was also doing the poor woman a good turn.

When we arrived at Layham Rectory the door was already open, and laughter could be heard from the parlour, accompanied by the booming jollity of Charles Walpole. After pressing the bell I decided to walk straight in, and escorted Mary down the short hall. Sure enough, Charles's housemaid was otherwise engaged in passing around glasses of sparkling wine on a fine silver tray, and I could see that this promised to be a lively occasion. When she next passed, I helped myself to two glasses and handed one to Mary, who was looking around in shy awe, the pleasure on her face unmistakable. Pleased to be the author of such happiness, I took her hand and led her over to meet our host.

'James, God bless you for coming!' Charles boomed. 'And you have a guest!'

I introduced Mary and saw that he approved. Clasping her hand in his own he told her, 'This recital promises to be most special, my dear! Young Jacob Harris is back from his studies in London and has promised to entertain us with something of what he has learnt. Let us hope that his tutors have taught him more than he has learned in the taverns of London! No, no, he is a good boy—I was his guarantor, you know, so I am eager to see what my protégé can do! But how rude of me! Please, Miss Teager, take a seat. You have had a long walk! Shame on you, James, you should have used a trap! You shall certainly have one for your journey home.'

Mary was about to protest when Charles moved on and was giving his hearty welcome to still more guests. We sat down and surveyed the room in companionable silence. I felt more content than I had for some time. I have not felt well recently, and even my laudanum lifts my spirits for only a short time. I am finding I need ever-more drops to stave off the melancholy that has plagued me for years. But this afternoon I felt, if not happy, than as close to it as can be expected.

In the corner of the room I saw Dr Badwell. I had last seen him at the Stowe's home, and he retained his sombre countenance. He saw me and nodded, but made no move forward. I reminded myself that he had not attended the Easter Service and wondered what denomination, if any, he favoured.

The American walnut clock on the mantelpiece chimed rhythmically, announcing three o'clock, and Charles clapped his hands as if to congratulate the hour on arriving. The dozen or so guests fell silent, and looked up expectantly. I could see Mary's flushed and fragile neck, her chest rising visibly as her hand tightly clasped the delicate stem of her glass. A mixture of pity and pride rose and fell in the instant, before I returned my attention to our gregarious host.

'Welcome, welcome my dear friends. I am so pleased that you all made the journey to be here this afternoon, especially those of you who have conducted Services this morning and may feel tired'—on saying this he looked to me and gave a warm smile—'but I feel sure that you will not regret this decision. I have the honour of introducing you to a young man with a prodigious talent, and whom I have known since he was a baby!' Laughter trickled around the gathering, and for the first time I noticed a neat young man dressed in a plain dark suit seated next to the fire. His eyes were fixed on his hands, which were held tightly in his lap. I guessed him to be no more than twenty. Oblivious to his obvious discomfort, Charles turned to the young man and motioned for him to stand. 'Jacob, dear boy, come forward so that we may admire you.'

The gawky student reluctantly obeyed. I glanced at Mary, and caught her looking in my direction. Shocked to find our eyes meeting, we both turned back to where Jacob diffidently stood with Charles's large hand planted firmly on his shoulder. 'Here he is! Our own musical protégé! It is to Jacob's parents' credit that they have supported his musical development, and I know that they are most proud of him, as of course we all are.' Pausing for a moment, he turned to the crimson youth. 'Am I talking too much?' Then, seeing the young man's discomfiture, smiled, 'I see that I am! Well, let us get along then. Ladies and Gentlemen, please make yourselves comfortable as we prepare to be delighted and entertained by the musical talents of Jacob Harris.'

Acknowledging the polite applause with a curt nod, the young man seated himself at the piano, coughed, and stretched his long fingers over the keys. He appeared to close his eyes, his head inclined to the ceiling, for such an uncomfortable pause that Mary glanced to me and others around began to shift in their seats. I thought this nervous young man had lost his courage but then, in a sudden motion, he brought his hands down to the keys and began to play. The music filled the room, a confident and strong rendition, immediately obliterating the previous image the boy had given. Even I, no great music lover, sat spellbound and not one cough or murmur interrupted the performance.

Silently moving between us, the maid refreshed glasses and offered light sustenance in the form of cucumber sandwiches. When Mary was offered the platter I turned to see if she was enjoying herself. Shaking her head at the offer of food, she turned to me and smiled before returning her gaze to the young pianist. In the half-light she looked almost pretty and I wondered what it would be like to kiss her, and if desire would follow.

And so the afternoon mellowed, the wine relaxing both of us, and conversation became easier. After the recital, Mary spoke of her parents, of her early life in Hadleigh, and by doing so relieved me of sharing my own story. When the trap arrived to take us back to Polstead at eight o'clock I think we both felt regret. As she stepped down from the carriage outside the Humphries' cottage, I took her little damp hand and kissed it. She gasped, which reaction confirmed her innocent soul. In short, I could not have hoped for a more promising distraction from the dreadful task that awaits me tomorrow—the burial of Daniel Stowe.

XXII

Despite the pleasant evening with Mary, last night I had the strangest dream. I was swimming in the village pond, the sun bright on the water. My arm was suddenly pulled back, and my right wrist became entrapped by a cord of some sort. I pulled a knife from my pocket and sawed through the cord, which I now saw was a bracelet of yellow hair. The water became shallow and, as I stood, Mrs Marten appeared and pointed behind me. Turning in horror, I saw the face of a beautiful drowning girl, her hair tight around my wrist. Ann Marten began to laugh, and I woke up.

I cannot account for it, and had a powerful headache, although my usual dose of laudanum had some effect. No remedy, though. My head still pounded with the knowledge that I must officiate at Daniel Stowe's funeral. It was still early, Mrs Bright had yet to arrive, and the house was cold. My dream had unsettled me and so I rose, awaiting daybreak, whiling away the dreary hours reviewing the notes for my sermon. The funeral was set for ten o'clock and was expected to last one hour. But why did I feel so anxious? Granted, it was my first burial but no one in the congregation was likely to consider my words too closely. I took another small dose of laudanum and readied myself for the day ahead. Most of the village was to attend, including Mary. And her cousin, Sarah.

The few times I had previously spoken with Sarah had impressed upon me that she is a most remarkable woman, and that her kind are not often to be found in rural backwaters. She seems to have such vivacity; she is more alive than anyone else I have met here. But I am also troubled by the feelings she stirred in me, and am not insensible to the fact that thoughts of her may have prompted my bad dream. I resolved to be strong, to remember my position. If only she did not look at me with those melting blue eyes, and make me wonder how it would feel to kiss those full cherry-red lips, then temptation would not have been possible. I reminded myself that there are two types of women, and one leads only to damnation. I thought of the evening I had shared with Mary, how her gentle company had been a balm for my restless thoughts. I thought of my job, my vocation, and was certain I could not be tempted from the path I had chosen.

And so, at just past nine o'clock, I walked to St Mary's, taking the path that crossed Marten's Lane, as I often do. It was fateful indeed that I saw Sarah's blonde head disappear into May Humphries' cottage. It would be most uncivil to pass by, given that I had only called the night before, and I had a duty to remind them of the hour of the funeral.

The door was ajar, and May Humphries was bending over her grandson, straightening his collar. Behind her stood Sarah, half hidden, her face upheld towards the sound of my knock. She looked surprised at seeing me, and coloured slightly, before offering me a smile.

Mrs Humphries hardly acknowledged my greeting before gushing; 'You must forgive me for not attending the funeral, Rector. I have agreed to look after Joshua so that Sarah may go. She is friendlier with the Stowes than me.'

I sympathised with the boy's struggles as his grandmother rubbed at his cheek with her apron, asking politely, 'And how is Joshua?' I intended the question for Sarah, but her mother-in-law answered.

'Oh, very well! I love to mind him, when I am able.'

Sarah turned to me and asked when I must be at the church. At my answer, she said, 'Well, you must wait and walk with Mary and myself, Rector. For we shall be ready to leave in just a moment. I shall call her.' I was about to sit down when I heard a deeper voice which with sinking heart I knew to be Sarah's husband.

Jeremiah Humphries stepped into the room, his ungainly bulk hunched under the low ceiling. He clumsily knocked past the table and collapsed into the sagging chair. I had not thought that he would be at home and was surprised how his presence irked me.

'Good day, Mr Humphries,' I said, as pleasantly as I was able. 'I am glad to see you back from Lavenham in good health. Do you stay long in Polstead?'

'Just for a night, more's the pity,' he growled. 'The wool trade is so strong right now I can't be from Lavenham for long. We're expecting to ship to Denmark any day, so I'm riding back this mornin'. I can't even stay for the funeral.'

He gazed hungrily at his wife as he said this, and there was longing in his voice as if his very heart was being pulled from his body. What agony it must be to have a beautiful young wife like Sarah, and to have to leave her alone so often! He is as far from beauty as a man may be, with his gruff features, dull eyes and boorish demeanour. The thought of him and Sarah lying together made me shudder.

Joshua, whose face was seared with hot tears, stared up at me. I could see that he was in a bad temper, and forced a smile, although I am ill at ease around children. As I moved forward to speak to the boy, Mary came tripping down the stairs. She looked straight at me and her happy smile told me that she was delighted to see me.

Sarah moved abruptly to the table and began wrapping a piece of pie and a few oatcakes. Folding the paper over the pie, she made sure that the corners held tight, keeping the meat fresh for her husband's lunch. As she pushed the cork in the freshly filled cyder jug, Mary showed Joshua the soft moleskin of her cloak, telling him of the animals whose pelt had made it.

Sitting heavily in his chair Jeremiah grabbed his boots and pushed his feet into the stiff leather. As he sat back Sarah diligently knelt and began tightening the laces with double knots. The old hide was tough and she pulled as hard as she could on the bindings. Suddenly he said, 'Poor Simon. I'd not be him today for all the gold I could carry!'

We all nodded as he went on to say that he and Simon had got drunk yesterday, and Sarah looked up sharply. 'He was at the Cock last night? How is he?'

'Bad, I'd say. He drank himself into a stupor and I had to carry him home. Rachel won't be pleased, I'm sure, as he's bound to have a sore head today.' The laces done, he stood and gathered himself to leave for Lavenham. From the window we could see a few others walking to the church, mostly women as the men still had to work. Mary nodded to me that she was ready to go and the three of us made to leave the cottage, before Sarah turned to speak. 'I wonder, May, if you would mind Joshua for a while longer than the service? I don't want to take him to the wake— it doesn't seem fitting. But I should like to attend and pay my respects.'

*

The funeral was sombre. My words sounded like lies as I spoke of the Kingdom of Heaven, and how God takes only the most precious souls early. Rachel's cheeks were raw though she could cry no more. Simon sat straight backed beside her, his impenetrable silence like a shield around him.

After the service the crowd began a slow walk to the wake to be held at the Stowes' cottage. But Sarah could not go. Her tears were too keen. On seeing her tears something inside me woke, a feeling unknown to me before. She was just like a fallen bird, in need of rescue. I stiffened my arms, which ached to hold her.

Mary said wretchedly, 'What shall I do, James? Sarah cannot go to the wake like this, but Rachel is a good friend to both of us. I at least should be there.' I nodded, knowing that I too should attend although I would give a great deal to avoid it.

It was Sarah who offered a solution. 'If I could just sit and rest, perhaps in the church, I will gain control soon, I am sure.' Both women looked to me, one with relief and the other with an expression that I had seen before but could not place. It made me feel uneasy, but I saw what I must do. I knew that I must get rid of Mary.

'I will sit with Sarah a while,' I said to her, 'and we will join you when she has recovered her composure.' Satisfied, Mary kissed her cousin's forehead tenderly and walked quickly to catch up with the funeral cortege.

Inside the cool church Sarah seemed calmer. Her tears dried, though she still held on to my arm for support. We sat side by side in a pew and she leant her head against my shoulder. The warmth and weight of her was strange but pleasant. I hoped that she could not feel the racing of my heart.

'Are you courting Mary?' The question was almost whispered, and I could not see her expression.

I answered from my heart. 'Mary is a good woman, and I enjoy her company. But she is not...' I fumbled, unsure what word I sought. Sarah's blue eyes were still wet from her tears. She hung on my sentence, urging me to complete it, but I did not say the word 'you' that was so dangerously on my mind. She saw it anyway, saw what I longed for and, pressing her hand to my cheek, she kissed me.

The shock of that kiss, the sweet dread of being touched again, refusing to allow memories of Catherine to poison this moment, the longing was beyond my power to resist. One thing is certain; it was she who was in control. It was she who guided my hand under her skirt, who moved against me, and who skillfully placed herself within my reach. I gave in to the temptations of the flesh, and savoured my sin like Adam had enjoyed Eve.

The dusty dry smell of the church gave way to hot cherries, Polstead Blacks, the smell of Sarah. Sweet, dark fruit. I had only known a woman once before, and then, as now, instinct took over from inexperience. I found myself pushing her down to the floor, her body crushed beneath mine and—oh, lost by then!—the flesh between her thighs and the moist secrecy, which threatened to swallow me…

We moved together and drowned together. When my climax came, my wrist became entangled in her hair, as if to imprison me forever.

It was only in the moments after, as our breathing calmed, that I heard the sound of footsteps hurrying away and the gate to the churchyard creaking.

XXIII

Rectory Journal
20th April 1851

It is 3am. I cannot sleep. I have spent four hours tossing in the sheets, my thoughts tumbling about me like waves. I could drown in remorse. What was I thinking? Ah, but this is the problem—I was not thinking, merely feeling as I do now, my heart pounding and my palms so sweaty I can barely grip the pen. Thank God I still have some laudanum left, although precious little. I will invite Peter to visit me, asking him to bring a further supply. But what will he say to see me so broken? For he has seen me like this once before, at Cambridge. If it had not been for his stern words and actions then, the business with Catherine may have become ugly.

Oh, I am weak. And women are devious. Did not Adam learn this in the Garden of Eden? And what of Abraham, seduced by his own daughters against his will? If men as close to God as these can fall, then how could I have been expected to resist? Women are the stuff of sin, and Sarah is disguised as an angel. The most beautiful women have the blackest souls. Think of Maria Marten and her whoreish behaviour. Can a man be responsible for his actions, against such scheming? Perhaps William Corder, by his black deed, did mankind a service.

But how can I think such things? I cannot command my thoughts—a fever is upon me. Another dose of laudanum should calm me. But then another thought—the day to come. In a few hours Mrs Marten will arrive, ready to tell more of the business between Maria and William. I can hardly bear to hear of immorality– my soul sickens with it.

Ann

Rector, I don't know how anybody has the will to do anything in this heat, which thickens the air and fills the throat. It is hotter than any April I have known. I sweat without moving, and my clothes tang with the damp that lingers in the air after a day's toil. I long for a summer dress, silky as feathers, like Ladies wear on days like this. If I had such a thing, I could bear the heat. Instead, I wear this tired smock. The wool scratches at my skin, which is already itchy. Every day has threatened thunder, but at least when the rain comes it will wipe the sky clean. I wish the break good speed, as even the short walk here has exhausted me. I was beginning to tell you how I came to meet with William in the graveyard. I knew that he and Maria were—what word should I use, Rector?—Shall we say, courting? And then I saw them in the Red Barn. It was a warm evening and I had a bit of time to kill, so I took a walk. I didn't want to meet anyone, so I thought I'd take the route by Corder's field, and see the kingcups, which are one of my favourite flowers. They were in full bloom then, and thick like a yellow carpet on the ground, very pretty. Maybe I picked a bunch, I can't remember now. I do remember how peaceful it was. Made a nice change for me, as Tom was teething and Maria was never any help!

I was enjoying the last of the sunshine, as it didn't vex me then the way it does now. The birds seemed so loud, what with them being the only sound, and I stood and listened to their song. I knew which bird was singing by name, as my Father had taught me these things.

The sun was so lovely that evening. It was like a piece of fresh orange all ready to burst and rain its juice on me. I have only tasted something so sweet once. The sky was all pinks and yellows, and what with the purple flowers and the birds, I felt as happy as I ever have. I could see the dark shape of the Red Barn up on top of the hill, which was named on account of the way it looked on evenings like that, flaming red like it was bleeding itself dry. I don't know why exactly, but it had a glow around it, like Jesus's halo in that picture in the Church.

I walked up to the Barn until I was in its shadow, as the best blooms grew all around its walls. The air was still so warm, and the day's heat had cooked the flowers around me, lifting the smell right up into the air. I like the fragrance of summer, and I pushed my nose into a simmering bunch of scarlet and pink cuckoo flowers, and breathed in; honey filled me, and I imagined that I could taste their sweetness. I closed my eyes and swallowed the season.

It was while I was knelt by the flowers that I heard something. I stopped where I was and listened; it was not voices but noises I heard, and not one but two people. I have good hearing and didn't have to strain to understand what the muffled sounds meant. You may say, but Ann, surely you knew that William and Maria met at the Red Barn? And I would say, well maybe I did, but can't someone forget and then remember only when it's too late?

I should have gone straight home. I could've turned quietly away and been none the wiser but I wonder—would you? I believe it was a natural desire that made me curious about what was happening in the Barn, but I'm still ashamed to say that I allowed myself to look for a crack in the timbering.

The breathless gasps could be heard clearly and seemed to come from beasts rather than people. Leaning on the timbers and holding my breath, fearing discovery yet compelled to look, I put my eye to the split in the wood.

My view was not straight, and hay was partly stacked in front, but I could see them lying in the deep straw. I saw Maria's dress and William's jacket hung over the steps. Oh, shame on her, to let a man see her naked! A smooth bare knee and the back of a dark head—that was all, but that was more than enough. I should have gone then, but I had never seen anything like the shadows cast on the wall, which told a tale familiar yet strange to me.

The shadows looked like a tethered animal trying to escape and pulling against its chains. Its curved spine was bucking against the tethering trunk, as it pulled back and was thrown against its prison again. The movements became quicker and shorter, as the tethering was tightened, and it was motionless during the final seconds of its struggle. As the image relaxed and the breathing levelled out I slowly and quietly retraced my steps some paces and then, once I felt sure I was out of earshot, I ran as fast as my legs could carry me, cloaked now in complete darkness.

It was after this time that Maria fell with child again. As she had already borne two children she knew the signs early and, as she had previously, she confided in me. She had not yet told her own father, or the father of the child, and she wanted my advice. Or so she said, though she'd never been one to listen and what's the good in bolting the stable door once the horse is gone? Anyway, I think she wanted to gloat more than anything, as she knew I was still hoping to have a child of my own. She didn't know that I was already carrying.

That evening had turned quite cool for the time of year. I was shivering as I moved around the kitchen, preparing a space where I could begin chopping onions for the next day's dinner. Thomas had already gone to bed, and I planned to follow him shortly, so

I made quick work of the onions. Maria had not joined us for tea and I could hear her moving around in the upstairs room and presently she came down the stairs.

She looked awful. Her face was hollowed out and her black hair had lost its gloss. I pulled a chair out for her and she sat down. I suppose I knew what the matter was, having seen her twice this way before, but I asked her anyway. Maria was never one for weeping, but she cried that evening as she told me she was pregnant. I didn't ask, and she didn't say, but I knew the father was William.

I remember Maria turning to me and reaching out, as if I was her mother rather than a woman only a bit older than her. For her part, she looked as vulnerable as a newly weaned child, and I did hold her, feeling her sobs against my hollow breast and her caught breathing as the tears fell.

There was no doubt that Maria was sorry then, and I daresay that if she could have turned back time at that moment she would have. For my part, I thought on how ungodly deeds had a way of finding us out for penance, and saw that this must be her payment for the pleasures she had already enjoyed, although I kept these thoughts to myself. I told her that we would talk some more in the morning and sent her upstairs to get some rest. I sat for a long while before following her.

I had gone to bed with a headache, and I got up with one. I had the foolish fancy that if I could only turn back time for one day then Maria wouldn't tell me that she was with child and all would be well. But time, as I know, moves in one direction only—except in dreams—and she was indeed carrying. I felt the weight of this news as heavily as I felt my own child, still my secret, within my womb. But I had a premonition, a feeling I couldn't quite place, both unpleasant and familiar like the news of a death. I did not examine it too closely, as there were practical matters to be considered and I would be looked to for the answers.

Although Maria was not my own child, and there was no bond of blood between us, the fact that she was carrying for the third time without a wedding band on her finger, would still reflect badly on me, more so than on her own father who could not be expected to advise a young woman on her conduct. The villagers would mardle over my lack of authority within the home, and say that I neglected my duty.

Then there was the problem of space. Maria shared one room with her sister, Anne, while my husband Thomas and I had the other. Tom was supposed to share with Maria, but usually he ended up with me and I was always pleased to see him. The new baby would have to share their room, although it was already cramped. It was true that she was often away, gallivanting in London with William, as she had been with Mr Matthews before him, so I would no doubt have to care for the new baby as well as Tom. Although I loved him as if he was my own, I was still holding my secret inside. I still hadn't had my monthly courses, not since May, although I had not said a word to anyone, the child was growing. How would we have space in the house for two babies?

One more thing. This was harder to think of but no less pressing. The subject of the father. William Corder had sired a child, and these ties would bind. I didn't know how I felt about this. Another man caught on Maria's apron strings, when she was the one who lured them astray, just didn't seem right.

It was September by then and the weather was fickle. One morning I woke feeling sick and decided it would do me good to get some air. As there was a good wind I decided to spend the day doing the laundry. As you will know by now it is customary in Polstead to wash clothes in the stream by the church, as it runs clean from the spring and there are many trees for laying garments out to dry. It's also a social occasion and I decided that I should spend some time with my neighbours, to discover if there was any gossip about Maria. Tom would also benefit from the outing, and he could entertain himself with the other children.

It was as I was reaching up to spread one of Thomas's shirts out on a branch that I had my first pain. I thought, that if I did not know better I would think it the curse, but held tightly to the knowledge that I had not bled for four months and had other signs of pregnancy besides. Although my skirts disguised it, my belly was rounded and I had begun to feel the babe quickening. So, trusting my body and God, I continued with the washing, and did not leave early. The sun was sinking when I left with all the laundry dry and folded. I held Tom's hand as we came down the hill. By now he was tired and he dragged along on my right side, while I balanced the basket on my left hip.

Once at the cottage I lit the fire and began to think about supper. It was only when I had everything straight that I went to the privy. It was too dark to see but, if you'll forgive my bluntness, Rector, I could smell blood. I knew what that meant. I think I sat for a few moments longer, but I cannot say what my thoughts were. Happen I was thinking that, after supper I should go early to bed for this is what I did.

I lost the baby. 'Lost' is a strange word in such a situation, don't you agree, Rector? For surely I did not lose it—it was taken from me. Only God, I suppose, knows the reason, but it was not only the child who was lost. I lost faith then, Rector. Of course, I believe there is a God, and I believe in His power, but to believe He is good and kind I cannot. What God is it that takes a child from a married woman who would love it, and plants it in the belly of an unmarried girl, who curses its existence? Where is the justice in that? I didn't think this on that night, of course. I only thought how I could keep the child inside me.

The next morning the wind was sharp as a blade. It thrust itself against the cottage, cleaved its way into the bedroom. As I lay in bed I listened to my breathing, trying not to think of the wetness between my legs. I normally rise swiftly, but I was more cautious that morning as I pushed the blankets back. I could see then the damp streaks of red staining my nightdress and the insides of my legs. I felt my tight belly heaving in a cruel mockery of childbirth and, putting my hand to where the child was coming, I caught the liver-like ball with my hand.

Thomas had already gone out, and Maria had left for London the day before. Only Tom was in the house, and he was still sleeping. Not knowing what to do, I think it was panic that finally forced me up to search for a rag to wrap what was left of my child. In the drawer were a bundle of rags already torn into strips for my courses, and I pressed them to myself before wrapping my precious package, my precious baby.

It was hard for me after that. I felt like every day was a struggle, sometimes just to get out of bed. This was the third child I had lost; Maria had carried two babies to term and now had a third growing healthily inside her belly. Around me the world seemed as it should, and no one seemed to notice that I was not myself. But if I was not myself, then who was I? Sometimes, Tom called me 'Ma' but I was not his mother or anyone else's. Maria confided in me like I was a sister, but I was not that either. I was a dutiful wife, or so it would seem, but I was not content. So, who was I? Time marched forward and I found myself wondering what had happened to yesterday, to the girl I was. I used to enjoy the changing seasons and watch for the colours with joy but even special times like the Harvest or Yuletide didn't move me. Instead, I seemed to glide over the days feeling less like myself, and older, so much older, than I was. I swear that had my child lived, this story would have been different. I would have been content.

I am an old woman, Rector, and now I see how losing that baby left a longing in me that led me to a place I shouldn't have gone to. Even now, all these years later, I still think of it. I still have dreams. I do not dream of my husband. In my dream I am telling a man that he is foolish, that he should have taken more care. He has my hand in his, and is imploring me. I turn, as if to leave, but he stops me. He catches my shoulders and leans to kiss me. The rest is hidden. It is my dreams that betray me, even now. I did not choose to desire another man. It was against my will that my heart stepped up its beat when I thought of him. After I saw him I was restless and could not calm myself. If we met suddenly, unexpectedly, I read other things into our encounter. I imagined a desire on his part, or a planning on mine.

Even now, all these years later, I do not allow myself to think of his hands, or to remember his voice. For what choice is there? To be a dutiful wife is the only option I have. I will not be judged by others as a fallen woman. I will not allow it. And yet I must tell you what happened next. I cannot leave this earth until it is done.

XXIV

Ann

As my life draws to a close, I find that I am increasingly living in the past. Perhaps it is talking with you that has awoken my memories, which now pull insistently at my thoughts. I think of those things that have been lost to me, and there is both sorrow and joy in what I remember. And shame. Always that, reminding me that I have not always acted as I should. Memories follow me as I move around the cottage, trying to complete my chores but just wanting to sit and rest. I have no appetite either; my dress hangs on me like a sack.

I remember one day very clearly. It must have been just after I lost the baby, as I know I was sad and I had to work extra hard at my chores to try to forget. Although it was a cold day I was scrubbing the step, and my hands were numb from the icy water and the cold wind. From where I was squatting I could see down the path and along the road, which leads out of the village, and I saw Maria returning once again from London. I remember this day most distinctly because she was walking quickly, for fear of dropping one of the many parcels in her hands. I watched her tussle merrily with her boxes and noted that, although most were in brown paper, there was a red ribbon hanging from her wrist that was tied round a white and red striped box, the kind used for storing fancy hats. I had seen these boxes before, when in service, but of course I had never owned one myself. I was surprised to see Maria with such a thing and, knowing my look as only another woman can, she laughed at my jealousy. She always looked forward to showing off her latest gifts from whomever she was courting. William may not be as rich as Mr Matthews, but she managed to get what she wanted just the same. In spite of myself, I was eager to see what gift he had bought her.

How my bruised heart railed against a God who rewards good deeds with loss, and sinning with luxury! If God does not punish sin, then how is it wrong if others take justice into their own hands? It seemed to me then, that He is blind and only those sinned against see clearly. It is women who are the guilty ones. Maria was right about one thing: men are fools.

William was soft clay in the hands of a girl like Maria. He may have had prospects and a fine education, but he was as naïve as a schoolboy when it came to love. I think he may even have married her if I hadn't talked sense into him, telling him that it was not Maria he loved. She was not the kind of girl who a gentleman should marry—although she thought differently. She was still hiding her pregnancy from everyone except me, and her trip to London, with the lavish gifts, had convinced her that William was hers for the taking.

When Maria spoke of the baby she always said 'he', and I don't think it occurred to her that the child could be a girl. Although she was not overjoyed at being pregnant there was an aspect in her nature that saw opportunities within all situations. Besides, her own experience had taught her that money could be gained from carrying a man's son, as Peter Matthews continued to send her five pounds every quarter for Tom—a considerable sum which saw us through many hard times. And now she was carrying William Corder's child, and he was son to the owner of the largest farm in the area.

As the weeks went by my own flat belly was mocked by her swelling one, although she was careful to hide it when she left the house and I don't think that anyone in Polstead suspected. At home it was a different matter, and I had to bite my tongue as she helped herself to extra slices of bread and cheese on account of the baby. As for William, he began to visit the cottage most nights. They no longer went to the Red Barn, and Maria was less careful in her attentions to him, perhaps thinking that her future was already secured. She began to retire early in the evening, and often she would be in bed when William arrived. It didn't seem right that she was so neglectful, but she probably learnt this from her father who would visit The Cock most nights, and did not feel the need to sit and talk.

William too would go to The Cock when Hannah Fandango, Samuel Smith or Thomas Wainwright were around and even then Maria would not join him. These were friends William had made in London, and I told you about Hannah Fandango telling my fortune at the Cherry Fair. But her main occupation was smuggling, and the three were notorious for dishonesty. I think they took William for a fool, and Hannah had been William's lover, which used to enrage Maria. But even her jealousy of Hannah had faded since she felt the first movement in her belly.

The first time I saw William with them I had gone to The Cock, telling Maria I needed to remind Thomas of something, not that she cared where I went and she had no reason to doubt me. But when I got to there I did not speak to my husband, who was supping with William Pryke and too bleary to see me scuttle by. It was curiosity that pulled me there. Instead I went to the back room, which was darker and I was right in supposing that this was where they sat. I did not want them to see me, but sidled up to the doorway, sitting on a low stool. It was not a usual habit for me to visit The Cock, excepting the times I had gone to drag

Thomas home, and I did not wish to be seen or remarked upon. I just wanted to observe for a few minutes. I have always been able to hide in the shadows.

William was in the corner, and sat close to him was Hannah, her hair loose, smoking a thin pipe. I could not see how she looked at him, 'though I had no doubt that there would be an invite in her eyes as that was her profession. He was so like a child, that he could not be responsible for any weakness at the hands of such a scheming woman. I knew I should be mindful.

Sat opposite were two faces I did not recognise, but I knew immediately which one was Samuel Smith, as he was known as 'Beauty'. He had dark curls, and a winning smile, and I could see instantly how young widows could be parted from coins easily by such a face. So the other man had to be Thomas Wainwright, the clever one of the group, and known as the cruellest. Between them they nursed jugs of liquor, but they spoke low with their heads close in. I could not hear a word they spoke, though a fear twisted in me as I saw how William nodded and shook Wainwright's hand.

I would have observed longer but I heard a too familiar voice close by; it was my own husband. For a second I though he was calling to me, but then saw that it was a general goodbye to all; I watched him leave knowing I had to reach our cottage before he did. This was not so difficult as the path was dark and I was able to cut around the back whilst he staggered slowly down the lane. What was hard was leaving so unsatisfied, and knowing nothing of what had been said.

Fortunately, William's friends visited but rarely and so most nights William and I would be alone, with Thomas out and Maria in bed. I became something of a confidante to him, for who else did the poor man have to talk to? He tolerated Maria's behaviour, and didn't even see how shoddily she was treating him until I pointed it out. It began to be a relief to him when she went to bed, as he grew accustomed to my quieter, kinder ways. Maria was becoming a nag and a shrew, and he can't be blamed for growing tired of her. So by day I was with Maria, and was a great support to her even if I do say so myself. But in the evening I was a friend to William, and this arrangement suited us both just fine. He helped me too; he knew that I wanted to better myself and would sometimes recite some poem or other that he had learn as a schoolboy, and then he started to show me how to make letters and write my name. He was a patient tutor and I learnt quick, always making sure that Thomas and Maria didn't know, as they would have mocked me. So, although innocent enough, this was our first secret. And one secret often leads to another.

I can't say how it first happened. I couldn't even remember which night; it was so natural and so gentle. We began to sit closer, and then we touched, and then we were more than companions. But I remember his skin, the softness of it. So pale and smooth. At first I was ashamed when he touched my rough body, my wind-scarred face, but he made me feel beautiful and young again. It was the first time since my father died that I had felt loved. These memories are my only jewels, which I take from their dark box and hold to the light only when I am alone. But now you know, Rector. William and I were lovers. Do not judge me—let he that is without sin cast the first stone.

I think you know by now, Rector, that life in Polstead is like a patchwork quilt, each piece linked to the next with jagged needle marks. It is only the watchers among us who see the whole pattern. I have seen that some are ailing, and I fancy that I know why. We are a small village, and I have reason enough to meet with everyone from time to time. And I have seen the spinster Mary Teager, getting ready for her outings with you in her best dress. She reminds me of myself from another time. She sometimes comes to visit me, to enquire after my health; she is a good girl. I have seen how she has dark moments, when she sits in front of her mirror, knowing that she is getting old and that she is not beautiful. I have read her thoughts, how she becomes so upset whilst getting herself ready that she thinks she can't go.

And I have seen her cousin Sarah; catching Mary's tears and whispering oiled words into her ear. I have seen her pull back Mary's long hair, not severely, making an intricate rope and knot. I have watched her take a red ribbon from her own hair and skillfully weave it into the plait. By the time she is finished Mary has stopped her tears, but Sarah's eyes are full. Mary thinks this is from friendly affection and hugs her tight.

But I know the ways of such women, for didn't I have the best teacher in Maria? And I think that you are beginning to know them too, Rector. Do you look at that red ribbon and think of another? Do you touch her while saying goodnight, your hand stroking her cheek and then taking that silky ribbon between your fingers? Do you turn away, thinking of a different woman?

I have become a silent witness. I care for Joshua often now. And I have seen Jeremiah Humphries sitting by the hearth. Seen how he sits without removing his coat, how he turns on hearing the door, hoping to see his wife, and how his face falls when it is only me returning with his son. I see his red face and smell the liquor on his breath.

And I have answered his questions. I have told him that Sarah must be in the village, or with his mother. Or blacking the grate and that she didn't want the boy here while she did it for fear he might swallow some of the lead. But then he looks at the grate. It is untouched.

And we have waited, her husband and I. Hearing the gate creak as she opens it. Watching her creep in the door with her hair loose, the red ribbon gone.

We all have our secrets, Rector. And you and I are both good at keeping them.

XXV

Rectory Journal
May 3rd 1851

Today I am tormented with those thoughts that have plagued me incessantly over the days since Ann Marten's confession that she and William were intimate. So dark that I can hardly write them down, as if the act of sealing them in ink would seal my own fate. How can I judge Ann Marten, for her revelation that she and William Corder were lovers, when I myself have so transgressed? I have found myself wanting for the second time in my life; at least with Catherine I had the mitigation of youth and naïvety. My liaison with her should have been lesson enough to avoid immoral entanglements, especially with a married woman.

The basest forms of human nature are evident in all mortals. This recklessness that I fail to control is the same feeling I have witnessed in others, notably my brother Henry, who often threw caution to the winds in his amorous affairs. Now it is my turn to hear the seductive coaxing of that inner vice, whispering perfidious reason in my ears. Urging me to the conclusion that, in experiencing the temptations of life, I can benefit my fellow man. That I can be a more sympathetic servant of God, by being a sinner too.

That the woman, Sarah, wills me to be so also is evident. Have I not seen her blush, her blue gaze studying my face when we speak? And did she not, only yesterday, find the most trifling reason to come here to the Rectory, when I was alone? And how weak against temptation I proved myself, yet again!

One thing my calling has imposed upon me is the importance of separating the spiritual from the physical. In my study of theology it is clear that one must rise above the desires of the flesh. I take heart that my ministry on behalf of the soul is superior to that which occupied my brother Henry, and it follows that whilst Henry dealt with the limitations of the flesh I must look to higher things. The physical needs of the body have been as unknown to me as the gates of heaven were to Cain, excepting my brief fall from grace when that seductress Catherine had me in her power. With God's help I rose above my earlier transgression and thought such things behind me, yet I now find that, far from satiating my curiosity, my body demands its satisfaction again and again. Is it the Devil that tempts me, or God's own test? He has helped me before, and surely I will not fail again. But I am a hypocrite. My thoughts are at best questionable, fracturing my sense of myself. I watch my actions like a commentator, my spirit strong but my body weakening.

This argument rails on until I am forced to conclude that I must take action. It has done me no good to enjoy the pleasures afforded me by Sarah Humphries; even my mother had remarked in her last letter that I sounded melancholic. She also commented that the frequency of my letters has dwindled, but she put this down to my working hard. If only that was the truth.

But there is yet some light in my darkness. Mary is also a frequent visitor, and I have found a comfort in her unassuming company. Like all good medicines, its taste is not as agreeable as her cousin's, but I feel soothed by her sweet nature. In her presence, I feel the satisfaction of discovering that I can really be the person she takes me for; it is like returning home.

Mary is impressed by knowledge and erudition, and understands enough herself to be able to converse on a reasonable level of theology. This morning, for example, we discussed the nature of religion. That is to say, she had listened attentively to my treatise on the state of Christianity in Britain.

'Of course,' I had proclaimed, 'the problem is that so many call themselves 'Christian' when they are nothing of the sort. Take the Religious Census last March, for example. Did you know that thirty-seven thousand people attended Unitarian services!'

Mary, who sat quiet and grave, as she is wont to do, was most impressed by my impassioned speech. She had asked, 'Were the results of the census favourable, James? Despite the Unitarians?'

To which I was able to reply, 'Frankly Mary, they were not. Only half the population of England attended a church service, and this demonstrates a shocking moral decline in the country. If we then consider that half of those did not attend Church of England services, but other so-called Christian denominations, including the Unitarians, then it really is cause for concern. It is as if people feel that they can exist without a God-directed duty or purpose. They do not see a religious faith as being fundamental to their lives. Do they think that alone they can do the right thing, to live moral lives, without the need for a deity? We are living in increasingly godless times. Do you understand me, Mary?'

And I believe she did. Yes, my meetings with Mary do me good. They steady my thoughts, and point them away from temptation. They keep me from dwelling on Sarah, from going over our couplings in my mind, from lusting after her yellow hair.

I must think only of Mary. Her Aunt, gossip that she is, has let fall enough for me to know that she is smitten, and has even speculated that winter weddings can be most lucky. She even went so far as to suggest to me last time we met on the green that the Rectory would benefit from a woman's touch. Of course she is trying to influence me, encouraging Mary's fledgling hopes, urging us both to believe that a marriage is possible. And I have begun to believe it too. Why should Mary not be suitable for a Rector's wife? She will do very well, visiting the old and the sick with her baskets of eggs and lemon curd. At Christmas she will invite all the village children to the Rectory and give them fruit cakes, one apiece, and maybe even an orange. Oh, how they will love her! And one day we will have our own baby, and she will jostle it on her knee as she sews, or lie it on the floor as she puts up trimmings or bakes a goose. She will make this chilly Rectory a happy family home and when my parents visit they will see what a success I have made of my life, and finally see that I have achieved something worthwhile. Mary will ensure, with her generous heart, that I do not regret my choice.

Perhaps my lecherous deeds are God's way of telling me that I should marry. If I were to propose to Mary straightaway, we could be married before the Harvest. I will ask Peter to be my Best Man.

I shall tell Sarah our affair is over when we meet tomorrow. On the hill, at the site of the Red Barn.

XXVI

Suffolk County Asylum,
Woodbridge, Suffolk.
17th May 1851

Dear James,

I have just received your letter—it arrived yesterday but as I returned late, my landlady handed it to me over breakfast. I was somewhat surprised by its condition—if I did not know better I would have guessed that it had been written by a drunkard, judging by the sloping hand! But, as you say, you are tired and I know too well how that can affect one. When I get back to my lodgings it is all I can do to eat some bread before I retire—my life revolves around my patients, as I'm sure yours must around your parishioners.

You did not give any indication of why you wish to see me with such urgency, but you mentioned having felt this way once before. Do you refer to that business in Cambridge? Oh, my friend, I do hope it is not more of the same slander! I am glad that the girl saw sense and kept quiet, after I had spoken with her. It was clear to me that she sought to blame you for the deeds of another man. You have not been led into a similar trap, I hope? You are too kind, James—you do not see others for what they really are. But I will visit, as you ask, and offer a friend's counsel, two weeks hence. I have already mooted the idea of a holiday to Dr Kirkman, who said he could spare me for a week. As to the medicine I gave you, I am pleased that you find it such a help for your headaches. Our medical superintendent does not like to fall behind developments, and so we no longer offer laudanum in a liquid form to our patients—Dr Kirkman has found injectible morphine much more effective. (It too is an opiate, like laudanum, and a marvellous cure. It has however three times its efficacy and works more quickly to calm agitated spirits.) I am therefore unable to do as you ask and bring a new supply with me, as the Asylum no longer stocks the vials and I doubt you would wish a needle in your veins!—but I'm sure you could easily procure laudanum from your local Doctor, if you are so minded.

So, shall we say that I will arrive on June 1st? Could you arrange for someone to meet me at Hadleigh? If you can confirm, I shall book my coach directly.

Your Friend, Peter

I was more dismayed than I had expected on hearing that Peter cannot bring any more laudanum—those little drops of medicine have cleared my head many times, and they ease the occasional shaking that befalls me when I am over-tired. But at least he is coming—it will do me good to speak with a kindred spirit. His letter made me remember Catherine. She was not virtuous. Like most women, she fell for Henry and then, after his inevitable rejection, turned to me. Like Sarah she was a temptress, leading me forward and then pushing me back, kissing me softly on the cheek and then pushing me away, saying it was my brother she loved. What a clever game she played, teasing my appetite until I lost all reason. Afterwards she cried, and said she had been a virgin—as if I could not tell a virgin from a whore! When she found she was pregnant she had come to me, not in tears or fury but with a calm resignation. She arrived at my lodgings with a friend, and fortunately I had my friend, Peter, with me, who dealt efficiently with her as befitted his medical profession. Taking one of Henry's books from the shelf, he had directed her into another room while I sat silently with her friend. When she emerged she seemed calmer, and held in her hand a piece of paper. She did not look at me as she left, but her friend shot me a look of sickening clarity; she despised me. After they had gone, Peter remarked that he knew of a way that she could cure herself of the baby, and had written a natural remedy to help her. I think I knew what he meant, but did not ask for details as he returned Henry's book of medicinal plants to the shelf. All I knew was that it was possible to get rid of a baby before its birth, but little else. Mrs Marten is expected imminently, but it is Sarah who fills my thoughts. I shall put an end to our meetings when I see her—I must be strong, even though she will appear to me as an angel. But she is also a temptress. And Ann Marten has intimated that she knows our secret—it must have been her footsteps leaving the church that day. But she will keep quiet—and anyway, who would believe her? There is just Sarah to deal with and then all will be as it should, and I will put the whole sorry incident behind me.

Ann

Now that we both understand one another I feel I can speak freely, Rector. You know as well as I that a forbidden desire is all the sweeter. So it was with William. And he was forbidden to me in so many ways. First, I was a married woman. Then, he was courting my stepdaughter. Perhaps, most of all, he was a gentleman, and as such was out of my reach. Also, he was younger than me. After bedding with an old man nightly, touching William was like being newly loved. I felt it was the one thing that God had given me, my one reward for my many hardships. And he felt the same, but it was not until later that I knew how much.

Although I had been married since I was seventeen, I felt I was totally innocent when he caressed me. And he touched me in a way that Thomas never had—as if I was made of glass, and might break, and then as if I was the thing for which he had hungered all his life. He left me raw, like an open wound, sensitive to everything he did. I felt completely alive for the first time in thirty-one years.

William was just twenty-four, yet he had learned much about a woman's desires. He understood my passionate nature more than I, who had never realised such ardour existed. His teacher in these arts was Hannah Fandango. He had met her when he was twenty-two and living in London, and he told me that since then he was under a spell from which only I had released him. She taught him how to please a woman, and for that I thanked her, but she also encouraged him to cheat at cards and obtain money from his father by devious means. William was so much like a child in some ways, and I could well imagine how the fortune-teller manipulated him.

In London he was involved in activities of which you would not approve, Rector, and things which I would not either, had I not known what it is to hunger for more food or the warmth of a good coat. Hannah was wild, and had wild friends, and I have already told you a little of Beauty Smith and Thomas Wainwright. They had unsavoury dealings all over Suffolk and Wainwright had stolen livestock from a nearby farm, and had been to prison for it. He was also Hannah's protector so William had to deal with him to get to see her. The woman was no better than a whore; though rather than money she favoured jewels and silk. As for Wainwright, he was a painter, and Hannah was his model. William had a miniature of her that Wainwright had painted, and it was a good likeness. I made him destroy it.

I was pleased that William was no longer thick with Hannah Fandango, but she and her two companions still came back to Polstead every now and again, planning some new scheme, and often William would drink with them. Maria was jealous of his continued association with Hannah but I was only fearful he would get caught up in some evil scheme and, sweet innocence that he was, would fall foul of the law. Although I do not have the power of prophecy like Hannah, I have a nose for such things. And wasn't I proved right?

It is as well to know things, rather than be ignorant, and I have always had a way for finding out secrets. There was a secret here, in this very Rectory, that became part of my story. Oh yes, Rector, Elizabeth Bright has reason enough for disliking me—and for resenting your arrival. Have you not noticed it? But you may not know about Rector Whitmore's wife. She has that type of illness which us poorer folk cannot afford, as it is a disease of the spirit, but she spent most of her time in this house laid in bed with smelling salts and tonics. I dare say Whitmore began to rely on his housekeeper, what with her being the only other woman in the house to tend to his needs. And as the Bible says, all flesh is weak.

XXVII

My head pounds. I feel sick to my stomach. I should like to lie in a darkened room, but there is too much to do. If only Peter were already here—I should like to have a friend to confide in, instead of this blank page. I ought not to write, I should keep my thoughts hidden. But they threaten to poison my soul, and must out.

I arrived at the site of the Red Barn early, which was deliberate. I like to see her approach from a distance, to savour the moment, and wanted this innocent pleasure one final time. Rather like enjoying the fragrance of a flower before plucking it. I could see her long hair, loose, lifted by the air as she lithely climbed the hill. I had already laid my jacket on the ground but remained standing. As she came closer I could see that she was not smiling. Her eyes were puffy as if she had recently wept. She fell into my embrace, the tight rise and fall of her chest against mine as she tried to control her breathing. The top of her head, which reaches just under my chin, was inviting and instinctively I kissed her hair, smelling cherries. Her perfume was headier than any liquor and I would have sunk further under her spell, had I not felt wet tears on my cheek. I asked her what was wrong, but she just clung to me.

Oh, I am a shameful man. I thought fearfully of Sarah's husband—had he found out? My career would be in ruins if we had been discovered. When she began to breathe more steadily, I guided her beneath the tree, lowering her down gently on my spread coat.

Sitting at her feet, I wondered how I had let matters get so out of hand. Slowly, and as if every word pained her, Sarah told me the terrible news; worse even than I had feared. She was with child.

She had been sick this very morning and her dress already felt a little tight. Her voice was like a plea. 'Oh, James, I feel the changes in my body. There is a new heaviness in my chest in readiness for the new baby. I am so very scared—what will become of me?' Once she had said this she took a long breath and waited expectantly, her hopeful blue eyes fixed on me.

I wanted to run away, and not look back. I didn't speak for some time; then I said, almost accusingly, 'Is it your husband's?'

Sarah's reply was to bow her head into her hands and begin to shake, saying over and over. 'No, no, no. It can't be. He hasn't touched me in months. I have not wished it. He has been away such a lot, and when he has been home I have pushed him away, pleading headaches, and he has borne it. If only I could love him as he loves me! He'll know it can't be his. It will kill him, James, I promise you. It will kill us both.'

She looked at me with her clear eyes, still beautiful, but no longer with any power to move me. I felt remote, like I was watching her from a great height. I felt something else too—anger. Why had she come to me that day, after the funeral, seeking comfort? I could give her no comfort now, but merely another time to meet. She expects me to solve her problem then.

And now I am so tired. I have dismissed Mrs Bright and told her that I do not want dinner. Even she can see that I am sick but if she was concerned she didn't say so, and left the house quickly. My headache has asserted itself more forcefully, a frequent and unwelcome guest.

So I am here again, at this oak writing desk. I unlock the top drawer, and my hand begins its daily pilgrimage to the medicine chest where my precious laudanum waits to cure me. Or so I used to believe. Recently it makes little impact on the pain and I am finding the need to take more just to feel something close to normal. And my supply is dwindling, with no prospect of renewal.

The key to the drawer I keep with me at all times. Mrs Bright will not know of the current use of laudanum in fashionable circles and I do not wish to shock her. But I am used to city life and have city tastes. I pull the drawer open, gaining satisfaction from the now familiar grind of wood on wood, the comforting closeness of the fit. Inside the drawer is a tin box and, like Pandora, I delve deep, welcoming the rush of anticipation. The tin box is not locked, but has a catch and I open this with the reverence of a physician opening a new phial of life-giving medicine.

Against the black background of the box, the glass bottle winks like an old friend. The liquid is too pure, and must be dissolved. I take the dropper and count to four as the tears join my thimble of water. Tasting the bitterness, I down this welcome antidote to this hellish day. I savour the last sparkling drop at the bottom of the glass, licking my wet finger with my tingling mouth. Soon the delightful numbness creeps over my swollen tongue. With luck my headache will ease in twenty minutes at the most, so I will assist my recovery with a measure of whisky. On a day like today, a little liquor is most welcome.

I sit in my usual chair by the cold hearth. I do not light a fire, as my body is now immune to the chill of the Rectory. I sink into green velvet and close my eyes. Although numbness has disassociated body from brain, my fisted heart still pushes blood around my heavy limbs. I refill my tumbler and attempt to steady my breathing. I must make a plan.

Perhaps there has been a mistake? Although I cannot claim to be familiar with the fertility cycle of the female, I know that a woman's imagination is an erratic thing. Could she be imagining this pregnancy? And how could she be so sure that I am the cause? After all, we have only been lovers a short time.

Women are devious creatures; she has got what she wanted and now she is making me suffer. My vocation, my very life will be destroyed if this were ever known. And what of Mary, and my plans for marriage? There must be a remedy. After all, many men are led astray by women. Take my brother Henry. He was destroyed by women's lust, infected by a scheming harlot. Poor Henry! I feel grief surfacing for the first time, for my brother and for myself, for the fragility of all men who are seduced and deceived and killed by women. If Ann Marten's hints can be trusted then even my predecessor was guilty of the sin; is no man safe?

Looking at my disjointed writing I can see that my mind is rambling now. Sarah Humphries is not Maria Marten, I am not William Corder. The paper seems to float before me; it is such a struggle to write! To my right, in the bookcase, I see my brother's medical books. They are calling to me a message of hope. It is as though Henry has come to save me in my hour of need. Oh forgive me, Lord.

I feel the leather spine, dust marking my fingers as I decipher the familiar titles. My hand slowly, inch by inch, moves along the shelves until one book, snugly tucked between two larger volumes, arrests my questing fingers. I grasp its binding with my shaking fingertips. The title blazes gold out of red leather. 'Poisonous Medicinal Herbs'. I take it down, sink to the floor with it cradled in my arms. My eyesight is blurred, my hands shake like an ague;

but it does not take long to find what I seek. There are drawings of plants, and this one looks innocuous enough; familiar, also. I feel sure that such a plant may be found in the Polstead woods.

I hold hope in my hands like a prayer.

Juniperus Sabina

A common shrub. The entire plant is toxic. Used medicinally to encourage the onset of menstruation. If dose is too high can cause convulsions, haemorrhage and vomiting. Should not be prescribed to women who may be pregnant, as the drug will instigate a spontaneous abortion.

XXVIII

Ann

I am coming to the end of my story, but also where it begins, where I begin. I had a different life before it happened and now I am wrapped up like a bandaged arm; the arm is wounded, but the blood or tear is invisible, and just the tight knot of fabric keeps it all hidden. That's how I feel, like I'm all wrapped up with only the bandage keeping me together, and a noose strangling my heart. If they come undone they will unravel until all that is left is a shrivelled old woman longing for death like a lover.

My story has become my life more than any person, and maybe it's all I am. Without it my life hasn't amounted to much. I've had no children who'll tend my grave. It's only by my story that I'll be remembered; it is my offspring, my child. But the story the world knows is a bastard child; it's not my story, the real story. Not the one I'm telling you.

And now I am handing my child over to you, Rector. You are my choice, though I am sure you are unwell; you are so pale. You should ask Mrs Bright to make some chicken soup, and save the bones so you may suck the goodness off them. That's what I used to do when Tom was sick, and he'd gnaw on those bones for ages, chewing like a dog! It took his mind off his poorly head or belly, or whatever it was.

It took me longer to walk to the Rectory than ever today, and I wondered if you might come to me again next time.

There was no one about as I crossed the village, not even May Humphries. She's probably indoors making the cherry pies and apple puddings which Joshua so loves. I don't bake any more, as there's only Thomas and me, and he's no more bothered with eating than I am. If Tom was to visit, that would be worth baking a cake for, but I gave up that hope years ago.

Who would have thought that the boy could have turned against me with such passion? Me, who was more to him than his own mother? And he was so young when Maria died. I didn't think he'd remember what happened at William's trial. For years he didn't say anything about it, but when he was twelve he suddenly started to have dreams and then he remembered fragments, little bits here and there, about his mother and the trial. It was like a broken jug being repaired, piece-by-piece, and I could only wait, praying that some bits would never be found. But they were.

After that I bitterly regretted telling him to speak in Court, and planting in his memory something that had no natural root. I would have given the world not to have seen the look in his eyes as he realised he had helped to hang his mother's lover. I can't bear to recall the words he said to me, as he got older, how he called me a liar and then, worse, a murderer. It was the darkest time of my life, and that's saying something.

After the trial people called me a witch, on account of my own dreams and the finding of Maria's body, just like I described. They thought I could tell the future, or lay a curse, and there may be some truth that I did both, but not through witchery. Some even came to ask for help; one girl wanted a boy to love her, one wanted rid of a rival, sick people sought a cure. One woman walked all the way from Hadleigh to ask me to cure her barrenness. She said how she knew witchcraft was ungodly, but she'd willingly sell her soul if it meant she could have a baby. I sent her home with her soul unpurchased and with no hope. I often wonder if it would have been kinder to take her money, place my hands on her flat belly and pretend a cure—she would have been happy for a while, and wasn't that what she came for? But I didn't do it. I have never been good at giving false hope. It would be worth the price of a soul, though, if I could. They even tried to say that Thomas's runty terrier was my familiar. I ask you! But he's always kept dogs to help with the mole catching. I can't stand the things myself. No, I'm not a witch. I may be many things but I don't deal with spirits.

Sometimes, I want to change my story so much that I almost believe it's different. I think that Maria is alive and living nearby. We could sit sewing and talk of what a fine man Tom has grown into. She would say, 'Oh Ann, how good you were to me. Better than my own mother.' And I would smile and all bad feelings would be long since buried. But what's the use in thinking like that? What's done is done and wishing doesn't butter any parsnips. So, here's the real story. This is what really happened.

I have told you that Maria was with child. When her belly began to show, William arranged for her to leave Polstead for the remainder of her confinement, and I found this a blessed relief. I hadn't forgot how she was when carrying Tom, sat all day like some Lady, expecting to be waited on. I had no desire to be at the birth on account of her cruelty when her poor little Matilda was born. Let some other woman be her handmaid! And, with her gone, it would be a blessing for William and me. Thomas was as blind to our courting as the moles he caught so I never worried about him.

So, on March 19th, 1827—that date, with others to come, is scored on my soul—William came to collect Maria, to take her to lodgings in Sudbury. There was much to do, what with packing and saying goodbyes. Tom thought his ma was visiting London and was begging for a present, but she pushed him away saying there would be no presents this time and she would be gone for longer too. This made him cry—whether it was the lack of a gift or the fact she'd be gone so long I'm not sure—but I comforted him, as a boy should not be treated that way by his own mother. But I could see she was scared, after having had such a bad time at his birth. William promised he'd visit her and fetch Ma Garner just as soon as she was needed.

Maria packed her bag with two loose dresses, and I wrapped up some things from the larder—a bit of fresh cheese, and a corner of bread with lots of crust, just how she liked it. And then she went off.

Neither Thomas nor I visited her in Sudbury, but of an evening William would come to tell me how she was. Of course he came for something else, too, but this was a good excuse for his visits, and no one remarked upon them.

He had found her a place in Plough Lane, he said, clean and simple, run by an old woman who was not choosy about who she let her rooms to, provided their money was good. She knew William Corder was the son of a wealthy Polstead farmer so she thought she had no worries on that score. But William's father was not generous, and he worried about how he would pay for Maria. He was so low, but I was able to help him. When Peter Matthew's postal note came for Maria I gave it to him. It was my money by rights anyway, as didn't I care for Tom more than Maria ever did? And why should the money not be cashed to pay for Maria's keep? I came to regret giving it to William later, but at the time it seemed such an innocent deceit.

In the second week of April Maria was delivered of a boy. Both mother and child were poorly and the woman thought it best they should come back to Polstead where I could care for them;

she didn't want any deaths in her house, especially an unmarried girl and her bastard son. So William had no choice but to fetch her home.

When she arrived she looked thin and ill. The baby had been delivered too early, he was so yellow, and covered all over in soft hair like a fledgling bird. I thought we would lose both of them, and set about nursing the boy as best I could. But Maria had always been strong and before too long she began to bounce back to health. She still didn't care about the poor little mite, who didn't even have a name. One evening, when she'd been back about four days, I was woken in the night by his crying. I lay listening, holding still in the bed so that I could hear any movement.

I willed Maria to pick the baby up. His crying, at first piercing, now turned to racking sobs—the child would lose his voice if Maria did not nurse him soon! I slid from the bed so as not to disturb Thomas, who was snoring loudly, and moved quietly to the other room. I stood at the door a few seconds before the heartbreaking cry of the infant drew me in. I felt pure pity at the sight. There was the sickly thing, thrashing against his swaddling, in the wooden drawer that served for a cot. Tom was sitting up in bed, sleepy and confused. But Maria was nowhere to be seen.

I picked the baby up, although it was well past being comforted. I whispered loudly over his cries, 'Tom, where's Maria?' I always called her this, never 'your mother', and it was only later that I thought how odd this was. He said he did not know where she was. She must have sneaked from the house when we were asleep, thinking to go unnoticed.

The baby was rooting for my breast, but he would find no milk there, so I rolled my sleeve up and offered my elbow. As he sucked desperately, I cursed Maria for her selfishness. All I could offer a sick infant was flesh and bone, not a mother's life-giving milk. And Maria was with William, I knew that for certain. After all that he had promised me. And I was holding a baby that was theirs, not mine.

When I got downstairs the baby was still howling. I didn't mean to put my hand over its face; I just wanted it to stop crying. And then it did stop; it stopped kicking and straining and was still. I shook it hard and its head flopped to one side. But it was still alive; I could feel its heart beating like a tiny thread.

I waited with the child on my lap until I heard Maria and William come in. Her face was puffy with crying, and I looked to William, but he shook his head. He had not told her about us. When he went to the larder she came to me, 'He won't marry me, Ann. He says he won't do it.' But she had worse news to come, when I passed her the sick boy, and she soon forgot her anger with him then, 'William, come quick,' she panicked, shaking the limp child and crying anew. William was back, and took the baby, then looked to me. For a second I thought there was accusation, but then I saw it was just fear, 'What's happened, Ann?' he asked me.

Maria was still looking to the boy but William looked to me as I explained how I had heard him crying and brought him down to soothe, but then he had gone limp, 'You should not have left him, Maria! A baby that weak cannot be without mother's milk for as long as you were gone...' I had hardly finished when she flashed at me, 'So are you blaming me? How can you say such a thing? I would not harm him. Why, its more likely you hurt him yourself you jealous old crow.' If it had not been for the grief she was feeling I would have slapped her, but William was quick to soothe her.

Maria wanted him to fetch Doctor Badwell, but what of the scandal? And what was the point in wasting money when it seemed all hope was lost? William sent her to bed with a glass of brandy, telling her that we would take care of the boy.

By midnight the baby's grip on life was very loose. I held the little bundle out to William, who took it tenderly. His eyes moistened. This vexed me; mine were as dry as dust. We both knew what we had to do. I unwrapped the shawl from my shoulders and held it out to him. He took this, too, and wrapped him up like a precious parcel. His tears fell, and for a moment I felt nothing but contempt for him—a grown man, weeping! But he knew it was the only way for him to be rid of Maria. He held the corner of the shawl over his son's head and then spread his fingers wide and pressed down, his big hand covering the little face. It didn't take long. It was all over in seconds. The baby didn't suffer. It was a kindness to end his pain. William said, 'I'll get Maria.' and left the room, climbing the stairs slowly, carrying the dead baby as carefully as if it were only asleep.

Later, we all sat together in silence. I poured myself some cider and gestured with the bottle to William, who nodded for me to refill his own glass. Maria stared at the floor, silent for once. William and I exchanged looks. We knew each other so well now, and I could read his face like reading the sky for rain. I saw a mix of emotions, guilt and pain but ultimately his relief at being free once again. Soon Maria returned to bed and William and I moved close together, to finalise our plans.

XXIX

Rectory Journal
1st June 1851

This is my testimony. My witness statement. Although I am not proud of my actions it is a record that my intentions have always been pure. My part is finished now.

I waited for Sarah to arrive on the hill where the Red Barn once stood. Standing at the foot of the elm I felt chilled despite the warmth of early summer. The sun examined my face without giving comfort. I clenched and unclenched my sweaty hands hidden deep in my pockets, nervous as a defendant in the dock. My heart beat erratically. Laudanum had not helped this morning, had not soothed my disordered thoughts. More would be needed. Taking the vial from my pocket I dropped some onto my tongue.

Sarah could save or damn me, and her decision was unknowable. Fixing my gaze on the brow of the hill, I watched for her yellow head to crown. She has never been late, and today was no exception, although as she gradually appeared she was not as light on her feet as usual. She was also dressed differently. Gone were the pretty colours. A loose sombre garment in funeral grey had replaced them.

As she approached I took in the pinched look around her reddened eyes, her pale cheeks. I observed, 'You've been crying.' She nodded, lowering her face as if to avoid my scrutiny. To comfort her, I reached forward, and she came willingly, collapsing into my embrace like a sick child. Holding her against me, feeling her small body shake, I have never felt more like a servant of God. I felt more in control than I have since my confirmation. New strength awoke in my soul. I believe God was speaking to me then, when He has been silent all these years.

When her sobbing had eased I drew back and looked into her face, as innocent as a lamb's, eager and yet afraid, yearning to hear my advice and yet dreading what I would say. Seeing this, and recalling the way I befriended Henry's discarded lovers in Cambridge I knew I was fit for the task. My mettle had remained thus far untested, but I would not fail in the task I had set myself. I would save us both, and she would give thanks for it. I knew at that moment that I had chosen the right course.

Sarah was terrified; she feared being sent to a workhouse, cast out by her own family. Her son would be taken from her and she would be abandoned. More than this, she said that she loved me. She called me wise and learned. She trusted me, and would do as I advised. Still, I chose my words carefully, as skillfully as any man who makes a living from delivering sermons. I said, 'I have been thinking about your predicament. First may I ask, does anyone suspect?'

She looked up with her guileless eyes, and whispered, 'I have told no-one but you, James.'

'Good. And can you be sure that the child,' I hesitated to speak of its existence, but steeled myself, 'is not your husband's?'

Something in this question seemed to light a spark in Sarah who replied with some force. 'I have not been with him for three whole months. The child can only be yours!' Desperate to stop any further displays of unnecessary emotion, I took her shoulders and steadied her.

'I have thought and prayed and I have a solution which will put an end to all your misery.'

She did not relax but her face became expectant. 'What is it? Will you be able to force Jeremiah to divorce me?' Something like hope illuminated her face, and I rebuffed that idea immediately.

'Divorce you? Why no, that would be the last thing that we would desire! We need him to remain in ignorance. No, Sarah, we must...' I hesitated again and then, as delicately as I could, said, 'remove the child.'

She gasped, 'Remove? What do you mean?'

'My brother was a doctor, and I have some knowledge of medicine. I know of a plant which will...' again I employed my words with care, '...empty your womb.'

'A plant?'

'A shrub—juniper. It grows here.' I showed her the plant, innocently laying on white paper. A small green branch with several new leaves, healthy even in this shadowy spot.

Sarah looked at it curiously. 'How would I...? Do I put it on my belly?'

'It must be swallowed. You must grind it up with a pestle and boil it in some water, and then drink it like hot tea. It is used to encourage a woman's courses, so that the foetus will be washed out with the blood. I would advise taking it in a hot bath, to minimise the bleeding and mess. No one will be any the wiser. In a short time all will be well.'

Sarah's tears came anew, but this time with bitterness. 'I can't do it, James. I can't kill my own baby—our baby.'

Impatience exploded within me, and I shook her quite violently. 'You can and will do it. How dare you think you can destroy my life! My reputation!' She was quite beside herself, crying loudly until I told her to be quiet. I thrust the plant into her hand, crumpled up the empty paper and returned it to my pocket. She was still weeping, but hopelessly, as if she knew there was no more to be said. I decided to leave quickly. I bid her good day and turned to walk from the site of the Red Barn.

XXX

Next I strode swiftly to Layham to call on Rector Walpole. I cannot describe my relief at finding him at home. I accepted a drink but refused his offer of a cigar. I wanted to clear my head, as my recent dose of laudanum had left me feeling slightly drugged. I was frustrated by Charles's chatter and listened impatiently as he bumbled on in his genial manner, which I now found intensely irritating.

'I have few vices, James, but the ones I have own me totally! Do you think it wrong that I should enjoy the luxury of wine and cigars when some of my parishioners lack meat with their potatoes? I often consider this, but then reason that what good would my sacrifice do? Surely a happy clergyman can do more for his flock than an unhappy one!'

It seems that the man can continue ceaselessly in this vein with minimal encouragement. But my restless demeanour must have impressed itself upon him eventually, for he suddenly said, 'Whatever is the matter, old boy? You look done in!'

I sat back, arms folded across my chest as though holding myself in. My eyes, reflected in the mirror opposite, were sunken and circled with mauve. I was shocked to realise that I was near tears and, being naturally compassionate, Charles sat closer and tapped my knee.

'When I first started out I was not the man you see before you,' he began in a kindly tone. 'This may surprise you, James, but I had a few doubts about God's purpose myself, and I had my dear wife for support, may she rest in peace. You're all alone in that Rectory, and Elizabeth Bright may be an able housekeeper but she's hardly congenial company for a young fellow such as yourself. It's natural that you will feel low, but things will improve. Why not go and visit your family in Cambridgeshire, hmm?'

I looked up. My voice caught in my throat, so I had to cough. 'I plan to go back soon.' Then I went on in a rush 'After the wedding.'

'Wedding?'

I think I smiled then. 'I have decided to marry. You met the woman, Charles, at your music evening a few months ago…'

'Ah! The resplendent Miss Teager! Well, my dear boy, you should have said…'

'I wasn't sure at first. I've been on my own so long, you understand, but it now seems like a good plan…'

'Yes, indeed. But, James—forgive me! You seem out of spirits! Surely you are happy?'

Seeing the deep concern on Charles's face made me want to weep. I answered solemnly, 'I'm fine. I have found an honest, dependable woman who will bring me comfort. Will you marry us? I can think of no one I should like better to perform the ceremony.'

This was all too much for my colleague. One minute he was watching his friend fight tears away, the next he was being asked to officiate at his wedding! Of course he was rather taken aback by the manner of the asking, and had to take recourse to the wine decanter.

'Naturally I shall be delighted,' he said, his composure restored. 'And when will the happy day be?'

'As soon as it can be arranged. Within the week, if you are able. And then I will take Mary to meet my parents. I see no sense in them travelling down just for the ceremony, which will of necessity be a small affair.'

Charles considered me for a moment, a knowing and troubled look in his eyes. He seemed about to say something, but then hesitated. When he did speak he had obviously chosen his words carefully. 'And what of your bride? Surely she has some say in the matter?'

'Fortunately, Mary is a woman with simple tastes. Her parents are dead, so there is only her old aunt to invite. I do not think she will mind if we exclude friends. After all, she is no longer in the first flush of youth...'

'But even so, James, she is female! Do you mean to say that you have not discussed these arrangements with her?'

'Not yet,' I admitted. I wondered what he would say if he knew that I had not yet asked the lady to marry me. 'But I know what her thoughts on the matter will be. Let us say the wedding will be in seven days. Does that give you enough time?'

'Well, yes, of course, but...'

'I have intruded upon you long enough. When we next meet I will have everything arranged.' I stood and Charles reluctantly echoed me.

I left swiftly, retracing my steps back to Polstead, but I did not return to the Rectory. Instead I carried on to May Humphries' cottage. It is a small cramped building and so I prefer Mary to visit me here. She is due to come to the Rectory tomorrow for dinner, but I could not wait until then. I banged on the aged wood of the front door. Receiving no answer I paused, listened for movement, and presently heard Mary's voice in the garden, talking to somebody.

Coming upon her round the side of the house I was pleased to see that she was in fact alone, but was talking to the chickens as she collected their eggs. She was stooped over, her hands moving with deft swiftness. She was wearing a black dress, plainer than the ones she wore when visiting me, and her hair was pinned up in a tight knot.

Engrossed in her chores, she had not heard me and I did not disturb her but watched, thinking again that she will make a fine wife. Domestic qualities are surely to be valued above beauty. I will enter this marriage with relief, like breathing out after holding on to breath. I will find peace.

Mary now had a full bowl of fresh eggs and turned, saw me watching, and blushed a deep pink. She was obviously aware of her unkempt appearance and distressed to be discovered talking to hens. She bade me welcome, brushing past with head lowered, to enter the cottage. Following her, ducking under the beamed door, I entered the kitchen. Despite the cramped conditions, its neatness was pleasing. There was a smell of fresh bread, rising in the oven. She is a homemaker, that much is certain.

She excused herself, and when she returned she had neatened her hair. However, she was still uneasy. I have noticed previously that her nervousness merely serves to relax me, as if our moods are oppositionally balanced. I did not sit down, and refused an offer of sustenance, but got straight to the point.

I began by saying how her friendship had been most welcome to me, making me feel immediately at home in Polstead. She smiled, and seemed to relax a little.

'I hope this does not seem sudden, my dear, but we are neither of us children, and you do not have a father I can ask. Perhaps I should speak with your aunt, as she is your guardian...'

'Aunt May has gone to visit Sarah.'

I shrugged, this news was of no consequence, and said, 'I think we have enjoyed each other's company?' She nodded vigorously. 'And a Rector needs a wife, a Rectory needs a mistress. I know you to be a sensible woman, and you should be aware that much would be expected of you in the community...' I felt I was advertising the post as one would for a housekeeper. 'But I feel quite sure that you are capable of all that would be required. If you consent. If you agree.' Silence. I had not been explicit enough. I took a painful breath. 'Will you be my wife?'

I think that we both breathed out with relief. I felt guilty at the broad smile that immediately transformed Mary's face. It occurred to me for the first time that she was in love with me. I had not mentioned my feelings. Nevertheless, she was delighted and, as it seemed the right thing to do, I moved forward and kissed her on the lips. It was our first kiss, and awkward.

'Oh, James, I never guessed! My aunt will be so pleased...' I do not relish the social niceties that follow engagements, and told my now fiancée, I fear rather abruptly, 'I would like the wedding to be soon. In a week, if you have no objection. Rector Walpole has agreed to marry us. And I should like my friend Peter to be best man. He is arriving this evening, and can only stay in Polstead for seven days.'

Mary looked stunned but still delighted. 'Oh, yes! Plenty of time! Why, I could borrow Sarah's wedding dress. It will not take long to alter it—she is an excellent seamstress. But—oh!—I will need some other things. I will need to go to town...'

'That is no hardship. Simon can convey you to Bury St Edmunds. I will see if he can take you and Mrs Humphries tomorrow.' As I took my leave she reached for my hand and whispered, 'Thank you.'

I left her to await the return of her aunt. Walking away, I felt a lifting in my heart, and dared to hope that all would be well after all.

It had all gone as planned, and the mistakes of the past would soon be behind me. I resolved to look forward to a bright future. As if to emphasise my change of fortune, I saw Simon Stowe's cart pulling away from the Rectory as I approached and realised with great joy that my dear friend Peter had arrived.

XXXI

Peter and I spent much of yesterday in conversation. It was good to be with my friend again, but his demeanour was depressed; he says he is tired and finding it increasingly difficult to please Dr Kirkman, who demands an almost religious devotion from his protégé. Peter did not speak of the wardens at the asylum, but his references to 'unkind methods' must refer to them. Despite Dr Kirkman's enlightened views, the wards are run by the uniformed staff, and Peter must mediate between the two. I asked about Maisie, the woman who had gripped my leg in such a frenzy of anguish, and he looked regretful. 'She took her own life, James. It should not have happened—she was supposed to be watched. But she took her own nightdress and twisted it into a rope. She hanged herself from the bell tower.'

I shuddered. I asked how had she managed to perform such a deed unseen. Peter explained that she had waited until a Sunday, 'when there are fewer staff, and patients are allowed to leave the ward and attend church. During the service, she climbed the bell tower. We heard her from the nave. Her neck broke like a twig.' Peter put his hand to his mouth, as if to stop any more words. I poured us both a drink and tried to judge if it was the right time to tell him about my imminent wedding, but decided against it. There would be plenty of time tomorrow.

Mrs Bright did not arrive, which was strange. I cannot say I missed her presence, or her food. I foraged in the kitchen and we dined adequately; Peter seemed content with the ham and potatoes that I found in the cold store. Over the meal Peter raised the subject of my recent letter and, resting his knife on his plate, said solemnly, 'In your letter, you mentioned some trouble that I might be able to help you with.' I had no wish to speak of Sarah, and anyway the problem was sorted out now. I was annoyed that Peter had raised the subject, and may have spoke harsher than I intended.

'You misunderstood, my friend,' I said shortly. 'It was nothing, just a trifling matter with one of my female parishioners. It is all forgotten now.' Peter said that he was glad to hear it, but there was a moment's uneasy silence before we regained our previous rapport.

It was late when we finally retired and I tried in vain to kneel on my red cushion and pray. It is often a struggle now, and I sometimes imagine my words are offered up into a vacuum, reminding me that I am desolate and alone. My only solace is in writing this journal, which I still do nightly. Abandoning prayer, I thought how I will enjoy sharing my life with Mary, of the balance she will bring to it, especially after all that has occurred recently. I am ready to commit to a steadier life. I will be a better husband because of it.

But then there was a voice outside—calling from the lane. Mary was standing below, wrapped in what seemed to be a white sheet, her hair tied in pieces of rag. She was calling up to me in some distress, but I couldn't hear, so I gestured that I would be with her presently. I pulled on my trousers and quickly tied my shoes, moving swiftly to the front door to let her in. Before it was fully open she had pushed into the hallway and fell on me. In a gesture that was more like a reflex I put my arms around her. She was dressed only in a nightgown, and I was dazed and confused at her display of emotion. Hearing the noise, Peter appeared at the top of the stairs. He too was pulling on his clothes, coming down to see what had brought Mary to the Rectory at this ungodly hour.

Gathering herself, she struggled out of my grasp and moved back towards the door, pulling me with her. 'It's Sarah! You must come quickly, James, she's so ill!' My heart became a stone and my mouth filled with bile. Peter responded with the speed of his profession, rushing upstairs for his doctor's bag, as Mary urged us to hurry.

I ran ahead of her and she struggled to keep pace. I rounded the corner and raced past the pond, up past the Corder house. My mind was tumbling, not coherent, my legs acting from some other instinct than sense and reason. As I neared the small cottage, I realised what a fool I was. How could I possibly see Sarah now? Tripped by my own fear, it was all I could do to steady myself.

It did not take Peter and Mary long to catch up with me as I stood motionless outside the house. Mary did not stop; now within reach of her destination, she ran ahead but Peter drew level with me and put a hand on my arm. 'You must go to her, James. A Rector is needed when someone is ill, as much as a Doctor.' His concerned expression told me that he guessed that I was afraid of what awaited us inside, but he could not know why. Mary turned and called to us again, and Peter pulled me on. I had no choice but to go with them.

On the threshold of the cottage I hesitated once again. The intrusion into Sarah's domestic domain bothered me more than I can account for. What concerned me, too, was that Jeremiah Humphries would be upstairs. I thought about turning back, but I knew I could not; I could not face Peter's inevitable questions and Mary's righteous anger. I knew I had to see Sarah for myself. Was she losing the child, was that why she was sick—was she now upstairs doubled in pain, after using the remedy I had given her?

Logic entered my restless reasoning. It is common for a Rector to be fetched when a person is sick, along with the Doctor. I would be expected to be there—my presence would not be remarked upon. Resolved, I climbed the stairs and stepped through the heavy curtain into the bedroom. A makeshift mattress on the floor, piled high with blankets, dominated the room. It was hot and crowded, the room inadequate for eight people. By the tiny window Jeremiah slouched on the floor with his head on his knees. When the heavy curtain swished back against the floor he looked up and, seeing me, attempted a greeting, which he failed to deliver before his face creased in pain. I saw his eyes just long enough to know that Sarah had kept her promise. He did not know our secret.

Also kneeling on the floor was Doctor Badwell, but he struck a different pose. I had not seen him since Daniel Stowe's funeral. Smartly dressed in his long black coat, his face was studiously sombre as he secured the brass clasp of his leather bag with a practiced motion. He turned and nodded to me, observing Peter's medical bag with a wry grimace, as if to say it was too late.

And on the bed lay Sarah, pale and still. I could only see her head, as a sheet was pulled up high to her neck. Her eyes were closed and her face contorted in silent agony. Either side of her sat May Humphries and Mary, each holding a cold hand. Mary's sobbing was the only sound, as May sat impassively considering her daughter-in-law. The three women formed a picture which froze in my mind, a trilogy of resignation, loss and death. Badwell stood and slowly placed a hand on Jeremiah's shoulder, before moving to the curtain, gesturing for me to follow him downstairs.

At the bottom, Badwell gestured for us to go to the porch. Here I introduced him to Peter, and they shook hands. Then, turning back to me, he said, 'A sorry tale, I'm afraid, Rector, I fear that discretion is needed. A case of poisoning.' He looked to Peter, identifying him as a colleague, and took from his own, rather more battered but identical bag, a sample container. Taking it, Peter closely observed the green debris at the bottom and asked if the leaf had been identified.

Badwell shrugged. 'There are many poisonous plants in this area, so it could be one of many. I daresay it makes no difference which it was—there was a large amount of debris from the fungus in her vomit. I felt it best not to inform the family—why cause more distress than necessary? To take one's own life is a sin and the whole family carry the guilt if it is known, isn't that so? My job's done here, I'm afraid. A sad day, to be sure, when a young woman chooses darkness over light. In your hands now, Rector. And God's.'

We stood, nothing more left to say. Peter was still holding the sample when the Doctor bid us goodnight. But he had no sooner left the cottage when Peter started and, as if a new thought had just occurred to him, called 'Wait!' and followed in his wake. Fear shivered through me. Had he remembered what I had said about a problem with a woman, which was now solved? And did he remember giving Catherine advice on a certain plant, within my hearing? I could not bear to think it.

It was only as I stood alone in the room that I saw Joshua crouched in the corner, whimpering softly. He was calling for his mummy. When he saw me he held his arms out, imploring me silently to pick him up, to give him comfort. I could not. I could not bear to stay. I left the cottage.

At the end of the path stood Badwell and Peter, bent in earnest conversation. Hearing my approach they turned and stopped speaking. I fancied that Peter considered me with an expression of disgust. I could not shake the notion that he was thinking of Catherine, of the advice he had given her. That he was remembering writing down the name of the very plant which he now studied in a sample glass.

I turned and fled. And where could I go? Not back to the Rectory, anywhere but there. And so I went to the only other place I could think of. To Ann Marten's.

XXXII

Ann

Rest awhile by the hearth, Rector. Don't worry about Thomas—
he is a heavy sleeper and will not wake before dawn. We can
speak freely.

This has been a terrible day—one that I would not wish to see
again. I am glad that it is now nearly over, and that night has
hidden all that has taken place.

When I first looked out this morning the ground shimmered
under a blanket of fresh dew, and the sky was pregnant with
clouds. I rose early, as I always do, and watched the sun push
tentative fingers through the night and begin her climb to watch
above the earth. The day stretched ahead, blank and untarnished.
Events, of course, do not merely unfold like a blanket brought out
in colder months, but tumble at us like thunder. Things happen
deliberately, as a result of something said or done, or because
of things hidden, and today was a day of reckoning, the day on
which a story turns, although it looked like any other. Such is the
uncertainty of life.

How strange that we sit now, in this darkened room. How strange that you have come to me this time, with your story pressing on your soul as mine has surely pressed me. It is your story that we must talk of now.

I have been looking after Joshua most days, and today was no exception. I have cared for the boy for two months now and have grown attached to him, although I have no such feelings for his mother. She fancies herself to be the heroine of a romantic story, but her tale is commonplace enough. Her story is not so very unusual. For what is it? A young woman, too pretty for her own good, trapped in a place that values her beauty but cannot reward it. Which makes her a wife and mother, but cannot give her a man she can love.

So, as her story goes, a stranger comes to town. Not as handsome as he could be, I think you'd accept, Rector, but pleasing nonetheless, and different from any man whom she has met before. A clever man, or at least an educated one, and she is in no position to tell the two apart. A man who sees her yellow hair and wants her for his own, who wants to know her as only her husband should.

I knew all this. I saw it all. It was in the way she brushed her hair sleek with oil, in the way she tied the rough silk at her waist just a touch too tight. For have I not seen it all before? Did I not watch Maria, and then see it in myself? I know the signs. And I have become part of the story. If I had not taken Joshua, then Sarah would not have been free to meet with you. She thought I believed her when she told me that she was going to the market, or blacking the grate, or doing the wash. But I knew different.

And I know something else. I know how you have suffered. I have seen your face hollowing over the weeks, your eyes sinking. A man destroyed is a pitiful sight. I have never been able to bear a man's suffering—a woman's is much more common and does not affect me the same way. But a shattered man makes the world seem unsafe. And so Sarah is the cause of your undoing. She is to blame for your unraveling. Two people drawn together by ill matched desires which, seeking love, they mistake for it. You have my pity, Rector.

I know it all. I see what others miss. I saw her swelling belly, her heavy breasts. I saw the roundness in her cheek and knew what it meant. I knew she was with child. I watched her with interest, wondering how she would make it right. Jeremiah would believe the child his. He is a foolish man, and smitten, so she was in no danger on that score. But her mother-in-law, May, has a sharper eye.

So this is Sarah's story. And it interested me, even whilst leaving me quite unmoved. For surely the tragedy is all the woman's.

So this afternoon I again went to her house. It was near two when I arrived and Sarah was taming Joshua's hair and kissing his head. When she heard me behind her she turned and I saw that she had been crying.

She offered me a brew but I knew she really wanted me gone and so I said that I had just had one. I took the boy by the hand—he comes to me readily now, smiling. My heart aches to see it. I looked at Sarah and thought that this child would have been enough for me, had I had one. I should not have risked him for the world.

Taking the boy's hand I led him here. I left Sarah to her own business.

Time passes quickly with a young child to amuse and it was soon after teatime, when I had agreed to take him home. Today Sarah had told me that she would be sewing—that she has to alter her wedding dress for Mary to wear. She did not seem happy at her cousin's betrothal, but then you and I both know why that is. She did not say anything directly, but when I noticed her wedding dress laid out with her sewing box she turned away, and said that Mary was to be mistress of the Rectory, and there was no joy in her words but a note of jealousy that I know well. Even though the white satin dress was piled on the table I knew she would not be working on it. As I walked back to the cottage I imagined what she would say if I asked her to show me the altered dress. For I thought, instead of sewing, she would have been with you.

I cannot think of what awaited me inside without my head aching. It makes me hot to think of how I walked to the door, not dreaming what lay within. Thinking back, I see now that she had thought of everything. She had fetched the heavy tin bath from the outhouse. No doubt Jeremiah would normally do this, and Sarah must have had to strain to lift its weight. She must be stronger that she looks. On the stove the pans were still bubbling, and the bath was as near to the stove as anyone would dare put it. The pans were heavy, as she had filled them to the top. The bath was filled deep. She must have thought it needed to be.

She had poured pans of hot water into the bath, and then refilled them—I suppose she was thinking that she might need more to clean up after her. The house was silent. No one around, Jeremiah was not due till suppertime, or even later if he stopped at the Cock for a jar. How would she have explained herself if he had arrived home early? Oh, I just slipped in the henhouse, and was cleaning myself up. Or; I felt a fever coming on and thought to sweat it out? She must have thought her purging would have been quick. She did not reckon on me arriving back early with Joshua.

The steam was rising from the bath, filling the room and making me sweat as soon as I walked in, The door to the next room, the one with the window, was closed so it was also quite dark. She had removed her dress, her petticoat. I was shocked for a moment to see her like that, quite naked. I think it's the first time I have seen another woman stripped bare. Even when Maria was in labour she kept her shift on. But Sarah was only covered in clear water, baptising herself to renewed innocence.

The water must have been near to scalding. Her skin looked like it had been cut, red mottling scarred her arms and chest. Her face was screwed tight in an agony of determination. She had forced herself low into the water, and was so locked into herself that she had not heard us come in. The shallow dome of her belly was not fully submerged but her hands were forcing water on this betraying part. It must have been like being on fire. Beside the bath stood a jug, of what I guessed to be gin. Later I smelt the empty jug and it was bitter and harsh—not gin then. She was quite still, held tight by the hot water and whatever it was that she had drunk. Suddenly she clasped her fists over her belly and yowled in agony. Bile came from her mouth, bitter to swallow, and she spat it out. Her hands moved to her chest, as if this was where the pain was worst, and held herself. I could see her heartbeat pumping fast in her neck and she was struggling to breathe.

I looked at her eyes, and she held mine. I could see it then. She had arrived in hell. And then I got a grip on myself. In an instant I hoisted up the boy, pushing his face into the rough itch of my smock, and carried him struggling to the outhouse, where I placed him on the floor with a rusk and told him not to move. I did all this with the same control that I have on all of my life. I am a woman who knows a thing or two, and I saw it all immediately. I knew what it meant; the hot bath, the strange drink. Sarah's tears. I knew that there was a baby and that it was unwanted. That the father was not her husband.

Returning to Sarah, I tried to pull her up from the bath, but such a violent gesture caused her to reel away and hot water splashed my face. I tried again and this time she flopped forward, her weight on my chest. She was fevered and drunk, her body shaking. She began to retch, her face to the floor, pouring out the poison along with her meagre lunch. Her slippery body cramped in on itself as she pumped up the violent protest of her stomach pouring forth its contents. I tried to steady her but she was unable to pull herself together. I could not lift her and she fell to the floor. Somehow I found the strength to help her into Jeremiah's fireside chair and, once she seemed safe, I reached for some clothes and shoved them into her lap.

Even though I could see how wretched she was I felt no pity; my only thoughts were for the little boy eating his rusk. I had known from the start that she was a bad one. Sarah is too pretty, too aware of her own beauty, too sure of herself to settle. And she is no lady, for all her airs and graces. But she thinks she is, or that she could be, and that's worse. Sooner or later a girl like Sarah always comes unstuck, just as Maria had.

I saw that she was slipping out of awareness and gave her a sharp slap, then another. She fell sideways with the blow but did not open her eyes. I grabbed her roughly, attempting to reposition her on the chair, but I had spent all my strength and was too weak to support her weight. I let go. Sarah fell again to the floor. As I knelt over her body, the door was pushed open and a little voice said, 'Mama!' I knew that I would need to get help soon or his mother would surely die. Grabbing his hand I ushered him from the cottage and down the lane. The day was gone now; it was early evening. I would fetch Mary, and she would know what to do.

XXXIII

Ann

Sit and rest, Rector. Try to gain control of yourself. Others have done worse than you and survived. You have to keep your wits about you. Let me tell you the next part of my story, that you may be given peace from your own.

I grant that today was a sad day—there is a different feeling in the air with death. There is heaviness, and it unsettles. It shouldn't feel like this, with only four days to go before you marry Mary. She is a good woman, and well suited to life in a Rectory. You see, Rector, life will go on as it always has. But you look pale; your forehead is waxy and damp. Are you sickening? Then close your thoughts to all but my sorry tale.

Maria and William's son was dead and we had to get rid of its poor little body. We couldn't give it a Christian burial, as if we'd told Rector Whitmore he could have informed the authorities. So it was decided that William would bury it in a field near Sudbury. Well, Maria insisted that she had to go. We tried to stop her, knowing that the death had unsettled her mind and she was not well enough to walk that far, but she would not be gainsaid. They both went in the end, carrying the body in an old sheet. I had expected them to be gone for a few hours, so was surprised to see them back within one. It seemed that Maria hadn't been up to the journey after all, and they hadn't even left Polstead. William had dug a shallow grave in the field by the Red Barn. Who would have thought that Maria too would soon be lying in that same field?

Just after the boy was buried Maria heard from Peter Matthews. She had told him that the money for little Tom had not arrived, and I kept quiet about giving it to William. Mr Matthews had paid a solicitor to look into the business of the missing five-pound postal order. He discovered that it had been cashed, after all, at the Post Office in Sudbury, and that Maria's signature had been on it. Well, on hearing this, she straightaway knew that William had forged it. After all, he had been in Sudbury during her confinement, and he knew what her signature looked like. So she was cunning. She didn't tell Mr Matthews of her suspicions but said she must have forgotten cashing it in Sudbury. He seemed to accept this. But that wasn't the end of the matter for her.

After the burial William wanted no more to do with Maria, but she was not so easily discarded. She insisted that he would marry her, 'or I shall tell the truth of what happened to the five pound order, and they will hang you by the neck or at the least transport you to the colonies.' William looked pale at that, and fear rose in me. I knew that Maria would do it. If she could not have William, she would make certain that no one else could either. I knew she would see him hang if he didn't marry her. And both outcomes filled me with fury. I did not see why she should have everything her own way. For once I had a man to love, who loved me back, and I could not stand by to see him transported or married to a devilish slut. I would not stand for it.

One night, about two weeks after we'd buried the boy, I lit the candle by the window, which told William it was safe to come. It was not long before he was at the door. He nearly fell on me, and I could smell alcohol on his breath, which was not like him. He normally smelled of herbs, especially sage, which was in the fancy soap he favoured.

He was so drunk that he didn't temper his voice, and I was afraid he would wake Thomas or Tom, but most of all Maria, but he was beyond caring. I took his jacket, and pressed my head to his pounding chest, trying to soothe him. 'Calm down, William. Hush, my love. I will not let harm come to us. Do you not know that I am your protector?' I said it and I meant it. And, believing me, William steadied slightly, though tears still wet his face. It sickened me to see him so broken, but when I heard what he had to say I understood. 'I know I am to hang, Ann. A rope in shadow is curled about my neck. I can feel it.'

I shivered, asking him what he meant. Was he to be arrested for the theft of the five pounds postal order? But William shook his head. 'Hannah was in the Cock with the other two. She said she saw the rope as clearly as she saw me. She had already told Smith and Wainwright that I was to die, and she told me the same when I arrived. She said she had dreamt of my fate on three nights. She said she also saw a woman's shadow behind me, even as I stood there in the Cock.' He clutched at me with a fearful passion; his face was ghastly. 'It must be Maria! She will be the death of me!'

'That witch!' I remembered the gypsy's prediction of my own fate, given at the Cherry Fair—that three bodies would lay dead across my life's path. 'But William, what is she doing back here? And what of those other brutes?'

Now William lowered his voice, which alerted me to the full import of what he was saying, and the news dawned like a groan in the pit of my stomach. 'They are to do one last job, Ann. They are stealing from two houses, one in Polstead and the other a few miles away. One will be empty for all next week except for an aged cook and three servants whose silence can be bought cheaply. The other will be empty for a good two hours. It's a big job—bigger than they can manage alone. But it's foolproof. They've set the day—it's to be next week, the day after the tithes are due.'

And now fear was all over me. 'Why did they tell you all this, William? Please tell me you are not to join them?'

He did not deny it. Instead he knelt me down on the floor, his cheek on mine, his breath in my mouth. 'This is our way out, Ann. Do you not see? It is our gift from Heaven. Just one wrong deed, from people who have too much anyway, and we will be free for the rest of our lives.' I felt my disgust weakening as I considered the sweetness of freedom. He said coaxingly, 'We could go anywhere; we could live abroad. Would you like that? I will finish teaching you to read and write; we could even set up a small school for ladies. You have so much to teach girls, Ann. It would be a success. And we could marry.'

The idea hung like forbidden fruit, unknown yet luscious. To think that I, who had never even left Suffolk, might go abroad! That I might sleep every night by the man I loved! No more scrimping and scouring. No more Thomas or Maria. And maybe even one day, a child of my own...One bad deed, and then a life of happiness. After all the wrongs that had been done to me, would God really begrudge me this one thing? I looked into William's expectant eyes, his cheeks now dry, his colour high as he saw me considering his words.

'I'll do it. When is it to be?'

He breathed out in relief. 'The next full moon is May 18th, which will make our journey from Suffolk easier. Hannah and the others will meet me at midday at the Red Barn.'

I pulled back from his embrace when I heard footsteps behind me. Maria had come downstairs and was rubbing her sleepy eyes, her crumpled nightshirt revealing her recent rising from bed. 'What's going on? What are you two plotting?'

I see the understanding in your face, Rector. You begin to see now. It is starting to become clearer, but you are still unsure what happened between William and I; what part Hannah, Samuel Smith and Thomas Wainwright had in my story, or how it was that Maria came to be murdered. I see the questions in your face, so dark that they dare not arrive on your lips. You want to know if I killed her. You want to know if I am guilty, or if William was rightly hung. Or maybe we are both guilty. The truth is always somewhere in the middle, as you should know after today. And I will tell you the rest of the story when we meet again. But it is nearly morning. Thomas will be awake soon, and I think you should return to the Rectory before Elizabeth Bright arrives to give you your breakfast. And look to her, Rector. She is not to be trusted.

XXXIV

Rectory Journal
June 4th 1851

I arrived back as the sun was rising, a red halo hanging over the Rectory. My walk was slow, but my thoughts buzzed like flies, torturing me with Sarah's death and, worse, the thought that Peter might think me responsible. But I had told her the exact quantity of the potion to take; how could I know she would take too much of it?

It was so early that I had expected Peter would still be asleep but, upon opening the unlocked door, I heard voices coming from the library. In my exhaustion, I could not place them. Unsettling thoughts entered my mind; could it be Jeremiah Humphries? I was tormented by the idea that a constable had come to arrest me for Sarah's death.

What I saw in the library stunned me. There, in deep conversation, were Peter, Mrs Bright and John Whitmore, my predecessor. At first I thought my sleeplessness was making me imagine things but then Peter turned and saw me, 'James, thank God! We have been quite beside ourselves with worry! Where did you spend the night?' Before I could answer he had ushered me to a chair, studying my face with the eye of a doctor. 'You haven't slept. You cannot carry on like this, James, you will destroy yourself.'

I could not speak. I was still staring at Rector Whitmore. He nodded to the housekeeper and she left the room with a sideways sneer in my direction. I recalled Mrs Marten's warning not to trust her.

John Whitmore cleared his throat. 'I am most grateful to your friend for being here when I arrived last night. If not, I should not have known where to place my head after two days' travel. You did not reply to my letter, James. I know that you received it, as Elizabeth was adamant she gave it to you.' It took me a moment to realise that he was referring to Mrs Bright, and I recalled what Ann Marten had suggested about their relationship. I could not remember any letter, but I could see there was no point in arguing. 'You have had us all very worried, young man. What were you thinking of, disappearing like that? We feared you had fallen in the pond, like the unfortunate Thomas Corder. Where did you go?'

My mouth was dry, but I managed to articulate that I had been at the Martens' cottage. He nodded. 'Elizabeth guessed as much.' Peter, who had not risen from my side and still held me in his gaze, urged me to retire and rest. Despite my feeble remonstrations, he helped me up the stairs and to my room. I was relieved to be out of Whitmore's presence, although my friend also seemed cool towards me, treating me in an almost professional manner.

'You mustn't mind John's gruffness,' he said. 'He seems a good man. It is concern for you that brought him here.' So they were on first name terms already.

I asked what he meant by 'concern'.

'It seems you have been acting strangely. Your letter about the Red Barn murder alerted him that all was not well, and then Elizabeth—Mrs Bright—told him that you do not sleep but seem obsessed in writing some journal...'

'What? She has been spying on me!'

'Hardly spying, James. Your fatigue makes you paranoid. She is concerned and worried. As we all are. Rest now—we will talk later.' He stood to leave, and I found that I did not want to be alone with my thoughts again. My head throbbed, and I longed for some laudanum. I had but one dose left. I had no choice but to ask Peter's assistance.

'Please, Peter, will you get it? Without telling anyone?' He nodded, and took the key to the drawer where the drug was kept, which I carried always on my person. It was only when he had left the room that I realised I had also directed him to my journal, which I kept locked in the same drawer. Would he read it? No, of course not. As he said, I was being paranoid. Peter would not betray me. Nevertheless, he did not return with the laudanum, and I was too tired to rise and fetch it myself, not able to brave another encounter with Whitmore. I was totally alone.

Sleep came in waves; dark images flashed across my blinking eyelids, waking me every moment only to plunge me back into nightmares again. I must have been like this for some hours because the next interruption was Mrs Bright, who carelessly placed some soup on the bedside cabinet. It must have been lunchtime but I could not eat anything. A short while later there was another knock and this time Peter entered. He felt my forehead and enquired if I had slept. It seemed I was his patient now. I grimly recalled that he was used to treating the mentally afflicted. He sat on the chair by the bed.

'Are you able to talk, James?' There was no warmth in his voice. I felt I was being analysed. Then came a deeper voice, from the doorway.

'You cannot ignore us, young man. We mean to have it out with you.'

And then Whitmore too was in the room. I felt trapped but also angry; how dare he come into my bedchamber! I had to squint at him, as the sun was shining into my eyes from over his shoulder. In a blunt, business-like tone demanded, 'Why are you so fascinated by the Red Barn murder? Did I not warn you to stay away from the subject?'

I forced myself up on the pillow, adding as much steel to my voice as I could muster. 'I told you in my letter. Ann Marten came to seek my ministry. All I wanted from you was more information about something that happened during your stewardship in Polstead.'

I could not see his face, but I heard the condescension in his voice. 'Information, is it? Well, it can do no harm now.' He reached into his pocket and took out a cigar, expertly cutting and lighting it. The sun had moved from his shoulder and now I could see his penetrating eyes considering me. 'Maria was missing for eleven months before her body was found; you probably know that. Do you know what happened afterwards?'

I shook my head, my interest aroused. He drew on his cigar, and said slowly, 'The body would not have been found without Ann Marten's dreams. Then the constable went in search of Corder. He was found fairly quickly. He was arrested as he breakfasted with his new wife.' I tried to dissemble what I was being told, that Corder had a new wife. Whitmore chuckled, no doubt amused by the idea of a man being handcuffed while in the middle of his breakfast. He looked at Peter, as if sharing an amusing anecdote. 'It seems that he had placed an advertisement for a wife in a newspaper! I never knew that such a thing could be done! No doubt she was as shocked as he was when they arrested him. She was heavy with child as well. I met her at the trial and she seemed sensible enough, although what kind of woman responds to an advertisement like that God alone knows. I brought it with me—here.' He again reached inside his coat, this time retrieving a folded sheet of newspaper, which he thrust it into my lap. It was the back page of The Morning Herald, the classifieds section, and one box was circled in black ink. Inside the box was printed:

MATRIMONY. *A private gentleman, aged 24, entirely independent, whose disposition is not to be exceeded, has lately lost the chief of his family by the hand of Providence. To any female of respectability who would study for domestic comfort, and willing to confine her future happiness in one every way qualified to render the marriage state desirable; as he is in affluence, the lady must have the power of some property, which may remain in her own possession. Should this meet the eye of any agreeable lady, who feels desirous of meeting with a sociable, tender, kind and sympathising companion, they will find this advertisement worthy of notice. Honour and secrecy may be relied on.*

Peter took it from me, also keen to see how such an advertisement might be phrased. I was unsure what to make of it. Whitmore seemed amused and looked closely at me. 'Corder placed that advertisement just two months after he left Polstead. And many women replied, not just the one he married.' Then, as if to himself he said, 'She held herself with great dignity at the trial.'

The trial! This was something of which I knew very little. All I knew was that it was held in August. Whitmore had been there. If he was finally willing to talk, then I would certainly listen. I asked if he would tell me about it.

'My goodness, but it was hot!' Whitmore loosened his collar, as if in sympathy with the memory. 'Steam rose from the land with the humidity. And the courtroom at Bury St Edmunds is terribly stuffy. The walls are all wooden, as are the seats, and that day it was like being confined in a larder laden with over-ripe cheese.' He coughed to stifle his laughter, and Peter too was smiling. It seemed just an amusing story to them. 'The Judge had to be carried over the crowd to reach his seat, and William's lawyer had pushed to his position, when the force of the throng took him all the way to the door again. The Red Barn trial was the attraction of the century.

No respect was given to the Marten family who had to push through like everyone else, especially Ann who had to suffer the indignity of hearing people whisper, 'That's her, the stepmother, the one that had the dreams', or even calling out 'witch!'"

Peter, no doubt out of professional interest, asked about the composure of the murderer, to which Whitmore replied, 'When they led Corder in, the crowd hushed. He seemed to be quite controlled, steeling himself probably. He was well presented, no doubt thanks to his wife, though there was some blood on his collar where he'd nicked himself shaving. He hardly looked around, but put his chin to his chest and kept his head down.

First to be called was Phoebe Stow, Simon's mother. Her cottage is nearest to the Red Barn, and she recalled one day in May, at the time that Maria went missing, when William had asked to borrow a spade.

Maria's father, Thomas Marten, was next in the witness box. He was a picture of sorrow, and could barely utter a syllable before his eyes welled up. He recounted how he had believed Maria and William had married and were living quietly somewhere in the country. He said he had received letters from them, written by William who explained that Maria couldn't write herself on account of a sprained wrist. He had never doubted the truth of what he was told until his wife had persuaded him that something was wrong on account of the dreams she had begun to have about Maria.

Ann Marten followed him into the witness box. She spoke of the baby boy that had died, about William's promises of marriage to Maria, which had came to nothing. How she had helped Maria to get ready to meet with William in the Red Barn on May 18th, and had never seen her again.

But it was Maria's son, Tom Matthews, who convinced the Judge as to Corder's guilt. He was so small that they had to put a box on the floor for him to stand on. Everybody leaned forward to hear what he had to say. Ann had made sure that he was clean and neat and he did very well, looking at her the whole time he was giving his evidence. He nodded when they asked if he'd seen William on that afternoon, carrying a spade to the Red Barn. And that he saw him later, just after midday, hurrying away from the Barn with his head low as if to avoid being seen. When he finished he returned to his seat and asked Ann, 'Did I do all right, Ma?' He had done better than all right—the sight of the murdered girl's son condemning her lover was what Corder swung on.'

Whitmore came to the end of his narrative, and added sombrely, 'After that the decision was made: guilty, of course. William Corder was hanged for the murder of Maria Marten.'

He stubbed out his cigar on the floor and came to the side of the bed, sitting on the blanket, imprisoning me. 'So there is your information, James. Now you must give us yours.'

We sat in silence; Peter gazed in concern at me. Only Whitmore appeared calm. 'I wonder if we should say a brief prayer?' He closed his eyes and sent his prayer heavenwards. 'Dear Father in Heaven, We thank you for Your understanding and benevolence. Lord, please give me the right words that I, your servant, may be blessed with understanding and compassion in all things. In the name of the Father, the Son and the Holy Spirit, Amen.'

I echoed the final word, my eyes wide open yet so blind. Peter looked awkward, and moved to the window. Looking at him, I saw the lines in his face that were normally reserved for fulsome smiles were pulled downward. He took a red handkerchief from his inside pocket and mopped his forehead, removing beads of sweat running from his hairline to his brow. He frowned and leaned forward as if to plead with Whitmore then, sighing deeply and visibly composing himself, stood silently by the window.

Whitmore sighed with impatience at my continuing silence. 'You were seen, young man, with the girl.'

Rector Whitmore shouted now, as if pushed beyond his limits. 'For God's sake, man! We know you had carnal knowledge of her in the church. Elizabeth was still there. She saw everything.' The footsteps that I had heard—not Ann Marten's, then. They had been my housekeeper's.

'And your friend here suspects that Sarah died in an attempt to miscarry her unborn baby.'

I looked to Peter, who was blushing but defiant. 'The sample in the glass, James. Juniper. An extremely toxic plant.'

So I was discovered. He had guessed my secret and told Whitmore, who now said, his voice devoid of any emotion, 'So, the father of the dead child was you. Will you deny this?' And then, to my horror, he revealed—from the confines of his coat— my journal. He had read my precious journal, and all that was within. And then I looked to Peter and saw that he too knew its contents.

'How could you, James?' His voice was sad. More terrible to my ears than Whitmore's accusation. 'After what happened in Cambridge. How could you be so..."He did not finish his sentence but turned his back, as if he could not stand the sight of me. I had betrayed him. He had rescued me once, believing me innocent. Now he saw me for the abject sinner I was.

I looked at my hands, and blinked back tears. There was no face of compassion to offer comfort. 'I fear that the Lord has quite forsaken me.'

But Whitmore would allow me no pity. He threw the journal into my lap and spat out, 'No, James. It is you who has forsaken Him.'

*

I had been left on my own for several hours, and although I had now risen and dressed I had no wish to leave my bedchamber and I lay idly on the bedcovers. It was growing dark when I heard the knock on my door. Expecting Mrs Bright or Peter, I did not respond and turned my back. I had no wish to see anyone.

But when the door opened and I heard my name I knew that it was none of the people I feared. It was Charles Walpole. He approached the bed on which I lay, and sat on the chair.

He was out of breath, 'Don't tell me you have come this far just to see me!' I hoped I sounded more lighthearted than I felt. 'What, without a flask of claret to help you along the way?' I think I may have even smiled, but he was straight faced as he struggled to regain his composure.

'I will not hide my feelings from you, James. I come on very grave business and I feel the heaviness of my duty as keenly as if it were a yoke around my neck. Do you have something which we may both partake of to give us courage before I begin?'

I gestured to the night cabinet, where there was a half-empty bottle of port and a used glass. He poured a generous measure and drank it in one mouthful. Removing his glasses, he rubbed his nose as if in pain, then lowered his voice, 'James, dear boy. This morning I had a visit from Mrs Marten.'

'From Mrs Marten? But why would she visit you?' My thoughts raced over what she may have told him.

'She told me a very sad tale, James. She told me of the tragic death of Sarah Humphries, dying in great pain, watched by her helpless husband and her little boy who has not yet seen his second birthday.' He said this in a soft voice, his eyes sympathetically on me, even though this revelation must mean he knows my part in the ghastly tale. I am ashamed to say that tears fell from my eyes, and I wept silently like a child.

Charles seemed desperate to say something to help. He made an open-palmed gesture as he spoke, 'It is terrible for a young woman to die, especially when she leaves behind a child. But she is with God now.'

I almost laughed at that, thinking of the sin that would surely weigh Sarah down to hell. The Rector frowned, watching me as I leaned back into my pillow, trying to master myself. He placed his hand on my arm and I could have cried anew, for here was the first pity anyone had shown me. When my oldest friend, and my own conscience, had deserted me this one person seemed to be on my side. He waited for me to still and spoke again, 'I can see your torment is terrible. Grief and guilt are painful emotions. But you are repentant, and the Lord will listen. He has already sent Ann Marten to me, that I may help you. She fears for you, James. She believes that if the village discovers your relationship the consequences will be grave. And she told me how you had run from Sarah's house like a guilty thing, after you saw her dead body. I believe we can save the situation, with God's will. Alas, I do not think that our colleague John feels the same, but I am hopeful that we may persuade him that forgiveness and Christian hope are necessary here.'

I clung to the words like a drowning man on a rock, clinging to Charles's faith rather than my own. But I could not believe that the situation could be salvaged; I had seen Whitmore's disgust and knew that he would tell the Bishop. All was lost to me.

'James, is Mary aware of any of this? Is the wedding still planned for Friday.'

I suddenly felt very tired, and shook my head. 'She doesn't know anything. Sarah did not tell anyone of our meetings. The blow will be too hard for her to bear when she finds out.'

And then I could bear it no more. The shame of my sin. Sarah's death. My betrayal of my friends. I propelled myself up, pushing off Charles's restraining hand. I threw myself at the door, flung it open to find Mrs Bright there, bent at the waist towards the keyhole. She did not even have the grace to withdraw, but I was past caring. I pushed past her, raced blindly down the hall and to the front door. In my anguish I yelped like a dog, running to the lane that led into the village as though the Devil himself were at my heels.

XXXV

Rectory Journal
June 4th 1851

My feet took me to the site of the Red Barn. The place where Sarah and I had met and laid down. Where she told me that she was with child. And later, where I told her how to rid herself of it. And now she is dead. The shadows around me were like the ghosts in my dreams, confused voices from my past. Henry, whose fatal flaw, has become my own. Catherine, who tells me of her broken heart, of the child she removed from her belly, after I wanted no more to do with her. Was she dead then? No, it is Sarah who is dead. But why do I live? If only I could lie down and give my unworthy body to the cold, hard ground, my perjured soul to God. This was the field where William and Maria buried their son. It was where Maria was murdered. Our stories seemed to have converged, William's become mine, Maria's become Sarah's. I needed to know the end of their story, that I might also discover what will become of me.

The candle was in the window when I arrived, as I knew it would be. When she opened the door I felt relief to be with her;

she alone does not judge me. And so I wrote down her story one last time. My final task. I have transcribed the final part of The James Version.

Ann

The wind is high tonight. I can hear its heavy breath blowing down the chimney. From where I lay before you came, Rector, I could see a bright moon in the sky, just as there was on that May 18th twenty four years ago. I felt then, as I feel tonight, like it was shining its light on me, through to my soul, and that the rest of the world will remain in darkness and asleep while I rise. Upstairs Thomas snores heavily, a noise that used to drive me to distraction but which I have come to find comforting. Tonight it made me smile. I saw his face, relaxed; the twitching of his eyelids as if he were a puppet with strings and Sleep was pulling them. His chest rose and fell in a smooth, easy rhythm, content in the knowledge that his life will go on for many more years, so there is no need to hold it so tightly. As I watched him breathe so steady, I knew he would outlive me. I have always known this. He has not been a bad husband; he could have been worse. He has never beaten me and only gone drinking after giving me money for food. He has done his duty, and I know many who would not, so for that much I am grateful.

But what of me? Have I been a good wife?

I have not. I have been too restless, and even now as I approach my death my mind is not gentle. The wind's howling soothes me, as I find no peace in silence, and never could. Would he have married me if he had known that I would never settle? That, although the dinner would be ready, it would be prepared with sighs, that although his shirts would be clean, they would not be pressed with love but with resentment? Maybe he would, but then he does not know how deep my restless spirit goes, how much I have wronged him.

You look tired. But perhaps now I can help you. I visited Layham today, and spoke with Rector Walpole. He is your friend and I think that all may be well for you, after all. I knew that he was the person I must see in order to save you from Elizabeth Bright and Whitmore. I knew that if he saw you, saw how tired and ill you are, he would help and you would not be alone. You have done no worse than many others before you. I do not judge you—how can I? I only care that you listen long enough to learn the truth. I just want one other person to share my secret, to carry the knowledge that has weighed heavy on my soul for over twenty years. It is a long time to carry such a burden.

I do not feel guilt, although I am guilty. I could regret too many things and so I choose to regret none. But to say the words out loud, to surprise myself by hearing the truth that I have not even allowed myself to think of, has brought me some peace. I am ready to die now, once my story is told.

The night that I agreed to leave with William, the night that he told me of his plan to go abroad and open a school, Maria interrupted us. At first I feared that she had heard us talking but I realised she could not have seen us embrace as she looked merely irritable, and the hand she placed on William's thigh confirmed it, though he shot me a look of dismay. He felt trapped, and I longed to free him. So we took a gamble. William told her that he would, after all, marry her. He said that he had been explaining to me that he had a licence for them to be married in Ipswich on May 18th. She was triumphant; thinking her threat of reporting the five-pound theft had worked. Then William took a greater risk; he told her, as he had already told me, that Hannah Fandango, Beauty Smith and Thomas Wainwright had planned two burglaries for that same day. If Maria and he went in with the others they would share the profits, which would set them up for life. Now Maria grew fearful. She may have had loose morals, but she was no thief.

I saw the way William was heading and helped to secure her willingness. 'Maria, you know I would not normally agree to such a thing. But just think how much money there would be, think how you could buy your own home and never have to toil ever again.' I appealed to her greed, not to her love for William.

So, on that fateful day of May 18th 1828 I helped Maria to get ready to meet William in the Red Barn. It had been agreed with the gypsy that they would carry out one burglary, he as lookout and she to go to the house dressed as a boy. Hannah, Beauty and Wainwright would do the bigger job outside of Polstead. I will not tell you any more of their crime as it remains unsolved, and I would not wish to put you in a difficult situation.

Of course, Thomas thought she was simply going to meet William, and be off to Ipswich to marry. We had to explain to him that we were dressing her as a boy so that the bailiffs wouldn't see her. I made up a story about Rector Whitmore obtaining a warrant for her arrest after he had heard of the death of the illegitimate baby. This was a lie of course—Whitmore could never have found out about that little body buried in unsacred ground. And even if he did know I doubted that he would get a warrant, as he himself wasn't a stranger to the sins of the flesh, and he'd already known about Maria's other bastards, Matilda and Tom. Why should he object to a third?

I helped her to choose which clothes and hats were to follow in her trousseau, telling her not to pack too much. Wouldn't she be weighed down with riches all too soon, I urged her, enough to buy many new things? I held the jacket for her to put first one arm into, then the other, then I pinned a cap over her dark hair. I saw that she was afraid of committing the crime and steeled myself against giving any comfort—even I am not such a hypocrite. And then I saw William's red and white spotted handkerchief and tied it around her throat, the knot resting where her collarbone dipped. She made a very handsome boy.

It was just before noon when she left to meet William at the Red Barn, where Hannah, Smith and Wainwright would also be, and from where they would go their separate ways. Hannah and her consorts would then head around the woods to their destination, where the servants had already been bribed and would be waiting with the silver and jewels. Hannah was to be watcher while the men collected the valuables and tied up the servants, lest it be suspected that they were in on the crime. Then they would head back to the Barn with the booty.

Meanwhile, William and Maria were to aim closer to home. I haven't told you this, as maybe I was a little ashamed—but they planned to burgle the Rectory. Whitmore had collected in all the tithes for the year so there was a tidy amount of money, and we knew where it had been hidden, as Elizabeth Bright often boasted of how she dusted the coins until they gleamed, and how Whitmore trusted her and did not keep them locked away. We also knew that he would be away from the Rectory for at least two hours that afternoon, as he had reason to walk past my cottage. I have told you that Whitmore and Elizabeth began to rely on each other more than they should and now I will tell you plainly that they were lovers. Most of the village was ignorant of this, as they remain to this day, but I had known for months. It was confirmed to me when Whitmore started the habit of visiting her cottage every Friday—after all, they could not use the Rectory with his wife there. I turned a blind eye, but now the knowledge would serve us well. With only Mrs Whitmore in the house, and her always in bed, the theft would be undisturbed. Our planning was very careful, Rector, and we thought nothing could go wrong.

After Maria left, Thomas went back to work and Tom went to play on the green, so I was alone. William and I had already agreed that I would be at the Red Barn at 3 o'clock. I should be all prepared, with all I needed packed, to go with him. Only then would he tell Maria that he would not marry her; that it was me he loved. As she would have recently committed a burglary she could no longer report him for stealing five pounds, and we guessed that her new wealth would sweeten her disappointment at being jilted. She didn't love William, that much was clear. I guessed that, with nowhere to go, she would return to our cottage and care for her father, son and sister, as she always should have done. And I would be with William. For once, fortune would be on my side.

And so, I readied myself for my new life. I went around the cottage, collecting what I needed. My possessions were few, but I comforted myself that soon I would have more and better things to call my own. For the time being they would do. I gathered my one other summer dress, my darned stockings and a shawl. I took the gold chain that had been a wedding gift from my mother, my one valuable possession. Then I took something for sentiment— the small wooden horse my father had carved for me when I was a baby. I took bread, cheese and beer for the journey. My hand shook as I pushed the cork in the neck of the bottle. Finally, from the back of my linen drawer, I retrieved the small book of poems gifted to me by William. I considered the small pile, which summed up my life, realising that I had no way to carry it, other than in my large laundry basket, which would be too cumbersome. A thought came to me, and I went to Maria's room, easily spying her most treasured hatbox, its silk ribbon tied in a neat bow. It was the one thing I stole from her, after all that she had stolen from me. My belongings fitted into it perfectly, and the feel of the silk against my wrist gave me courage.

Finally, I went to straighten Tom's bed. My eyes stung with the thought that I may never see him again, feel his warm sticky hand in mine. It was hard to leave him, but if I didn't go I would be held forever, in that cottage, in that life. And I hoped to have a child of my own soon—mine and William's. I was being given a chance to escape, and I had to take it.

I closed the door for the final time; my bonnet tied swiftly, the hatbox hanging from my wrist. I turned to the path that cut up to the Red Barn, my hopes high. But then something terrible happened. Walking towards me was Elizabeth Bright. I was so shocked that I stopped, my hand to my eyes as if to chastise them for what they saw. She walked past me, greeting me as she passed. Then, noting my ashen face she stopped. 'Are you unwell, Ann?'

I shook my head, and the silk ribbon slid from my sweating hand. Elizabeth caught it before it fell. 'It's not like you to have a hatbox—more Maria's style I should say.'

I stood dumb like Lot's wife, unable to turn away. When I found words they tumbled from my dry mouth like stones in a landslide. 'What are you doing here? Where is the Rector? Why isn't he with you?'

She stared at me, puzzled at my aggression, before a realisation came to her; that I knew that they were lovers. She licked her lips, wondering how to answer. Pride overcame modesty. 'John is unwell. He's in bed with a fever. I am going to him now.'

I took a sharp breath, my forehead beaded with sweat. All was lost, then. She couldn't know that Maria would be entering the Rectory at any moment, with Rector Whitmore in the house, and William outside as lookout! I knew I must warn them. I began to run down the lane and up the hill to the Rectory, with Elizabeth Bright hurrying after me.

At the gates of the Rectory was Maria. I shook her shoulders and asked impatiently, 'Where is William? He was supposed to be here!'

'He's inside…'

I stood aghast. 'But you were meant to go in, he was the lookout…'

Maria looked down at her shoes. 'I got scared and couldn't do it.' Then she raised her head and said defiantly, 'He's just left.'

Then Maria saw Elizabeth Bright, panting up behind me. 'What is she doing here?' I ran round to the back entrance of the Rectory knowing that William would have left it open for a speedy exit. I hoped he would still be downstairs, and hurried along the corridors as swiftly and silently as I could, not daring to call out his name. And then, rounding a corner, I was grabbed from behind and a hand clamped itself over my mouth.

'Ann!' It was William, thank God, standing in the shadows. 'What are you doing here?'

'Whitmore's upstairs,' I gasped. 'We must leave.'

And then Elizabeth pushed past us and ran up the stairs, calling, 'John! John! Are you all right?' He appeared, in his dressing gown, at the top of the stairs and she ran to him, putting her arms about him. Whitmore remembered to push her away, but not before he had kissed her face. Looking down, he saw that William and I had both seen him. Then a frail voice called out, 'John? Is something the matter?' He paused for just a second, taking in the scene, Elizabeth still shaking in his arms, before he replied, 'Nothing to worry about, dear. Go back to sleep.'

We did not wait to see any more, fearing the alarm would be raised in moments. All was lost. William grabbed my hand and we fled from the Rectory, past Maria who yelped like a startled deer and followed behind us. We did not stop running until we were inside the Red Barn.

XXXVI

Ann

Inside the Red Barn, I put my arm around my lover's neck and sobbed. It was not until I had cried myself silent that I saw Maria, standing there with a look of horror on her face, holding in her hand the silk-ribboned hatbox.

She saw it now. She saw what we had kept hidden for months. She began to back away. 'You wait until I tell Father, you wait until it all comes out...'

William let me go and slowly walked towards her. 'Maria, we never meant to hurt you. It just happened. We meant to tell you today...'

'So I see! You were going to leave together! And what of me?'

'You would have been well cared for. The money from the Rectory...'

'But there is no money! And I did nothing! But you—you went in the Rectory!' A crafty look came over her face as she saw her salvation. 'They'll be calling the constable now. You'll hang for this, William!'

At that his face turned ashen. He was close to breaking point. All that he had suffered recently—his brother Thomas drowning, the death of his son, Maria's threats, Hannah's terrible prophecy;

and now the threat of the hangman's noose. He collapsed to the floor and sobbed, a broken man. All of our plans were in ruins before our eyes. I froze, shocked at his weeping, until love overcame disgust and I was able to go to him. I put my arms about him, offering futile comfort, but he was wracked with pain, and could not surrender to me. His coat hung open, his pistol pressing against my thigh.

And then I heard the cruellest sound I have ever known. She was laughing, wallowing in his misery. Her face was shocking; masklike, her eyes and mouth stretched wide in hysteria. Her evil laughter filled the barn, echoed round the walls, cracked open my skull and jangled my brains. And it must have been the same for William. He could bear it no more; what man could? He reached into his jacket and, pushing me aside, he fired his pistol at Maria. There was a split second of recognition in her eyes, before the bullet hit. She fell to the ground, blood pulsing from an eye socket. Screaming, her mouth a perfect circle, she was bloody, wounded, but alive.

William reeled back, throwing the pistol aside. We knew that at any moment Hannah and her two accomplices would come in. William was a condemned man. And all because of that selfish, spiteful whore. How could any woman bear it? How could I stand by and watch the man I loved be destroyed by her? I seized on the hatbox, opening it to reveal, stabbed into the skin of the cheese, a paring knife. I drew it out. Maria was lying on her side, her hands to her face, whimpering. She did not see me approach, but William did. As I lunged at her chest he came behind me and grabbed my hand. 'No, Ann!' he cried hoarsely, pulling me back. The knife had stabbed her in the chest, but came out too shallow, cutting her across the cheek and neck in the struggle. She screamed anew, writhing on the floor. Still she was not dead.

I turned to William, fierce that he had held me back, shouting, 'We will both hang now. We are finished.' He repeated his curse, that he would hang by the neck, over and over: Well, I told him,

'I'll be damned before I let her hang me", but the bitch would not die! It was as if the evil spirit inside her was too strong. I watched her writhing, her blood staining the ground, with no pity in my soul.

Around her neck, the spotted red handkerchief was straining against the taut muscles of her flung-back throat. I put my hand on the knot (the one I had tied just a few hours before), and pulled it loose. She gasped at the sudden release of pressure, but in the same moment I reknotted the handkerchief tighter. Her face flushed dark, then ashen, her hands banged against my chest, still strong, surprisingly strong—until inevitably she weakened through loss of blood and lack of air. But it took so long to do. She didn't want to die. The life had to be throttled out of her. Still I twisted the knot, pulling the noose tighter. With one last gasp, a convulsion, her body finally stilled. It was over. She was dead.

We had to act quickly then—I say 'we', but William was no help. He knelt over her lifeless corpse, and stared at me with an expression of horror and reproach. It should have been gratitude. Why is it always women who know what must be done? There was a spade and shovel in the barn, and it didn't take long for me to dig a shallow grave in the dirt of the barn floor. I pulled her by her shoulders, surprised at how heavy she was and once she was laid in the hole I did one more thing. A superstition from my childhood.

The dead can haunt us if their spirits are not at peace. I knew Maria's spirit would enjoy tormenting me, so I took an iron stake that was propped against the wall and thrust it through her body, pinning her to the ground by her hip. And then I filled the grave in and covered it with straw.

I told William that we couldn't leave together now. I would return to the cottage; he must leave with the others. When they arrived with their plunder he should tell them about the aborted burglary at the Rectory, and go with them to London. And finally, after a few weeks, he would come back for me. He agreed to my plan, grateful that I was taking control. I told him that we would be together one day, just not yet. I don't think I believed it even then.

So there is my story, Rector. You know the rest. That he came back to Polstead often at first, to visit me, saying he loved me. But after a few months he stopped coming. He had cooled towards me since Maria's death, and then I felt he was nervous around me. Finally, he never returned and I feared he had a new life. I was tortured by the idea that he might love another woman, that he had forgotten me and all our promises. I told of my dreams about Maria, about where she was buried. Once the body was found, I made sure Whitmore was sought. He'd kept quiet about the attempted burglary at the Rectory because of his affair with Elizabeth Bright and I knew that he would not cast doubt on my story, lest his own be revealed. I had a power over the pair of them and Elizabeth never forgot it. But they both kept the secret; if it came out that they were lovers it would destroy both his career and her reputation. And so, when William was arrested, Whitmore supported the view that he'd killed Maria; after all, why should he doubt what everyone else believed? I believe that he wanted William hung, then there would be only me alive who knew his secret. But now one more person does—you. And this knowledge will save you. Whitmore cannot judge you for a sin he himself has committed, and for a much longer time. And he is married, which makes his guilt heavier.

So you know now that William and I share the guilt of Maria's death, although it was my deed that finally did it. William signed his confession the night before they hanged him, but he never named me. After all, it was his gun that started the murder. From the time he fired the bullet there was no going back.

To take another's life is a mortal sin. So if it's such a damnable deed then why did God not strike me down years ago? Why did I stand in the crowd, watching William's body jerk like a puppet on a string, and walk away unpunished? I saw them cut him down too, but I couldn't stomach the next part. They butchered him into four parts. They say it's so that the body can't come together again, so that the soul can never return home. It's a punishment they save for the very worst murderers, like covering a book with his skin, and hanging his skeleton on display. But he didn't kill Maria. Where has his soul gone then? Does his spirit live forever in between heaven and hell, with no resting place? They say that he haunts Polstead, and maybe that's why.

But I don't believe in hauntings any more. After all, if his ghost did return surely it would have come to me, and I have never felt such a thing.

I used to think it was Maria that kept us apart. It turned out that she was what bound us together, even after she died. And now they have both been dead for over twenty years and still it is William and Maria who crowd my life and fill my dreams.

When I am dead I don't expect to meet them again. I no longer have the faith. But what if I am wrong, and my blackened soul is weighed down with its deeds, so heavy that it falls to hell?

There is no use in pretending any more. I am no better than Maria, but surely I am no worse. Now I can rest. The truth has finally been told. I can close my eyes for a final time and sleep. And, if there is a place beyond this one, maybe I will find William again, whether it be in heaven or in hell.

XXXVII

Rectory Journal June 5th 1851

Today should have been my wedding day. I should have awoken a bachelor for the final time. The early sun creeps in through the curtains and mocks me. It is going to be a beautiful day. I would not have left my bed but I need to pack my belongings. It should not take long—I have few possessions, and no one that I wish to bid farewell to. I have not seen Charles since our last interview. It saddens me that I shall never see him again.

Whitmore has made it clear that I must leave Polstead immediately. If I do not resign my position and leave the Church he will, he says, be forced to speak with the Bishop in Bury St Edmunds. I do not know what will happen to the post of Polstead Rector. Whitmore is to return to Kent today, taking Mrs Bright with him, he maintains, as his housekeeper. Of course I know this to be untrue, but I have held my tongue. I have been judged and found wanting. I have no choice but to leave both Polstead and my vocation in the Church.

I shall catch the Norwich coach at noon. Mother is not expecting me until tomorrow, with my bride, so she will have a shock to see me alone. I cannot spend another day in this Godforsaken place.

I will find another occupation—I am still young enough. And as to marriage, I want nothing more to do with the female sex. My flesh crawls when I think of them. I will find it a relief to be celibate. And here on my desk is my journal, the memoir of my meetings with Ann Marten. My sympathy for William Corder is absolute, now that I have heard the truth. He is no guiltier of Maria's death than I am of Sarah's. The victim writes her own epitaph.

There must be many people who would pay good money to know the truth about the notorious Red Barn murder. Maybe I do not have to search for another career—I could publish a book. I could reveal Ann Marten for the fornicator, adulteress and murderess that she is. And what of Thomas Marten, her husband? Surely he should know what kind of woman he has married?

The more I think on this, the more I see how perfect this solution would be. The book, The James Version, would tell the truth about the Red Barn murder of Maria Marten. But now I hear knocking at the door. Mrs Bright has already departed with Whitmore so I must answer it. I pray it isn't Mary. I have not told her that our wedding will not take place. I pray that Charles— poor Charles—has undertaken that unpleasant duty.

*

And so, God's hand intervenes again. When I open the heavy oak door, here is Thomas Marten, hat in hand, looking agitated. I know without asking why he is here but he tells me anyway. 'Yes, Sir, she died in the night. Quite peaceful, like. Her face looks— well—like she's asleep. I wanted to do the right thing by her, and she'd left this note, see. She knew she was dying. She told me to give it you straightaway.' I close the door and return here, to the library, the letter in my hand. There is no seal, but the crease is deep, and when I open the paper I am surprised to see that Ann Marten's hand is confident and bold. This is what she writes:

Dear Rector Coyte

I hope you have thought on what I said yesterday. You must see that nothing is without purpose. You were meant to hear my story, and I shall help you with yours. I shall save you, just as you have saved me.

Polstead needs you; the village needs a man to take it to his soul. You must resign yourself to living here, for where else could you go? Mary Teager will never believe you guilty of an immoral act, and May Humphries would not wish it to be known that her son's wife was a whore. She will keep quiet. She will have her hands full with Jeremiah and Joshua now.

Rector Walpole is your friend and will forgive your sin. As to Rector Whitmore and Elizabeth Bright, you now know their secret, and it mirrors your own. Whitmore will leave Suffolk and I doubt he will show his face again.

The way is clear to you now. May your life be long and prosperous.

Ann Marten

I read the letter just once, before throwing it on the remaining cinders of last night's fire. I watch the flames consume the words, and feel my own transgressions being cleansed by fire. Has Ann Marten set me free? Can I marry Mary, even though my flesh crawls at the thought, and settle to a long, cloistered life, atoning for my sins by a dutiful allegiance to Polstead? Dear Lord, you move in mysterious ways.

My penance might yet be my salvation. So be it.

AUTHOR'S NOTE

This novel is an entirely fictional account of the notorious Red Barn Murder. Whilst I have honoured the known significant details of the case, I have taken an author's liberty of creating characters that are entirely fictional even if their names are authentic.

As to the truth of who killed Maria Marten that has been buried along with the people who played a part in this sensational case. At the time of the murder it was widely accepted that Ann Marten's prophetic dreams, which led to the discovery of Maria's body, were genuine. The modern reader, however, is less likely to accept such an idea and it is from this initial premise that the novel began to take shape.

In writing several books have been useful, most notably Peter Haining's *The Murder in the Red Barn*. I am also grateful to the Bury St Edmunds Registry office for allowing access to the original transcript of the trial and the significant records from the relevant dates.

Lightning Source UK Ltd.
Milton Keynes UK
178424UK00001B/71/P